Nemesis

THE RESURRECTED QUEEN

JAYCE CARTER

The Resurrected Queen
ISBN # 978-1-83943-789-2
©Copyright Jayce Carter 2022
Cover Art by Kelly Martin ©Copyright April 2022
Interior text design by Claire Siemaszkiewicz
Totally Bound Publishing

THE
RESURRECTED
QUEEN

Dedication

To all the reverse harem authors out there, since if not for their books, the neighbors hearing me through our thin walls would be the closest I'd ever get to an orgy.

Chapter One

Nem

Nothing stays a secret forever.

I stood there, covered in blood, facing four men who I was hopelessly bound to, who now knew I'd been lying to them, and who might just kill me for it.

Carlos' body still rested on the floor behind me, and I'd have put a bullet into Rune — mostly because he was the biggest target — if I hadn't run out of ammunition.

Which was part of the reason I couldn't blame them for the seething anger they stared at me with.

"Kelsey?" Dane asked, as if he might have misheard the entire conversation. His gaze didn't stray from my eyes. Was he trying to see the girl he'd known there? Trying to see if he could catch a glimpse and recognize me?

Good luck, buddy. That girl died ten years ago.

I nodded, dropping my arm since the gun was heavy and useless at the moment.

"How?"

"I'm pretty sure you can work that out for yourself."
I risked glancing across the four men, not meeting their
eyes but searching for a reaction from each. Mostly,
they wore shock, as though they had to replay
everything that had happened between us to come to
terms with the idea that I wasn't who they'd thought I
was, that they'd already known me.

Colton took a step toward me, and I took a big jump
backward.

He froze, his expression hardening as though he
didn't care for the reaction. *Too bad.* Only an idiot
would trust them, especially now. They had every
reason to kill me, even if they hadn't before.

Still, he didn't argue, didn't try to reassure me.
Instead, he glanced around the room, sliding into a
familiar 'all business' mode. After a second, he nodded.
"We've got work to do. Five bodies downstairs, one up
here. There's too much blood and not enough time to
clean it properly. Let it look like the hit it was—just
make sure no one knows who did it. Let's get rid of any
evidence."

"There isn't any," I snapped.

Colton gave me a chilling look, one that reminded
me of why I'd backed away earlier. The man was
terrifying when he was calm like that. "How about the
bloody handprint on the banister? That left a good set
of fingerprints. Or perhaps the video footage?"

"There isn't any footage. I made sure the power was
off before I got in front of any cameras."

"For this house, sure. You failed to notice that the
camera at the neighbor's house watches their RV and
also gets a look at the front door of this place. Also, did
you bother to find out if he has any universal power
supplies hooked up to his camera feeds? This was
sloppy, Kelsey, no matter what you want to say."

Jayce Carter

The criticism sucked, but it wasn't nearly as painful as the way he said my name. That took the breath from my lungs, threatened to connect me back to the girl I'd been, to the life that had been stolen away.

"I can help," I said, rather than trying to argue with him. The reality was that it had been sloppy. It had been impulsive and foolish, and I still had too much alcohol in my system to pretend I was on the best footing.

"Not a chance." Colton looked over at Bray, who still hadn't said a word. "Get her back home with Dane. Rune and I will clean up this mess."

A moment of hope hit me, the idea of getting a moment alone, of figuring out a way to put everything back right again, before I'd managed to royally fuck up the entire plan.

It fled, however, when Colton landed his heavy gaze back on me. "And when we get back? We're going to have one hell of a talk, *Nem*."

I had a feeling I wasn't going to enjoy the sort of talk he meant…

* * * *

Dane

There were moments when life liked to really kick a man in the balls. I'd experienced plenty of those, when everything lined up perfectly to fuck me over.

And this was sure as hell one of them.

I sat in the backseat of the car beside Nem — *beside Kelsey* — and couldn't get my brain to catch up. Me, who never shut the fuck up, couldn't figure out a single thing to say.

Now that I knew, I wondered how I'd ever missed it. How couldn't I have seen it before?

9

The same nose, even the same smirk when she didn't want to laugh but couldn't help it, the same damned eyes.

Sure, she'd grown up. The last time I'd seen her, that morning before it all went down, she'd been seventeen, that age when kids thought they were adults and were only too quick to want to prove it. She'd started to fill out a bit, to lose some of that gangly stage girls went through when they got taller but lacked the curves that came with adulthood.

A flash of Nem naked hit me, a memory of just how much I enjoyed those curves coming over me.

How could it be her, though?

A memory from ten years ago, from a night I never wanted to remember, came back to me, aided by the way the streetlights flashed inside the SUV as we passed them...

I couldn't breathe, couldn't think, couldn't do a damn thing beyond putting one foot in front of the other. Getting news when I could do something, that was one thing. Adrenaline hit a person, put them into fight or flight so they could solve the problem.

If I'd gotten the news when I'd been in town, I'd have been at the house within ten minutes, running into the damned flames myself, uncaring that they still roared. I would have happily burned alive in that house if it meant saving Caroline or Kelsey.

Instead, it had taken three hours to get back, and by the time we did?

It was all over.

The fire was out, the house nothing but charred remains, blackened supports and soot.

Caroline was dead. Kyler had called and told us the news. The drive back, not wanting to tell Kenz, had been torture on a level I hadn't known existed. Kyler would tell her—it wasn't our place to do so.

After dropping her off, we'd come to the house. Why? Maybe some stupid vigil, some sentimental desire to stand watch over what we lost.

Kelsey...

As much as Caroline's death hurt, it was nothing compared to Kelsey. She'd been too young, too sweet for this to have happened. It was as if some hollowed-out piece of me remained, something she'd taken with her, had burned away beside her.

I remembered when she'd tried to kiss me just weeks before, her young want, the foolish romantic notions, and how I'd set her aside. It wasn't that I hadn't wanted her...

Fuck, I had.

I'd just cared too damn much to let it happen. She didn't know what she wanted, was too young to have a clue, and I wasn't about to let her keep going with that stupid fascination.

Kelsey had a real life ahead of her, a chance at a family, at a home, at all the things she deserved. She'd get none of that if she pursued the idiotic idea of some romance with me, with my brothers.

She'd get none of that now...

Yet, staring at the ash, the rubble, it wasn't just the loss of her that dug at me. It was the loss of the stupid fantasy I held on to as well.

An idea I kept locked away except for the brief moments it broke free, usually at night just before I fell asleep, when I thought...*what if?* What if she grew up a bit more, figured out her life more, then...

It didn't matter anymore, did it?

She was gone. Gone because someone had targeted her to get back at Kyler, gone because someone had been a coward and killed an unarmed child.

I followed Bray around the house, to the backyard. I didn't need to ask him what he was looking for.

Bray was quiet, but he held hope the rest of us had lost a long time before. "She knew where the safe room was."

"The safe room is ashes," I reminded him. It had been created to hide a person, not to protect them from flames.

Even if she'd made it there, she'd have been trapped inside while she burned. That was a worse thought than her taking a bullet or two.

Still, I let him hold on to the idea. It would get torn free soon enough.

In the backyard, the blackened grass hid signs of anything. I was caught by the patio swing there, the cushions burned, the metal like a skeleton left over. I remembered how Kelsey would sit there in the mornings, watching the sky as the sun rose. I woke early, so I'd usually been the one out there with her.

We didn't talk much, one of the few times I could just be silent, where I could rest. She'd been too fucking good for me, for any of us, for the whole damned world we lived in. She'd given me a sense of calm I'd never found in any other place.

I pulled my gaze from it, trying to bury my reactions, trying to take the pain that shot through me and shove it down beneath everything else before it consumed me.

On the back wall, where the safe room had been, was...nothing. The fire had eaten it away, leaving no evidence there had been a hidden space there at all.

Jayce Carter

Bray dropped to his knees, placing his hand on the foundation there, in the ash that was the only thing left. He hung his head forward, his eyes closed.

I got that feeling, the pain, but I didn't let it take over.

Instead, I turned to find Colton coming around the corner, Rune on his heels, their matching expressions hard.

"Anything?" I asked, even though I knew the answer. What was I hoping for? For him to explain how it hadn't really happened? That it was all a big mistake?

Colton shook his head, a quick jerk that screamed anger. "It was Cantor Lorris."

"You sure?"

"Kyler gave me the name. The body they found out front, just outside of the fire, is Cantor's second. Seemed to take a slug when they were coming in—guess the security tried to do something."

I struggled to understand it, to believe it. I'd done some horrible shit in my life, all in the name of duty or power or loyalty, but I'd never slaughtered innocents.

Spouses and kids were off-limits—always.

Of course, expecting others to live by my rules would do nothing but cause heartache. The reality was that other people in our world weren't as principled as we were, and this was more proof of it.

"Why kill them and not Kyler?" I asked.

"Kyler got a text message from Caroline this morning, after we left, saying Kelsey wasn't feeling well and asking him to come home."

A frown touched my features. "Caroline wouldn't ever do that..." Caroline was tough and independent. She wouldn't call for help over something as trivial as Kelsey not feeling well, and she sure as hell wouldn't have called Kyler home.

13

"Exactly. Near as I can figure, they broke in around nine in the morning and must have taken Caroline's cell and sent the text message. They were probably hoping Kyler would speed home and they'd get him too — take out the whole family in one swoop. Hell, I bet they thought Kenz was there, too."

"And when Kyler no doubt answered that he was busy, they decided to cut their losses," I added.

"Looks like being a selfish fucker saved Kyler's ass again." Rune didn't look at anyone else, his voice a mess of fury, as if he were just looking for a target for all that aggression.

"So what now?" I asked though we all knew the answer. It had been our job to take care of Caroline and Kelsey, to protect them, and we'd failed. We hadn't seen this coming, hadn't been able to stop it, and now two of the only people in the whole fucking world who mattered to us were gone.

Colton answered, a darkness in his voice that reminded me of how dangerous the man was. The rest of us, we could kill — would kill — if we needed to. Colton specialized in it, enjoyed it, relished the part of him that took life with such skill. "We didn't save them, but we'll fucking make sure the people who did this suffer for it."

And that was a plan that I could get behind...

Nem twisted her head, her familiar eyes locking with mine and pulling me back to the present.

All that pain, all that fear, all that guilt I'd carried all this time, and she'd never been dead at all. Where had she been? Why hadn't she *told* us she was okay?

I wanted to wrap my hand around her neck and demand answers, to force her to let me into her head and figure out what exactly she'd gotten herself into. Where had she been for ten fucking years? What had she been doing? Who else knew the truth?

I knew better, though. She was even more stubborn than she'd been before, and now wasn't the time.

So I sat back, tearing my gaze from her even if that was the last thing I wanted. Some part of my brain screamed to not look away, to stare at her, to memorize every detail. I wanted to strip her down, now that I knew the truth, and kiss each freckle on her lying body, to nip each one and bask in having her back.

There would be time for that later, though. The reality was that even knowing it was her didn't really answer shit. It only gave me more questions, more uncertainty.

Nem was a bomb, and if I went poking around with it, it might just blow up in my face. It meant I had to play the game, still, and if there was one thing I knew for sure…

I needed all four of us if we had any hope of untangling the disaster of a woman beside me, because she was too fucking dangerous for any of us to face on our own.

* * * *

Nem

The shower was hot, but even as it turned my skin red, it didn't sear away the memories, the questions, the doubts.

Back at the men's home, I'd retreated to the bathroom to wash the blood off. Bray had taken my clothes, and I hadn't even fought him on it. I loved the outfit, but it was covered in blood. The safest choice was to dispose of it—probably by burning it.

Red ran down the drain, from both the dye that leached from my hair and the blood that I washed off. Most of it had dried, so I used a washcloth to scrub it clean.

And yet, even with all the unknowns, even with the frustration about Kenz, about Kyler, none of that was in the shower with me. Instead, it was *them*.

Would I walk down that hallway and find a bullet with my name on it?

No, that would be too impersonal, and by the looks on their faces, they were feeling rather personal about this.

I tipped my head back, letting water run through my hair, trying to block out the memories that threatened to consume me.

It was like suddenly, now that they knew who I was, I struggled to keep a wall between who I had been and who I was now. They'd shattered that separator, and I had no idea how to build it up again.

I felt like *her* again, like the young girl who was too stupid to see the world for what it was.

You aren't her anymore! You've grown up, gotten stronger, smarter.

If they thought for a second that I'd be an easy target, they had no clue who they were dealing with.

That was the point, though, wasn't it? They didn't know. They'd seen a glimpse, one I'd chosen to show them, but they didn't have a clue how deep my hatred ran, how determined I was, how strong I'd gotten by sheer willpower. They hadn't seen me crawl out of the burning building, hadn't seen the blood trailing me, hadn't watched as I'd built myself into what I was now.

I turned off the shower and squeezed my hair to try to get all the water out I could. I wrapped a towel around me before pulling open drawers quietly, searching.

Finally, below the sink, I found it. They'd taken my gun—another fair thing to do, but I didn't care for being unarmed—however it was nearly impossible to keep a determined person from finding a weapon.

A button-up shirt sat on the counter, along with a pair of underwear. I slid on the outfit, then tucked the straight-edge razor I'd found beneath the sink into the waistband.

If they wanted a fight, I had no problem giving them one.

After getting dressed and procrastinating as long as I could, I found myself in front of the four men who I couldn't read.

Well, Rune and Colton looked tired. Then again, cleanup work wasn't the easiest or most fun part of a job. Guilt tugged at me, but I refused to let it get a foothold. I hadn't asked them to clean up my mess, to take care of me.

At least some of their anger had seemed to dissipate. Maybe it was like disasters. Hysterical screaming could only last for so long before people accepted things as the new normal. The men had gone through their shock, and that sort of emotional level couldn't be kept up for long.

Rune and Dane sat on the large couch, while Bray had pulled in a chair from the kitchen and Colton remained on his feet, leaning against the bookshelf. Colton always did that, was always silently watching from the outside.

One more seat rested in the room, a chair in the center that made it clear it was for me. I almost laughed as I remembered times they'd done this before, when they'd tried to scare me into admitting where I'd snuck out to the night before.

It hadn't worked on a sixteen-year-old girl. Did they really think it would now?

Still, I took the spot meant for me, ignoring how little I wore. That was another purposeful step, no doubt. During an interrogation, a person wanted to highlight the difference in power. Make the suspect uncomfortable, make it clear they weren't in charge, remind them how little control they had.

If they thought giving me one of their button-up shirts was going to do that, they were sadly mistaken. We could have done this with me naked, and I'd still have been fine.

The alcohol had faded away, leaving a headache behind but putting me on solid ground for going toe-to-toe with them.

"What happened?" Rune asked, surprising me by speaking.

They normally let Dane do the talking.

"When?" I asked, going for casual, as if none of this mattered all that much to me.

"You were at the house with Caroline when men arrived, judging by what we heard. How did you escape?" Rune spoke as though my mouthing off didn't bother him, as if he couldn't be shaken.

Still, interrogations were a matter of giving the right information while keeping the wrong to myself. "Carlos thought I was dead. He figured the three bullets he put into me would take care of the job. Shelia had taken Caroline's phone, so she couldn't call anyone, and Geoffrey shot my mother. Lucky poured gasoline around the house and lit a match. While everything burned down around me, I dragged myself to the safe room in the closet."

"The safe room was destroyed," Bray said, his tone still untrusting.

"I kicked the vent cover off and crawled out."

"That vent was tiny."

I let out a soft laugh, recalling how I'd pulled myself through, how the smoke had made me cough as I'd struggled—or maybe it had been the blood in my lungs. "I got cut up trying, but I managed it. Seems like when the world is burning around you, you're capable of some surprising things."

Colton spoke up from his spot. "You had three bullet wounds, Nem. You couldn't have walked anywhere, didn't take any of the cars. How did you get out of the backyard?"

It was hard to think about, to force myself back to that night, to the fear and the pain. I did it, though, making myself reach for what had happened. "I got to the bushes before I collapsed. The men who did it didn't stick around—fires attract a quick response. Someone showed up who helped me."

"Who?"

I shook my head. "You don't get everything in my head. All I'll say is that it was a friend, and I'd be dead without them."

Dane pressed his lips together, as if the answer was unsatisfactory, but he knew better than to push. "Why didn't you tell anyone you were alive? Why pretend you were dead? Why let us all think Cantor's men had killed you?"

"It wasn't Cantor."

"Of course it was." Dane spoke with such certainty, but that wasn't the only thing I heard. Even after a decade, it was the anger that shone through. "He tried to trick Kyler into showing up so he could take out the entire family. When we caught up with him, he was on the run. Not much more proof needed."

"He was fleeing because anyone who had you four after them would run. I lived through it. I took out every fucking person involved except the one who planned it. I know exactly what happened, know who was behind it, and trust me, it wasn't Cantor."

"So who was it?"

I met Dane's gaze head-on. "You want to know why I didn't come back? Why I let everyone think I was dead? Because Kyler set up the hit. He hired those men to kill my mother and me, and I had no goddamned idea if you four were in on it or not."

And that sure managed to shut them up.

Chapter Two

Nem

That I slept at all surprised me, but having a fucking nightmare wake me didn't. The last few days had shaken up my entire past, stirred up ghosts that I'd thought had already crossed over, and now my brain was playing jump-rope with every horrible thing I'd gone through.

So bolting upright in bed as I clawed at the scar on my chest felt on trend for everything else.

I'm not bleeding. I had to tell myself that, over and over again. The wounds had healed many years ago. I wasn't bleeding out.

Fuck, why was it so hard to believe it, even as my fingers traced the raised, healed skin?

"I wondered what the nightmares were about." Colton's voice was soft, and it took a moment for my eyes to adjust and spot him seated at my desk in the dark room.

It had to be daytime, but the blackout curtains worked wonders.

I tried to slow my breath. "Why am I not surprised that you watched me sleep? That's creepy, you know?"

"You think you're quiet, but you're not. You let out a soft cry before you wake up, and I've heard it most nights. I guess I don't have to wonder what they're about anymore, do I?" He dropped his gaze to my chest, and I realized I was still rubbing at the scar, despite it being covered by the shirt.

I forced myself to leave it be. "Is there a point to this little visit?"

He tilted his head, as if even he wasn't sure. "Did you really think we were behind your attack?"

"Why wouldn't I? You just happened to leave the day it went down. You told me I couldn't come with you guys and Kenz. That wouldn't strike you as suspicious?"

"Yeah, it would," he admitted. "You should have known us better than that, though. You, your sister and your mother were our entire lives."

"Well, I've learned loyalty doesn't mean as much to some people as we like to think. It's flexible when it suits them."

"Your safety has never been flexible to us."

I shook my head. "If you're here to rehash old arguments, you don't need to. I'm pretty clear that you all didn't know about Kyler's plan." Saying it out loud was surprisingly helpful. It gave me the chance to accept it, to hear the words and admit…yeah.

I still didn't trust them, didn't know where exactly their alliances were, but they'd been too shocked to see me, too surprised at the truth, too sure Cantor had been behind the attack to have been involved.

They might have been hard to read, but the four of them could never have faked that reaction.

"So, are you going to turn me in?"

He furrowed his eyebrows. "What?"

"To Kyler. You're devoted to him now, right? All that loyalty you talked about, that all goes to him. So, are you going to tell him about me?"

Colton leaned forward, his elbows going to rest on his knees. "You think that we're sworn to Kyler?"

"Of course. You protected my mom, my sister and I, and now you help protect him. You said—"

"We said we were honor-bound, but we didn't say it was to him. It was to your mother."

"And she's dead, so you seem to have moved to him."

Colton shook his head. "With you and Caroline gone"—he gave me a meaningful look, as if scolding me for my deception—"our only purpose was to protect Kenz."

"So why are you working for Kyler?"

"Because Kenz was a child. The best option for keeping her safe was to keep Kyler safe and in power. Working for Kyler has only ever been a means to an end for us." He moved off the chair and sat on the bed in front of me. "If you think we'd turn you over to him, especially after what you said, you're not paying any attention."

I stared at him, trying to find some proof in his expression that he was lying. I wasn't sure if he was telling the truth or if I was just so pathetically desperate for it to be the truth that I'd accept it.

The nightmare had taken down my defenses, stolen my good sense, because all I wanted right then was to kiss Colton. I wanted to crawl closer, into his lap, and lose myself in him.

I wanted to erase the memory of the nightmare, to replace it with what I knew Colton could give me.

I didn't know if he moved on his own accord, because he wanted me as much as I wanted him, or if he did so because he read what I needed on my face. Either way, I found myself flat on my back, his demanding lips against mine.

He kissed me with a passion tinged with anger. It was as though he wanted to punish me for lying to him through his kiss.

Fine by me. I'd take whatever he wanted me to, revel in it, in the honesty of it. He was angry and frustrated and well fuck—so was I.

He undid the buttons of the shirt I still wore, and this time, I let him. I wasn't ashamed of the scars I bore, wasn't afraid to let him see them now that he knew the truth.

After he'd gotten the shirt open, when it parted to expose all the bare skin and the pair of panties I still had on, his fingers skimmed my heated body. He brought them up over my stomach, my ribs, then cupped my breast in his warm hand.

I cried out against his lips at the touch, at the way it somehow felt more overwhelming than before. Was that because he knew who I was now?

He released my breast, but when his fingers found the scar there, he broke the kiss and lifted his body so he could stare down at it.

His dark eyebrows furrowed, as if he couldn't understand it, as if it made no fucking sense to him.

"This shouldn't have happened," he said before dropping his head and kissing the old mangled scar.

"If you try to make sense of why anything happens, you'll drive yourself crazy," I told him.

"I know why it happened — because I didn't see Kyler for what he was, because I was too damned busy ignoring you to see the risks." His breath warmed my skin around the scar, since I had no real feeling on the actual mark.

"Ignoring me?"

He darted his gaze up, even as his lips hovered over my skin. "You were too fucking young, and way too tempting."

"Not that tempting, since you turned me down."

"You were a kid, Nem, and one I was supposed to be taking care of. Pretty sure that didn't include putting my dick into you."

"You don't seem to mind it now." I lifted my thigh, the one between his knees, and ground it against his erection.

He groaned then shuddered. "Well, in case you haven't noticed, it's been a long time, and you aren't a kid anymore."

Fair enough. I didn't feel like a kid, not when I looked at him, not when he kissed the scar again then moved down farther. His lips seared me, leaving a trail of burned nerve endings in their wake. He wasn't rough, didn't nip me, didn't leave marks, even when he sucked on the undercurve of my breast.

It felt strange, almost romantic, like he was trying to form something between us that wasn't possible anymore. It also felt really fucking dangerous.

I wanted rough. I wanted to be driven so crazy that nothing else mattered. I didn't want any of this stupid romance notion.

I shoved his shoulder, and he lifted his gaze to mine, confusion there.

"Knock it off," I said.

"You seem to enjoy it."

"I want your dick and maybe your tongue, so long as you don't use it to talk."

"And what do you call this?" He traced his tongue along the point of my hip above the waist of my underwear.

A broken moan left me at the touch, but I wouldn't let him throw me off. "You said it yourself — I'm not a kid anymore. I don't need this bullshit romance thing."

A frown touched at his features. "Romance? You think me walking in here fucking you like this is romance?"

"You don't need to pretend this is anything other than what it is — sex. I don't need you to act like you give a shit about me. We're both killers — let's not act like we aren't."

He stared at me for a long, silent moment. It was intense to peer down my body, to see his dark eyes locked with mine. He shook his head as if disappointed. "You might be older, but it doesn't seem like you're any fucking smarter than you used to be."

I would have argued, but when he wrapped his fingers in the waist of my panties and tugged them off, anything I would have said faded away. It pulled me down a few inches from the force, but that only made me want him more. Maybe I should have been afraid when he moved over me again, his size and weight pinning me down.

Colton was a killer — no two ways about that. He was merciless when he wanted to be, and he had plenty of reasons to be angry with me.

Maybe closing my legs and telling him to leave was the smartest choice, but he'd always managed to make me choose the stupid one, because I wrapped my leg around his hip.

He closed his teeth on my bottom lip, each touch like another punishment, like a way to remind me of how damned pissed he was.

Fine.

I was pissed, too. Angry about what had happened, angry about him knowing the truth, about him turning me down for so long before this had all happened.

Hell…I was even angry at him for not recognizing me, for not knowing I was still alive, no matter how unfair such anger was.

It seemed we wanted to punish one another, and this was the perfect way to do it. It reminded me of that first time, when he'd shown up and fucked me on the stool.

Colton, the man who usually chose his actions so carefully, seemed the reckless one when it came to me. It fit, somehow, that he'd been the first to have me, and now was the first to have me when he knew who I really was.

He sank two thick fingers into my cunt, but it seemed a cursory touch, as if just to ensure I was wet enough to take him. I knew how good he could be with those fingers, which made this feel like yet another punishment, yet another way to get back at me for my lies.

His cock felt like fire when he pressed it against me, pausing to break the kiss and meet my gaze. It was intense, full of years of questions and anger and pain. He stared at me as if he wanted to make damn sure I knew it before we went any further.

I tightened my leg around him, trying to pull him in closer, wanting to feel that delicious edge of pain of him sinking into me.

He didn't look away, didn't try to hide anything as he plunged his hard cock into me.

I arched up at the sudden fullness, at the way he took me over entirely. It was painful and perfect and beautiful in an ugly way — just like us. Like our history and our lives and our whole damn relationship.

He shifted to his elbows, bringing him closer, letting me feel the heat and firmness of his body against mine.

He paused, frowning, turning his gaze to the side. The flash of silver, and he held the razor I'd stolen from their bathroom, the one I'd hidden beneath my pillow and that he'd made me completely forget. "Really?" he asked.

"Can never be too careful." *Why does my voice have to sound so breathless?* Probably because I was being fucked by Colton, which seemed like a good enough reason, even if it annoyed me to show any sign of weakness.

He shook his head and tossed the razor to the floor. "You don't need weapons against us — against me. You're a fucking weapon on your own, Nem, and I've got no doubt you cut far deeper than any blade."

I opened my mouth to argue, but he leaned in and stole my words with a kiss. It wasn't the sort of kiss people wrote about, or one like those in the movies, full of all these sweet things. It was a claim, as if he could wipe away the past decade, as though he could make it so I understood something he didn't want to say.

But I didn't. I didn't fucking understand anything he felt or thought or wanted me to get through my head.

This was just stupid attempts to make hormones into something deeper, just people trying to pretend they weren't animals driven by primal urges, so they told themselves things like love and fate are real.

They weren't.

I wrapped my arms around his shoulders, clinging to him, returning his kiss with every bit of pent-up angry lust I had. He could say all he wanted at the moment about something more, and I could remind him it was nothing but bodies and stress relief.

Colton let out another one of those deep groans, letting me sample the mint on his breath from his toothpaste. He pulled back, then snapped his hips forward. He fucked me wildly, just as he had the last time, but I was more used to it this time.

It made it better, let me move with him, let me lift my hips toward him to urge him on. I wanted more.

Harder. Deeper. Faster. Whatever he gave me, I only craved more of it.

And Colton didn't disappoint. He broke the kiss, wrapped one of his arms beneath my lower back and held me tighter. It made it so each roll of his hips not only sank his thick cock deep into me but ground his pelvic bone against my clit.

I curled my fingers in so my nails dug into his back. This felt different, but I didn't want it to.

I didn't want to feel something new, something more. Now that he knew who I was, now that our entire history was between us, everything seemed to mean more.

I struggled to shove that away, to simplify it, to make it just about sex again. Even as I gasped, as my body rushed toward an orgasm I knew would shatter me, I told myself over and over that this didn't change anything.

I had a plan, one that was going to end with me dead for good. There wasn't a future, and no amount of sex — no matter how good — would change that. I needed to accept it, to hold that truth tight so I'd never forget it.

If I forgot, I would risk everything. If I let myself think for even a second that there was anything important between the Quad and I, if I thought I could have some sort of future, I'd second-guess everything.

The truth was that the only way to ensure Kenz's safety was to kill Kyler, and I wasn't foolish enough to think that I could walk away from that.

So I tattooed that on my heart, even as I let myself fall into the crushing orgasm Colton forced from me, as I lost myself in his touch and his body and the moment of absolute bliss.

But even when I knew how things would go, that one moment between seconds, when my higher thinking switched off and I was nothing but sensation, but feeling and instinct, I did the one thing I knew was more dangerous than any plan I had.

For that one second, I loved Colton, even knowing it would destroy me faster than Kyler ever could.

Chapter Three

Nem

Somehow, each time I returned to the mansion, it felt even more imposing than the time before.

It wasn't the decor or changes Kyler had made — those things made it nicer, if anything. Maybe it was just recognizing what the mansion really was.

A prison.

It was nothing but a way to trap Kenz in a life she had no say in. It made me wonder... If Kyler hadn't tried to kill me, would this have been my future as well? Would I have ended up married to some old man who Kyler wanted to buy favors from?

Would I have gone along with it?

I wanted to say no, but I wasn't the same girl I'd been back then. If Kyler and my mother had told me I would marry some man, I wasn't sure I would have said no.

A hand touched my back, making me jump before I realized it was just Rune. He stared at me, the same hard to read expression he'd had since he'd discovered the truth. We hadn't spoken much, but that wasn't surprising. Neither of us were 'in our feelings' sort of people.

Rune had been the only one to drive me today, claiming Colton, Bray and Dane had other things to do. They were probably busy trying to dig up information on me.

Good luck.

I'd hidden my real tracks well. I'd made sure my fake history was easy to follow, at least on paper. I'd planned this since opening my eyes after surgery and realizing I'd survive.

I'd spent ten years setting up my identity, learning, growing.

If the Quad found anything I'd tried to hide, they'd earned it.

I swallowed and nodded, as if to let Rune know I was okay. Even that hesitation shouldn't have happened. I needed to keep my head in the game, not let the men distract me from what I needed to do.

We didn't knock since I had keys and security codes to the house. Kyler's car was outside, and he'd already called me that morning to ask me to meet him there.

Inside, the house was coming together well. The walls were all patched and repaired from running the cables needed for the cameras and motion detectors. In fact, at first glance, it would have been impossible to realize any work had been done recently.

Then again, I'd made sure to hire the best.

Well, the best who I knew Jarrod had access to, meaning their security systems would still allow *us* to bypass when we needed. Every bit of advantage we could get was needed.

Kyler walked in on his cell phone, his expression one of annoyance — at least until he spotted me. The way he smiled made my chest hurt. It was stupid, like some reflex from childhood that had craved seeing that exact look, one where he actually appeared *happy* to see me.

Instead, I'd gotten disinterest at best.

Then again, from what Carlos had said…

Kyler might have known all along I wasn't his. A man as obsessed with bloodlines as he was wouldn't have taken that too kindly.

He gestured toward the sitting room, then nodded at his phone, his meaning clear.

Go sit in there, and he would be in when his call finished.

Once he'd walked out again, Rune peered down at me, his eyebrow lifted.

I wasn't sure if I was just an expert at reading men or if the ones I dealt with simply expected me to read their faces far too often, because his meaning was just as clear.

Be careful.

With the cameras, he couldn't say anything out loud, but that didn't stop the demand from chafing.

I'd taken care of myself for a long time without them. I didn't need Rune holding my hand and telling me all about the dangers of life.

We were about a decade too late for that talk.

Instead of giving him even a glare in return, I turned on my heel and headed for the sitting room.

No doubt Rune would go check out the security plans, perhaps visit Kenz. Keeping up appearances was important, especially since the Quad and I hadn't actually discussed my plan or why I was there.

Maybe it was obvious enough that we didn't need to. There weren't a lot of reasons someone showed up after ten years to face the person who had wronged her.

Revenge was a hell of a thing.

And yes, revenge was a *part* of it, but it wasn't the core issue. Though, even if the Quad hadn't been in on killing me, I didn't trust them enough to tell them about my plan for Kenz. They might want her safe, but that didn't mean they were willing to go against Kyler, that they'd be willing to get her out of the life entirely.

They hadn't thus far, so who knew what they felt was *best* for her?

A few minutes later, Kyler walked in, sliding his phone into his jacket pocket. "Sorry. An associate in Texas made promises that it seems he isn't capable of keeping." His tone said the person would be paying that debt with blood, no doubt.

Disappointing someone or not living up to the things they promised was a quick path to the bottom of a very deep hole.

"Is everything up to your standards?" I asked as I gestured around the house.

"Yes. I have to admit, you're probably the most capable associate I have at the moment." He undid the button on his suit jacket before sitting on the couch across from me. "It's nice to know the tasks I give you are handled."

"I try," I said, pretending that the praise did a damn thing for me.

Though…a terrible part of me *did* enjoy it. It wasn't the reaction when the Quad were pleased with something, and I suspected it was just a holdover from still seeing Kyler as a father. He might have been a terrible one, but for seventeen years he'd been the only one I had. *I guess we never outgrow wanting Daddy's approval...*

It reminded me of why 'Daddy issues' were such a thing.

"Actually, I called you over because I want your help with something else."

"With what?"

"I told you this place is being given to Mackenzie when she's married, but that isn't the only reason I picked it. I wanted something where she could live beforehand, and a place to hold the wedding."

I frowned. "Why not use the vineyard you bought for that?"

"Because that is too touristy. I need somewhere private where no one will raise eyebrows about who comes. A wedding like this will have a lot of people in attendance who are understandably private. This place has enough room, enough security and enough privacy to work for the venue."

I peered around the space, unable to argue with his assessment. "You'll need to rework the furniture situation, have a party planning company come in. They'll have access to the rentals for what you need and trained staff for the actual event."

"I thought you could handle that."

"I'm not a party planner," I said, my words slow. Pissing him off wouldn't get me what I wanted, but neither would getting stuck in a job I knew I'd fail at.

He shook his head. "I'm not asking you to plan it. Hire a company for that. I'm only asking you to coordinate with Mackenzie and the planner on the specifics. You know this house, you obviously are familiar with security. You can also bring in the Quad for security information and access to guards."

"Parties aren't my thing," I pressed.

"I'm busy, and Mackenzie doesn't have a mother to help her with this. I know it's asking a lot, but you'll be well compensated for it. Honestly, I think you're wasting your talents by focusing only on real estate. You would be exceptional as a personal assistant or business manager."

Which made his reasoning clear—he was interviewing me yet again for a position I hadn't asked for. Though the idea of being any more involved with Kyler turned my stomach, at least it would position me in a good place for the final blow. The more I could get him to rely on me, the better.

And working with Kenz would also make it easier when it was time to pull her out. It could help to gain her trust.

"Who is she marrying?" I asked, now that I could focus on the issue instead of my own feelings.

"His name is Torrance Narst. He is a capable business associate who can offer her a good life."

I hadn't heard the name before, didn't know him off-hand. While I knew many of the other important families in the area, there was no telling how close he would actually be. "I've never heard of him."

"He lives in the San Diego area."

Ah, close enough to be useful but not so close as to step on each other's toes. Again, Kyler's scheming was more detailed than I'd have expected. Still, the name would allow me to find out more if I needed to.

Kyler's phone rang, and he didn't wait for an answer from me. Instead, he rose and spoke to me as he pulled his cell out. "Why don't you go upstairs and talk to Mackenzie? You can start gathering details for what she wants. I've already moved her in here."

With that, he was gone, and I had a new job I'd never intended.

And…I was about to go have my first private conversation with my sister in ten years…

Knocking on the door to Kenz's room was the oddest thing I'd done in a while — and I'd helped cover up a few murders recently.

Back when we'd been kids, I hadn't ever knocked. I'd just walked into her room when I wanted to talk, or more often than not, she'd ended up in mine. Funny how many times that had annoyed me, how I'd been tired of my little sister constantly wanting to trail me around. I had loved her, of course, but like any teenager, I'd wanted my space.

How much I'd give up if I could just go back there again…

Instead of a decade ago, however, it was the seventeen-year-old Kenz who opened the door, looking every bit her age and then some, since teens always strove to look older.

"Nem?" she said, frowning as she peered past me.

So, Kyler didn't mention his plan, huh? Why am I not surprised that he wants me to do his dirty work?

I smiled, trying my best to appear disarming. "I met with your father, and he wanted me to come up and talk to you some."

That seemed the exact wrong thing to say, because Kenz's expression snapped shut, as if she realized she suddenly couldn't trust me. It seemed whatever relationship she had with Kyler wasn't all rainbows.

Then again, if anyone knew what Kyler was like, it was me. He might not be outright horrible, but he had a way of dismissing a person until they felt like they didn't matter at all. Hell, he'd moved her into a mansion rather than allowing her to continue staying with him.

I filed away the reaction as I did every other little piece, like the lack of decor in her room, the books about art on her desk, the easel in the corner, the septum piercing that was flipped up so it was hidden in her nostrils.

"You mean he hired you to plan the *wedding*, and now you're here to see what I want?" She moved back to let me enter, then closed the door after I did so.

"Well, it's your wedding. It should be however you want it." I swallowed down my revulsion at having to utter those words, at mirroring what Kyler would have said. I didn't care for feeling as if Kyler were manipulating me, yet I couldn't ignore his demands, either.

Kenz sat on the foot of the bed, then brought her legs up and crossed them, hunching forward. I could almost hear our mother in my head, wanting to escape through my lips and tell her not to slouch. "It isn't *my* wedding. It's my father's."

"We could make it yours."

"Not unless you can call it off."

I kept my mouth shut on that one, even though what I wanted to do was lean forward, take her hand in mine and swear she'd *never* have to worry about actually marrying anyone she didn't want to.

Instead, I answered, not bothering to hide my pity. "I know it isn't ideal, but we can make the best of it."

"*Make the best of it?*" She gave me the sort of look a teenager gives an adult when the adult tells them, 'you're a kid, your life isn't so hard!' "I'm being forced to marry a man who is almost *sixty* years old, all because it will help my father out."

"He said—"

"That it was for my safety. Yeah, I know, I've heard that a lot in my life. He likes to say it because then he gets to be the good guy. I'm not ready to marry anyone at all, but I'm for sure not interested in marrying a man as old as my father. I want to go to art school. I want to start my own life, to do what *I* want to do. I've spent my whole life being shuttled from one place to another, all for my 'safety', and I'm tired of it. If I marry Torrance, it just leaves me here in that same place, for my whole life."

My chest hurt at the pain in her words, at remembering how I'd felt at her age. It hadn't even been as bad for me, because at least I'd had my mother, had Kenz, had the Quad. Kenz had spent the last decade on her own.

It strengthened my resolve, that I'd fix this no matter what, especially when I got details about this man's age…

"Look, Kenz."

She frowned at the nickname. "No one calls me that."

"Sorry," I rushed out, trying to cover for it. "I didn't mean to overstep my bounds."

She shook her head, her expression having shifted to something almost…nostalgic? "It's okay. Only one person ever called me that—with who my dad is, only one person ever dared. It's nice to hear it again."

The words tugged at me, but I shoved the reaction down, moved on so I didn't get off track. "I know you don't want this wedding, and you can still work toward talking your father out of it. There's still time, you know? But at least if you start to plan it, you'll keep him in a good mood, make it more likely he's willing to listen to you. I've found sometimes the more you dig your heels in, the more someone drags you through the dirt. The best plan is often the subtle one."

She blew out a slow breath, and I could see the plan running through her mind. Kenz had always been smart but naïve. She could think through anything, but always thought people would do the right thing, always expected too much of them.

That was clear in that moment, when she agreed with me, when she thought for even a second Kyler would ever do something that wasn't selfish, anything that didn't directly benefit him. "Okay," she said softly. "We'll plan it, but there's one rule."

"What's the rule?"

She gave me a smile I'd missed, one filled with so much optimism it almost hurt. "No roses. I hate roses."

Chapter Four

Nem

A coffee shop was the sort of place that reminded me of how different my life was from most people's. I watched the patrons inside, the customers who went up to the barista and ordered a multitude of complicated drinks that said they came often enough to understand the menu.

Along one wall, where single tables sat, a row of people clicked away at their laptops. A woman at the end chewed on the eraser of her pencil as she stared at the screen of hers, and beside her a man with headphones on typed quickly.

"What are you thinking about?" Dane sat down at the table I'd taken, one that overlooked the entire shop, and placed two cups on the table.

"What it would be like to be one of them." I nodded at the woman.

"A failing author?"

I didn't bother to give him a side-eye. "Normal," I clarified. "Someone who wakes up in the morning and gets to decide what they're going to do, just because it's what they want to do." I paused, then sighed. "No, further back. Someone who got to decide what they wanted to do from the start. I wonder what that would have been like."

"Everyone decides what they want to do," Dane countered before he took a slow sip of his own drink.

"You say that because you don't get it—you don't know what it's like to be trapped by who you're born."

"That's bullshit and we both know it. Who you are now sure wasn't in the cards when your parents first looked at you, I'd bet."

I tore my gaze from the people who worked and moved it to Dane, meeting his eyes and the way he studied me as I spoke. "That's different. I wouldn't be who I am now if it wasn't for Kyler."

"Kyler might have given you the shove, but you were always difficult, always stubborn, always too smart for your own good. You make the life you're going to lead—no one else."

I shook my head. He didn't get it. It was easy for other people born without the last names that mattered to say those things. It was a nice story for the unimportant to tell themselves, but we legacies knew the truth.

It was like Kyler had told me, that names were a curse. They dictated our future, our worth, and even when we fought against them, they never quite let go of us.

I'd watched myself struggle with it, saw it in Kenz's face just the same. Dane wouldn't ever understand the weight of that, so I let the conversation go.

Arguing with someone when I knew I would lose was the epitome of wasted breath.

"So what are you really here for?" Dane asked.

"That should be pretty obvious."

"You could have gotten revenge the first time you met him. Hell, given the fact that list of yours is full of dead people, you probably could have crossed him off without playing this whole undercover game."

"That would have been too easy. A bullet is too good for Kyler."

Dane snorted softly. "Revenge is just justice with more pain."

It was hard to argue with that point. Then again, justice had never mattered to me. Justice was a lofty goal thought up by idealists, by people who believed in karmic balance. I'd lived too horrible of a life to think that was true.

The only karma was that which we created, and justice had to do with balancing shit, with making someone get what they deserved. I preferred to give them what *I* wanted them to have—fuck karmic alignment.

A drop of my coffee escaped the cup and landed on the table when I set the mug down, when the drink splashed over the side. I rose, then went to the station at the far wall that had creamer, sugars, napkins and stirrers.

After grabbing a few of the napkins, I turned when someone ran into me. It was a kid, a boy no older than fourteen, headphones over his ears and his eyes down.

"Sorry," he rushed out, then turned to take off.

I grabbed his arm before he could, my gaze hard.

He lifted his face to mine, his expression pure bravado.

Well, false bravado at least. It was easy to tell the difference if a person knew how to look. The giveaway was the tension in his cheeks, the twitch of his left eyelid.

I held my other hand out, just staring at him.

"What?" he asked, then tugged at my hold. "Dude, let me go."

"Give it back," I said, not needing to explain further. He knew *exactly* what I meant.

He narrowed his gaze, that defiance almost adorable.

At least, until his eyes locked on something behind me, and I knew damn well what it was.

Dane.

People didn't look at me with that sort of fear, even though they should have.

The kid reached into his pocket and fished something out. When he held his hand out to me, my watch rested in his palm. "I'm really sorry," he said in a rush.

I took the watch, then nodded at the table Dane and I'd been sitting at, the meaning clear. The kid, probably realizing he had no options, followed the direction.

He sat on the inside seat, the one against the wall, with Dane and I flanking him.

"What's your name?" I asked.

He kept his gaze down, on the table. "Ether."

I lifted an eyebrow. "*Ether?* That sounds like either a fake name or your parents hated you."

He let out a soft snort. "That's what I've gone by for a long time. My real name is Carlton."

"If your parents named you Carlton, they hate you anyways."

"Are you going to kill me?" His words trembled at the end.

"Over a watch? No, Ether, I don't plan on it."

"Maybe you should," Dane added. At my look, he shrugged. "Kid is stupid enough to try to steal from someone sitting here with *me*. Maybe it's a favor to the gene pool to take him out of it before he can reproduce. Last thing I want is to have his stupid kids trying this same shit twenty years from now."

"I recall you once tripping over a step in the backyard and spraining an ankle. I'm not sure you get to talk about the shallow end of the gene pool," I pointed out.

Ether moved his gaze from Dane to me, then back again, as though he couldn't fathom making that sort of joke about Dane. In fact, the way he stared told me Dane wasn't just a scary-looking man, but that Ether knew exactly who he was.

Which meant Dane had a fair point about him being stupid.

"Fine," Dane said, sitting back as though pouting. "We'll just rough him up in the alleyway to make the point."

Ether's eyes went wide.

"Ignore my bloodthirsty companion. Men have a tendency to want to prove the size of their dick by how many stupid ideas they can come up with. As you can see, Dane here is overcompensating."

"Wanna bet?" Dane muttered beneath his breath.

Dane wasn't wrong—there wasn't a thing wrong with his cock. That wasn't a conversation for today, though, especially in front of a kid.

"How long have you been stealing?"

Ether shifted in his seat, as if a conversation was the last thing he'd expected. "A few years."

"Who taught you?"

"No one."

Clearly.

"And you want to do this? Do you think I can't hear it in your accent that you've spent a lot of time in some very prestigious boarding schools? Plus, you aren't nearly good enough at stealing to have made enough money to buy the clothes you're wearing. You aren't stealing because you need to but because you want to. This line of work can be lucrative, but it's also dangerous. Are you just some bored rich kid looking for a laugh, or is this something you really want to do?"

He paused, as if he'd never considered it. Then again, few people did. We moved around on autopilot, and even in those times we moved in the right direction, we rarely thought much about why we did it.

After a long moment, his eyebrows drawn in concentration, he spoke softly. "Yeah, I want to do this. There's this rush, this feeling of power, of outsmarting someone. It's like, for that one second, I matter."

I got that. I understood how insignificant a person could feel, how everything in the world could seem too big.

Ether didn't stop there, though. "I've got two older brothers, both training to take over the family business, but me? I'm nothing. Oldest brother is the heir, the next is the spare and me? I'm just forgotten. I already feel like I'm living in the shadows of other people, so why not take advantage of it?"

I nodded, studying him. I could have asked what the family business was, but in this area of town, it could only be something bad. There weren't honest people, not here. Whatever it was didn't change anything, either. I didn't believe in bloodline grudges, in blaming one person for the sins of another.

Fuck knew I didn't want to have to pay for Kyler's or Jarrod's crimes.

I reached into my purse to pull out a business card and a pen. I jotted down a number and a name, then pushed the card across the table. "Call them."

"Who are they?"

"A middleman who can find someone to teach you what you need to know so you don't get yourself killed. Stealing isn't a bad line of work, but you need to get better at it or you won't do it long enough to make it worth a damn."

He frowned. "Why are you helping me? I tried to steal from you. Most people wouldn't let me walk away from that, let alone help me."

"Because I've been there, stuck, wanting to be more but not knowing how to start. I understand what it's like to fumble and not know what I need to know. I had someone who helped me, who taught me. I figure this is paying it forward."

He tucked the card into his pocket, a reverence in his motions, as if he had no more prized possession than what was written there. It gave me some hope for the kid. Thieves were like any other profession—they had amateurs who made the work into a joke and they had masters.

Ether had the ability to become a master—even with his stupid name.

"I'll give you your first lesson right now." I waved the barista over to take his order. "Slow down and pick your targets better. You should have noticed Dane there, and hunting in areas with known connections to crime is a bad idea. If you'd gotten the wrong person tonight, you'd have been lucky to just lose your hand. When you're ready to practice, hit the fancy outdoor mall in Glendale. It's full of rich soccer moms who have more money than good sense, and because it's outside, even if you're caught, there are a thousand different exits and places to disappear."

Ether nodded, soaking up the information as if he'd been waiting for someone — anyone — to take an interest in him.

An hour later, Ether had taken off, leaving Dane and me in the shop alone.

He stared at me. "Why?"

"Why what?"

"Why help that kid? He was a stranger, and it wasn't like helping him did shit for you."

I wished I could sit there and say it was some altruistic streak inside me, a part of me that gave a damn about other people. That was the right answer, wasn't it? That I just really wanted the kid to be okay, that I cared what happened to him. Hell, even that I got something out of it, that maybe someday he could help me in return, that he would owe me something.

None of that was true, though.

I stood up, having already finished my coffee. "Because I was bored," I answered. "Besides, incompetence is annoying. If he's going to steal, he might as well do it right."

Dane's gaze was heavy on me as I headed for the door, as if he didn't quite believe me.

Hell, I didn't, either. Why had I helped Ether?

Because I remembered being just like him, and it had taken dying for anyone to give a damn. I wasn't some selfless do-gooder — as proven by how I'd just taught the kid how to steal better—but it seemed even I couldn't just turn my back, not when I could offer that kid the one thing I'd wanted.

Someone to give a damn.

* * * *

"You look different." Jarrod stood across from me in my room at the Quad's house. He'd broken in, and, while that didn't surprise me, it still felt strange to see him there.

It was like mixing worlds that didn't normally touch.

Still, I couldn't blame him. With how closely the men watched me, meeting elsewhere had become all but impossible. Still, him being able to bypass their security impressed me. It was easy to forget just how capable he was some of the time.

"Did he call?" I asked, ignoring his statement.

"The stray you picked up? Yeah. Why'd you give him my number?"

"He needed some guidance."

"I'm not a thief."

"No, but you can connect him to someone who can teach him. We both know you have more than enough connections."

He made a sound that neither confirmed nor denied it. Funny that the two of us, who were as close as two people in our world could be, still had so many of our own secrets. We had our own contacts, our own safe houses, our own bank accounts because even we didn't trust each other entirely.

Still, Jarrod would help. He'd connect Ether with whoever he needed to, no matter how much he bitched.

He might not be a charitable person on his own, but he tended to do what I asked.

Was that fatherly concern?

Maybe guilt?

I doubted it was either of those. My best bet as to why Jarrod did anything for me was out of a feeling of owing my mother. It was his penance for not having saved Caroline.

It wasn't about me, but then again, I'd found few things really were.

I'd take what I could get. No reason to turn down something useful just because the person giving it didn't give a damn about me.

"She's grown up," I said, not preempting the words with anything.

Jarrod could keep up all on his own, could figure out who I meant.

"Kids do that."

"How do I do this?"

He shrugged. "Plan hasn't changed. Whether or not Kyler wants to marry her off, we can get to her. Before or after, doesn't matter in the long run."

"We are not waiting until after. You're not an idiot — you know what will happen on the wedding night. A man like Torrance wouldn't just let Kenz say she wasn't ready."

"And Kenz is a big girl who can handle her own. Rushing in there without a plan isn't going to help either of you. As I recall, that was the exact behavior that got you outed to the Quad, wasn't it?"

I pressed my lips into a tight line. He was right, which I hated. I'd gone off half-cocked, angry, not thinking and more than a little drunk. It had allowed the Quad to follow me, to figure out who I was, to complicate everything.

"I'm not going to do anything stupid—" *Again.* "But we can't wait. Not only is the wedding night an issue, Torrance could take her anywhere. I finally found her—I'm not going to let her slip away again."

Jarrod nodded, leaning against the desk. "I've made sure we have access to all the security systems in the house. Untraceable backdoor that will let us shut them down. No alarms, no cameras. The guards inside are still an issue, of course."

"From what I've seen, there are a lot of them. Not to mention, if we start shooting people Kenz knows, she isn't likely to trust us. Maybe the right choice is an in between place?"

"Do you think Kyler is going to allow her out of that house? Seems like he's on high alert right now."

"Maybe," I said, considering it. "If she gives him the right reason, maybe he'll approve it. It'd be far easier to get her from a public location. Fewer guards, more exits, less ability to track it."

Jarrod nodded, the way he tended to do when he agreed with the general idea but still had doubts about specifics.

Which was fair, especially since I didn't have any specifics. That was the worst part of planning things that revolved around other people. It was hard to nail anything down, to predict every little decision.

Jarrod peered at the door, his gaze hard. "Can you handle them?"

"Yeah," I answered with more certainty than I felt.

"You sure? Because so far, they've outsmarted you, caught you in your own plans and have generally fucked up your life—again."

"If anything, this is an improvement. I don't have to try to keep up the game around them. I don't have to worry about them getting the wrong idea, of them figuring out who I am. They know who I am, and they're fine with it."

"Fine, huh?" He made a derisive sound in the back of his throat that said he knew that was a far too simplified word. "And they're just happy as fuck for you to kill Kyler and steal Kenz?"

"To kill Kyler? Yeah. Stealing Kenz is another matter, which is exactly why I didn't tell them about that part of the plan."

"So you're still lying to them?" That lift of his lips said my not being entirely honest pleased him.

"Yes," I assured him. "Only an idiot puts all their cards on the table, and I'm no idiot. The Quad are useful—they have access and information I can't get anywhere else. You don't need to worry. I'm not confusing them for anything other than what they are—tools."

"You know, I remember saying that once. I met this girl—beautiful and smart and completely out of my league. I needed to do a job and she had access to the building I needed to get into. I wined and dined her, told her whatever I had to to get her on my side, all the while swearing up and down that she was just someone I could use then throw away."

"And what happened?"

"Life happened, that thing that likes to fuck up all my plans. Be careful, Nem, because tools have a habit of getting under your skin before you realize it, and when they do? They stop being useful and start being a fucking pain in the ass." He stood, pushing away from the desk and heading for the open window.

"What happened?" I asked again, wanting this piece of Jarrod's past, especially since I knew so little about his life. Despite all our time together, he'd been surprisingly unwilling to tell me much of his past.

He paused, his back to me, then let out a soft, tired laugh. "Well, that tool ended up tearing apart my life, Nem. Only thing I got from her was a lot of fucking heartache and pain."

"Nothing good at all?"

He turned his head, but he didn't look at me. Instead, it only highlighted his face in profile. "Maybe—I got you out of it."

With that, he slid from the window, leaving me there with his advice and revelation. He'd been talking about Caroline, about how they'd met, about how it hadn't gone the way he'd wanted it to.

And he was warning me that the Quad were no different. If I wasn't careful, they'd end up destroying me just as Caroline had him.

Love is a dangerous fucking game.

Chapter Five

Nem

I wasn't sure I'd ever read as much as I had in the last few weeks. I was used to continuously honing my skills, to working toward my revenge plan. Everything over the past ten years had led me to this place, but now that I was here?

It was a lot of waiting, a lot of downtime, a lot of quiet.

That meant I'd raided the men's libraries, each of them offering different books. Dane had ones on psychology and body language, Bray technical manuals, programing guidebooks and biographies, Colton books on warfare, ancient history and philosophy. And Rune?

His was an odd mix. He was the only one to have fiction, and tended to prefer either mystery, thriller or sci-fi novels. His nonfiction, however, seemed to be pilfered from the others, as though he went to their libraries and grabbed items for his own shelf.

Did he read them? Did he not have any hobbies of his own?

I slid the sci-fi book I'd borrowed back onto the shelf where I'd gotten it from, giving the book a solid B. It had been engrossing, but I'd found the characters lacking and shallow.

"Finished already?"

Rune's voice didn't make me jump—I'd grown accustomed to having them shadow me all the time, to the way their voices would break into my thoughts without preamble. It was strange how easily I fell into the routine of having them trailing my every step.

"It was a quick read," I said.

"I like that one."

"I figured that with how cracked the spine is. The story was good, but the characters weren't great."

"No?" He frowned, crossing his arms over his wide chest. "I liked them."

"Of course you did. The main character was a man who got everything he wanted, and his love interest was some damsel in distress who cried six times during the book."

His lips tipped down, as if he hadn't considered that before. "She wasn't helpless," he pointed out. "She outsmarted the bad guys when they took her hostage."

"Yeah, she outsmarted them so *he* had the chance to swoop in and save the day. You like it because you see yourself in the hero position. Imagine seeing yourself in her place? Imagine not getting to see someone like you be the hero, having to just get by until someone else can fix it all."

His frown deepened, but he didn't respond. What was there to say? I was right. It was easy to love a book when it fed my ego, but it was exhausting to keep reading and keep seeing people like me expected to sit down, shut up and wait for someone else to make it all better.

Fuck that.

"You know, I never figured you for someone who was interested in the history of the Byzantine Empire," I said to change the subject, pointing one of the books on the shelf.

Rune's expression flattened, as if my words had slammed shut any openness he might have been feeling. "Why not? I read."

"Clearly you read, but that doesn't seem like your type of subject."

And clearly I was picking all the wrong things to say, judging by the way he stood taller and lifted his chin.

Talk about sensitive…

"I can do more than just punch things," he snapped.

"I never said you couldn't. Reading things that aren't of any interest sounds boring, though. I don't remember you ever sitting out with a copy of…" I squinted as I read another of the books. "*The Advancement of Computer Programming in the 1980s*. That is clearly Bray's book, so what's it doing on your shelf?"

"I borrowed it."

"Along with books on old empires, narcissistic personality disorder and—" I spotted a small book at the end, then laughed. "*Beekeeping for Beginners*. This one was mine."

His gaze softened when it rested on that brightly colored green book. "I remember the presentation you did to convince Caroline that you were ready for a hive of your own."

"I think she was going to agree, but I'm sure it was Kyler who said no."

"Actually, she said no."

"What?" I scoffed. "And here I was blaming Kyler this whole time. I'd worked so hard on that presentation."

"What you didn't bother to ask about were allergies. Dane is allergic to bee stings."

I frowned as I thought back and I considered that. "So Dane was the one who said no, huh?"

Rune shook his head. "Dane went out and bought epinephrine then assured Caroline he'd be fine. Caroline decided risking his life wasn't worth it for a hobby, but she didn't tell you because she didn't want you to blame him."

I considered that, thought about Dane carrying around medication just so I was happy, so I could take up a stupid hobby I'd probably get bored of after a few weeks. It was strange to get flashes like that, to recall how happy I had been.

"What are you thinking about?" Rune asked.

"I've spent the last ten years focused on getting back at Kyler for what he did, planning it, obsessing over it. It's weird to think about the good times, to remember that life wasn't all bad."

He nodded. "Life was good. It wasn't perfect, but it was good. Losing that…" He let out a soft sigh and didn't continue.

What was there to say after that statement?

Losing it would have been hard on anyone, and the Quad had lost all the people they'd spent their lives around. Caroline and I were thought dead, and Kenz had been packed up and moved away, leaving them alone.

I lifted my hand and rubbed at the scar on my chest. It itched every time I found myself drawn backward, lost in the past, in the pain of when it had all been torn away.

Rune dropped his gaze to the mark. "Let me see," he said, his voice low.

I could have argued. He'd seen at least some of it from when I'd shown it to Carlos, when he'd been there to find out who I really was. This was different, though. The lights were on, giving me no place to hide, no way to pretend or dismiss anything. It wasn't in the moment, when Colton had seen it but when we were both distracted by passion.

Yet…for a reason I couldn't quite place, my fingers went to the shoulder of my tank top. I pulled it down, exposing the scar. My bra kept my breast covered, but with the tank top out of the way, he had a full view of the bullet wound.

He came forward, his steps heavy and loud in the silent room. It was one of the times I was made aware of just how large and intimidating he really was. It felt like a bear lumbering toward me, and me? With my scars on display, I felt more vulnerable than I had in a very long time…

He stroked his fingers over the scar, a reverent touch. A soft sound left him, almost as though he were trying to reassure me.

It made no sense until I realized I was trembling.
Pull it together, damn it.
But telling myself to do something and managing it were two different things. He used his thumb to trace the outside of the mark before reaching for the hem of

my shirt. It seemed he wanted complete access, because he tugged it over my head, then discarded it on the desk behind me.

If I'd thought just showing the one scar was difficult, it was nothing compared to Rune seeing them all.

"Three?" he asked.

I swallowed hard, the gulp loud. "He shot me in the chest first, then twice more when I collapsed."

"One," he said, touching the mark on my chest, then waited.

I set my hand over his, moving it to the higher of the two wounds on my side. "Two." I shifted his hand to the last one. "Three. The last two were in through the back, exited in the front."

"Explains why the scars are larger on the front side." He turned me, then lifted his hand to the long, thin scar on my back. "Surgery?"

"Getting shot in the chest isn't like taking a bullet somewhere else. There's a lot of important things there."

"These almost killed you, Nem."

I nodded, remembered the pain, the weakness as I'd bled out, as I'd dragged my body through the smoke-filled house, through the grass in the backyard. I turned to face him again. "They did."

He paused, dragging his gaze from the old scars to my eyes, a question there.

I kept my eyes locked with his as my words slipped free. "The girl I used to be, she died there. You all want to know why I never told you I was alive, why I never came back before, and that's part of it. That girl, the one you knew, the one who wanted to keep bees and be a fucking veterinarian when she grew up? She died there.

She bled out just like her mother and turned to ash in that fire."

"Then who are you?"

"Me? I'm what clawed my way out of her grave. I picked the name Nem because it's short for Nemesis, a goddess who exacts vengeance, because that's all I am now."

He kept his fingers moving over that scar, teasing the skin and my senses. "I remember when she kissed me, that girl, back when she was just a teenager."

"She was an idiot," I whispered.

"I don't know about that. She was sweet, smart and fucking mouthy." He leaned closer, his lips a breath from mine, keeping me off balance with the way he still stroked my scar. It disarmed me, made it hard to think. It felt like him touching some connection between who I had been and who I was now, and I didn't care for those two things to feel so close together.

"You turned her down," I reminded him.

"Yeah, I did. She was too young for my taste and not nearly ready for the things I wanted from her." His lips *finally* touched mine, though the kiss was far sweeter than I expected. It wasn't the angry, rough sex I'd grown used to with these men, with *my* men. He teased my senses with his lips, with his taste, with the gentle stroke of his hands over the scars that had changed everything for me.

When I tried to deepen the kiss, to take more, he pulled back until he could look into my eyes again. "Like it or not, she's still there, inside you."

"How do you know that?"

"Because I loved her in a way I ain't never felt before, never since — except for with you. Ain't no way she isn't still there, because if she were really gone, I wouldn't feel the exact same way about you," he admitted.

The words would have sent me running, but as if he knew it, he slid his other hand behind my neck and pulled me in for the all-consuming kiss I'd craved.

Suddenly, his little declaration didn't matter, not when he pressed against me, when that fire inside me started up. It could burn me and his stupid words.

What a way to go.

Rune

Fuck, would I never get enough of this girl? She felt like an addiction, like a drug, and no matter how much I got, it only made me crave more.

Most women I could kick. I indulged a time, maybe two, then moved on. They were passing distractions I quickly grew bored of.

Nem, though?

Each touch, each kiss, each word from her only strengthened her hold on me and made me want to escape less and less.

And no matter how stupid my words had been, they were true. I'd known it before, when she'd been far too young. I'd loved her, even if I hadn't thought I could ever have her. Now, though?

Now I could have her. I could touch her, taste her, take her in every way I wanted, and she'd only demand more.

She was flighty as fuck, but that was fine. I didn't mind chasing, didn't mind catching her.

She tasted of sweet tea, the sugar lingering on my tongue. The roughness of the scars pressed against my fingers, and she tensed each time I traced the raised mark over her heart.

I loved and hated the fucking things. They were proof of my failure, mocking reminders of what she'd suffered because I hadn't been good enough, fast enough, smart enough. At the same time, they were the evidence of her survival, of where her body had knitted itself back together when others would have given in. They proved exactly how tough she was.

Her words ran through my head, how she thought she wasn't alive anymore. Obviously she was, because I'd seen a lot of corpses over my life and none had ever been on fire like this.

I broke the kiss to taste her pulse, some ritual from me, a need to reassure myself that she was alive, that she was there with me. I spoke between the press of my lips to her soft skin. "You were so shy when you tried to kiss me that time, so fucking unsure. Adorable, really. Guess you grew up, didn't you?"

She let her head fall backward and set her hands on desk behind her, leaning against it, surrendering to me.

And I fucking loved that surrender.

"I'm not some naïve kid anymore," Nem said.

I laughed before teasing a kiss to the top of her breast, beside the scar and just above the line of her bra. I wanted to lavish attention to the wounds themselves, but I knew her well enough to know it would drag her right out of this moment.

I wanted this moment. I wanted to fuck her when I knew exactly who she was, when she knew who I was, when there weren't any secrets between us. "Practice a lot, did you? Was that with whoever the fuck saved you? Well, maybe that'll be enough that I won't gut him for having touched you."

Even the idea of some other man with his hands on her made my pulse speed and my vision cloud. I hadn't ever been possessive, but I fucking felt it then. I wanted to spread her thighs, to lick her until she was screaming *my* name, then fuck her until she could remember no other name at all. I had no idea who this asshole was, but he was enemy number one.

Sure, he'd saved her, it seemed, but that didn't do much to ease the anger inside me at the idea that he'd heard Nem make those passionate little gasps, that he'd seen her when she came.

"We didn't..." Her words trailed off into a hungry moan when I pushed the cup of her bra out of the way and took her pebbled nipple between my lips. I tongued it, then raked my teeth across.

"Didn't what? Didn't fuck? Well, you sure must have picked up those skills somewhere," I teased her, alternating between rough touches and soft ones, ensuring she could never quite keep up, never figure out which way I would go, what would happen next. It was the only way to get the upper hand when it came to Nem, I'd learned.

She was too smart, too determined. The only thing the girl couldn't seem to manage was her own emotions and the reactions her body had.

"I didn't," she said on a gasp. "I never —"

I stopped, pulling away from her now wet nipple, to meet her gaze. She hadn't trailed off that time — she'd stopped dead in her tracks to keep in whatever she was going to say.

And what it sounded like didn't make a bit of sense to me. It felt impossible.

Is she telling me she was a virgin before us?

My cock was beyond hard at the idea, but I forced myself to focus.

She was twenty-seven now. There was no fucking way she was innocent, not after so long...

"You trying to tell me you'd never been fucked before us?" Maybe I could have gentled that statement, but my brain refused to get on track with the whole thinking and talking thing, not when Nem was spread out before me.

She tore her gaze away, trying to hide.

Not a fucking chance. I caught her chin, forced her silver eyes back to mine. "It ain't possible that you were a damn virgin."

"I'm not some innocent little kid." She snapped the words out as if she could think of no worse insult, which said she didn't understand shit.

"Oh, trust me, it's pretty fucking clear you ain't a kid anymore." I reached for the button at the waist of her slacks. "But just this once, give me an answer — a true one. After all these years I spent mourning you, you owe me that much. You never slept with anyone before you came crashing back into our lives?"

Nem shook her head, as though the answer were so shameful, she didn't want to say it out loud.

Which made fuck all sense to me, especially as it really hit me that no one else had tasted her, no one had seen her lost to passion other than my brothers and me. It made that possessiveness inside me worse.

"Are you going to turn me down now that you know?" she asked, challenge in her tone. "You did it before because you thought I was too naïve."

"Yeah, well, that was before. I've fucked you already, Nem. I've had your lips wrapped around my cock, and I've seen you get fucked up the ass. You're anything but innocent anymore, but you know what? The fact you ain't never been taken by anyone but us? We were your first? The only ones to ever have you? Well, fuck, Nem, that's about the hottest thing I've ever heard, and I'm damn well ready to take you again."

I undid the button to her slacks, then shoved the fabric down. They weren't tight, so they slid off her without any work. She was barefoot, making it even easier to get her naked.

She arched her back and reached behind her, unhooking her bra, then slid it down her arms. It left her in just her panties, and I was reminded just what a sight she was.

Her long red hair was loose, cascading down her back with a few strands hanging over her shoulder. The black satin of her panties was dark against her light skin, and even the scars didn't change how pretty she was. If anything, they just added to the sight, to how beautifully lethal she appeared. Her breasts weren't large, tipped with peach-toned nipples, and the sight was like a plea for me to take one between my lips.

Her hips were larger, that pear shape women hated for some stupid reason. It was the sexiest damn shape for a woman in my opinion, a place for me to grab on to, to hold her still while I fucked her. Full thighs that would feel about perfect pressed against my ears, an ass that could easily drive me to my knees, and all the heaven between.

I ran my thumb across my bottom lip as I stared openly and took in every perfect detail of the woman who had haunted my dreams for years.

"Why are you looking at me like that?" Nem asked but didn't cover herself.

"Because I'm about to show you just how adult I think you are."

Nem

Rune's promise made me burn brighter, made me need more. It was one of those times when I was willing to go with whatever he wanted.

He'd proven that I'd like whatever he did.

He set his hands on my hips, dwarfing me with the size of them, then reminded me just how strong he was when he moved me. He shifted me until I was on the desk on all four, though even that wasn't enough for him.

Rune pressed his palm against my back, between my shoulder blades, until my chest hit the desk. The wood was cool against my bare breasts, causing me to inhale sharply at the sensation.

He chuckled darkly before pulling off his shirt then undoing his jeans with a flick of the button. Each inch of his tattooed skin that came into view made me wetter, made me more desperate. I could think of nothing else, nothing before this point and nothing after it.

When he got his zipper all the way down, when I caught sight of his cock, I let out a shameful, desperate moan.

He rubbed his thumb against my back, where he held me in place, as if to reassure me. It made my cheeks heat, knowing just how depraved I looked — *how I look? Fuck that, I am depraved.*

Rune wrapped his hand around his thick cock. He was tall enough that even with me on the desk, I could reach him. He moved his other hand to my hair, taking it in a tight grip before running the head of his dick along my waiting lips. "You have the prettiest lips."

I let my gaze move up, to meet his green eyes, just as I opened my mouth and flicked his cock with my tongue. Staring into his eyes while I did it drove my need to another level, and the lust in his gaze said he felt it, too.

"Fuck," he growled out, his hand in my hair tightening. "You're something, Nem. What it is, I don't got a fucking clue, but I know you make me crazy, make me feel like I can't breathe around you, like nothing else in my life ever fucking mattered before."

I felt that, too, that all-consuming bond. It had been there before, but only a shadow of what it had turned into. Was it age or time or trauma that had thickened it? I didn't know, but instead of thinning over the years, it had acted like the scar tissue of my bullet wounds and had only grown, strengthened, until I had no idea how it could ever break.

And no desire to break it…

He pressed forward, sinking his length past my lips, into the waiting heat of my mouth. I had my head turned to the side, so my body was lengthwise before him. I must have looked small, like a creature he'd caught.

Then again, as I hollowed my cheeks and took him deeper, I didn't feel caught at all. It was a sense of power, especially as he flexed his hands, as his hips rocked forward and he rumbled out more of those primal, almost feral noises.

Feeling like I had the upper hand didn't last long, though, not with Rune. He leaned to the side and ran his free hand down my back, then up and over my ass, which was still up in the air because of how he'd positioned me.

He slid his fingers over my panties, then delved into the warmth hidden beneath. His fingers were thick, but I was more than ready when he plunged two of them deep into my pussy.

"Fuck," he said, his voice low. "Hard to believe you've never had anyone else. I swear, your cunt is heaven. And here I have you, pinned between my fingers and my cock. I figure it's a pretty damn good place for you."

I couldn't argue with that—both because it was true and because of his dick filling my mouth. I never would have figured I'd enjoy this, always assumed I'd find it confining, degrading, yet that wasn't the case. Maybe it was the edge of affection in Rune's tone, or maybe I just enjoyed the sensations too much to care what came out of his mouth.

Rune must have enjoyed my silence, because he wouldn't shut up. "Normally I like to come inside your pussy, to fill you up good and full, but I don't feel all that willing to pull out of your talented mouth. Hell, I swear, the next time I've gotta sit through some fucking bullshit meeting, I'm putting you on your knees under the desk and using your mouth the whole damned time. It'd make the meetings downright pleasant."

I shivered as I pictured just that, as I thought about the passing words between Rune and whoever he had to meet with, how he'd have a hand beneath the desk, pushing me farther onto his cock. I'd try to distract him, because I was a lot of things and none of them included being a good girl. The battle of wills there sounded about fucking perfect.

He groaned and thrust deeper into my mouth. It caused me to gag, but he didn't relent. "You can take me. You manage to do every other fucking thing you put your mind to, so I'm pretty fucking sure you can handle a little cock."

I scoffed at the term 'little' and how untrue that was. He didn't need his ego stroked, but he wasn't close to lacking in that department.

Even still, his words did what he'd meant them to, no doubt, and made me determined to rise to the occasion. I closed my eyes, tried to focus on what I was doing, on breathing through my nose, on relaxing my throat. It wasn't all that easy, not with the way he fucked me hard with his fingers, the way my body was caught between focus and mindlessness, between his pleasure and my own.

"Hard to imagine it could ever get any better that this." His voice had dropped again, so deep it sounded more beast than man. "But you'll get used to it, figure out how to deep throat us without problem. Can't think of a better way to spend time than training every last hole on your sexy little body, especially knowing we were the first and the fucking last." He shuddered, one that screamed of barely held control.

I was determined to make him come first. It was a stupid game, one no one else was playing, but I wanted it. I wanted him to come undone, to have me—a girl with so little experience—bring him to that release first.

My cunt tightened around his fingers, a warning that I wouldn't be able to draw myself back from that edge for long. He knew what he was doing, and he played my body with ease.

I pressed forward without his urging, swallowing against the way his cock sank deeper into me, past my back of my throat, knowing that tightening would tease the head and bring him past the point where he could resist.

He let out a string of curse words that made the rest of what he said seem church-safe, and the kick of his cock, the way it jerked against my tongue, told me I'd won.

I went to pull back but he kept me still with the hand on the back of my head, kept his length buried as deep as it could go. I was trapped, stuck on his cock, forced to relax into the feeling of him coming down my throat.

A moment of panic hit me, but somehow it only turned me on more. In fact, when I struggled against the hold, when he had those two thick fingers of his filling my pussy, I crashed over the edge of my own release. It surprised me, hit me so fast and so hard that my reaction probably seemed like I was fighting him instead of myself.

His groan went straight to my cunt, as if my orgasm only fed his more, as my body tightened down, as each muscle knotted in place before snapping free, taking every bit of my energy with it.

Rune finally pulled back, allowing me to cough before I gasped in deep lungfuls of cool air.

I collapsed, my muscles unable to hold me anymore. I'd have probably fallen off the desk and crashed to the floor—and I probably wouldn't have cared a bit if I had—but Rune caught me.

Though, that was when the reality hit me.

I hadn't cared or worried, not because hitting the floor wouldn't have sucked, but because I was sure in some stupid part of my brain that I wouldn't fall. Even then, in my oxytocin-muddled brain, I'd been so damn certain that Rune wouldn't let me fall, that he'd catch me.

Which was foolish and dangerous.

The last time I'd trusted him, trusted any of them, I'd died.

The Quad had proven they wouldn't be there when I really needed them, and if I wanted to survive long enough to save Kenz, to get my revenge, I needed to remember that.

They're tools. Nothing more.

Chapter Six

Nem

I knocked on the front door to Kyler's house, unsettled by how comfortable I was there already. It was like I already knew the place, already had an ease there.

Colton stood behind me, having driven me for the impromptu meeting. I'd lied to him—or rather, chosen to tell a partial truth—and said I needed to discuss wedding plans with Kyler.

It was true, but Colton had no idea how that led into my real plan. Still, he'd had little room to argue. A call to Kyler had given me the go ahead to come over, and Colton could bitch at me all he wanted, but he knew better than to disregard Kyler's orders.

Kyler opened the door himself. After those first few times, his staff never interacted with me. I got the feeling they had been a buffer for him, a game. Now, however, he acted more...human.

It was unnerving, as though he considered me a friend now. It made my job easier but seeing him as a person felt wrong. It wasn't that I wouldn't do what needed to be done. I wasn't afraid I'd see some side of him that would make me change my mind. There was nothing I could learn about Kyler that would change him from what I already knew he was.

Rather, it felt like seeing a dog walk on two legs, something some deep part of me knew wasn't right. Kyler was a monster, so watching him act as if we were friends, as if he were some normal person, unnerved me.

Kyler moved aside to let me enter, and a nod sent Colton off to the guardhouse.

That was fine by me. I'd already had Colton in my ear the entire trip warning me to be careful, to not be reckless, to realize that Kyler was more dangerous than I understood.

It was a stupid thing to tell me. If anyone understood just how dangerous the man was, it was me. Last I had checked, only I had lost everything, had bled out because of Kyler's actions.

I knew *exactly* how dangerous he was.

"How are the plans going?" Kyler asked as I followed him through the house and to the backyard.

A swing sat there, one that made me pause. I was sure it hadn't been there before, and it appeared brand-new.

Did he get this after he saw me on the swing at the Quad's place?

The thought only added to my discomfort, to a worry that things were happening I hadn't predicted. Being close to Kyler was a benefit plan-wise, but it also increased the risk he might figure me out.

I took the spot on the swing he gestured to, finding a cup of coffee on the side, made exactly the way I liked it. Instead of allowing the questions and confusion to show, I answered what he'd asked. "Good. It's a lot, but the planner seems capable."

Kyler nodded and picked up his own cup. "She came highly recommended. I don't believe there is a well-connected person in this state who hasn't hired her for a large event. And Mackenzie? She's cooperating?"

I walked that line between truth and lie. "She's nervous about the wedding."

"Children like to think they know what's best, and they always rebel against the things their parents do for their own good."

"She's just so young."

"She seems younger than she is. After her mother's death, I fear I've sheltered her and indulged her too much. She hasn't had to grow up because I've protected her against anything that could hurt her. Sadly, I think a lot of her rebellious nature is my fault." He paused, then shook his head. "That isn't entirely true, I guess. Her mother, Caroline, was rebellious as well. I think it runs in her side of the family. Caroline had it, and even though I loved her, it was hard to deal with it some of the time. She tended to do as she pleased no matter how I felt about the issue. She knew how to play the game, but she always wanted to play her own game."

The way he said he loved her made me pause. I didn't hear a lie in it, didn't feel as if he were being dishonest, but the idea he'd ever loved her didn't seem possible. How could someone kill the person they loved?

Then I thought about when I'd pulled the trigger on the Quad, how the only reason I hadn't put a bullet in any of them was that I'd been out.

Maybe, in the end, we'd all kill someone if we felt we had to—love or not. That seemed like more proof that love was bullshit.

He took a deep breath, as if trying to shake the conversation off. "Mackenzie will do what she has to, because she knows her obligations. Her mother was stubborn, just like her, but they both understood responsibility. Just like Caroline got married for the good of her family, so will Mackenzie."

"You know, the wedding would go easier if we could get her more excited about it."

"Excited? I've written you a blank check for the event, the ability to plan it in whatever way she wants. What exactly could she want that isn't included in that?"

"I brought her magazines with dresses in them, so she could get a feel for what she liked. She mentioned wanting to go dress shopping."

He went still, which wasn't a promising reaction. "The planner mentioned stylists coming to the house and bringing any items she is interested in. Tailoring can be done in the same manner. There's no reason to put her at risk by letting her go anywhere."

"I know they can do that, but I think she's feeling trapped there, and it's making her dwell on what sort of future she's got—nothing but more cages."

"Everyone has cages, Nem, and as far as cages go, she's got a nice one."

I sighed and dropped my gaze, playing up the 'unsure' card to the best of my ability. "I'm not trying to argue with you, Kyler. You know best, I'm sure. I just thought, if anyone could make it safe for her to go, it would be you. Maybe by giving a little bit here, it'll show her that she still has things to look forward to, that her future isn't as dark as she thinks it is. It's like any negotiation — even if you hold all the cards, even if you can force it, it'll go easier if you can make the other person think they're getting something they want."

I lifted my gaze to find Kyler staring at me, his hard, blue eyes locked on me. Pressing a point was always dangerous. If I didn't push hard enough, I could get bounced back with nothing. If I pressed too hard, I risked breaking them — and my chance.

"I'm sorry. I didn't mean to overstep my bounds." I set the cup down and stood as if to leave.

"Sit." The command was sharp, and it gave away nothing about how he felt.

I followed his direction, curling my shoulders in, trying to look nervous.

Which wasn't hard because he *made* me nervous. Or, to be more accurate, what he could do if I fucked up made me nervous.

I went to apologize again, but he raised his hand to silence me. "Okay."

"Okay?"

He nodded. "You're right. Fighting Mackenzie on every little detail will only exhaust me and cause her to fight more. It will only make things more difficult. It's a better idea to give in to things that are less important, to make her feel as if she has won on the easy, safer things, and will make her less likely to fight against the more important ones."

"So, she can go dress shopping?"

"Yes. It will be just the one day, so make sure the place you choose will have everything she could want in stock. Alterations will be done at the house. When you have chosen the place — no plane rides, it must still be within a few hours' drive — send me the information and I will arrange security."

"The Quad can make sure it's safe."

He shook his head. "No. I'll hire others for it."

I frowned but didn't ask.

He let out a soft sigh, as if he wasn't used to explaining himself but still wanted to for my benefit. "I took the Quad off her security after the death of my wife and Mackenzie's sister. I trust them with you, but their personal feelings get in the way when it comes to Mackenzie. They often let Caroline and Kelsey get away with things they shouldn't have, so I will ensure the security detail is able to do the job without such distractions."

Doing it that way was probably for the best. Outsmarting the Quad would have been far more difficult than some random security force. The last thing I needed was for anyone getting in my way or fucking up the plan.

Finally, I saw an opening, a chance to do what needed to be done.

I could get Kenz free during the trip, and, when she was safe, face down Kyler and kill him.

For the first time, I could see the end, and that I wouldn't walk away from it didn't matter at all.

The memory of the men, of the fire that filled me each time they touched me, of that yearning for something I didn't understand hit me for a second, as if to rebut my statement.

None of that can matter, I amended. If I focused on what would happen to me, I might stumble, and I didn't have the luxury for doubt.

* * * *

Dane stood beside the limo, his arms crossed and his expression hard. It was the face of a man who was royally pissed off.

Worse, a man angry about something he couldn't do a damn thing about. That was the root of *real* anger, though. Anyone could get mad, but it was the impotence, the helplessness that made a person see red.

And Dane was seeing all red at the moment. I shouldn't have liked that as much as I did, but it was as if that part of him called to me.

Beside him were the other men, all of them looking at me with similar expressions that said they didn't trust me a bit.

The limo was in front of their place, waiting there for me to join Kenz for the dress shopping outing.

"What are you planning?" Dane asked, his voice low so it wouldn't carry into the limo.

"Wedding dress shopping." I offered a smile I knew he didn't buy.

Which was fine. This was almost over. None of them needed to believe me anymore. Wasting my time selling him some convoluted story would have been pointless.

Everything was in place. Jarrod was at the dress shop already, waiting. He would get Kenz out of there, take her some place safe, and in the confusion afterward, when Kyler met with me to figure out what had happened, I'd kill him using the blade hidden in my shoe.

It meant this was the last time I'd see any of them.

Somehow, seeing them pissed seemed right. If I'd spent our last moments together with them doting on me, it wouldn't have felt right. This was us, though. Broken and fucked up and full of anger.

Part of the security detail Kyler had hired already waited for us at the dress shop about two hours away, and the other two cars who would ride with us sat on the roadway, waiting.

I wanted to press my lips to Dane's, to taste his anger one last time. Hell, I wanted to bury my face in Rune's throat, to feel him rumble out that deep voice, to have Bray threaten me once more, to run my fingers through Colton's hair.

None of that was possible, though. There were far too many eyes around for me to let down my guard. If I gave in, if I had one last kiss, I didn't want to share it with random security.

So, instead, I gave a smile — a real one — to the men. "You worry too much."

"That's because I know you," Dane responded. "I know when you're lying."

"You said you couldn't read me."

"Your mouth is moving, so you're lying," he said.

"Don't do anything stupid," Colton added.

"I never would."

Bray snorted and shook his head. He probably knew better than to outright question me — what was the point in that?

Rune darted his gaze toward the street, toward where the other cars were. "I'm serious, Nem. I got no idea what angle you're playing right now, but watch your back. If you get yourself hurt, I'm going to be pissed."

"No need to worry," I assured them. It was easy to do so, because I *was* sure. I wasn't walking into this uncertain about how it would go.

That wasn't because I knew it would be fine, but because I knew I'd die at the end. There was a sense of security in that, a level of acceptance.

"It's been fun," I said instead of any of that 'see you later' bullshit lie.

Dane narrowed his eyes, but I didn't wait for any more conversation before opening the limo door and sliding into the car. We could go back and forth all fucking day, but that wouldn't change a single thing.

I'd made my plan, and now it was time to follow it through to the conclusion.

But fuck… I was going to miss them…

* * * *

Seeing Kenz in a wedding dress about made my heart stop. It was the first time I really had to come to terms with just how much older she'd gotten over the years.

Her dark hair was pulled up into a bun, and the white of the dress made the freckles on her nose stand out. She'd picked something far more risqué than was usual for wedding dresses, but she was young and trendy, so that wasn't a surprise.

Well, it was, but it shouldn't have been.

"You look wonderful," one of the five saleswomen said.

It was far too much help for one person, but Kyler had had the entire shop closed down so he could properly secure it. It meant their employees had nothing to do but fawn over Kenz, and judging by how well they did that, Kyler must have paid them a hell of a lot.

Kenz gave the woman an indulgent smile, as if she knew she needed to be polite but didn't really give a damn about her opinion. She looked my way, though, and smoothed her hands down the lace top. "What do you think?"

I stood, then walked closer, the entire moment surreal.

This was my little sister? The girl I'd thought about every damned night had grown into a woman in the years since I'd been gone. She looked more like our mother than ever.

"You look beautiful," I admitted, the words true.

She paused, as if uncomfortable by the praise. I tried to dial back my little meltdown, reminded myself that to her I was some woman her father had employed — nothing else. My breaking down would seem out of place.

"Sorry," I said with a shrug. "Weddings get me every time, I guess."

The suspicion left Kenz's expression. "Well, this isn't the sort of wedding to get all choked up over."

"Maybe it isn't what you planned, but that doesn't mean it can't still be good." I wasn't talking about the wedding, of course. Rather, I was talking about my plan for her, about the future she could have. Even if she didn't understand my real point right now, I was trying to ease her in, to give her something to remember later, after she was free and I was gone. "I never expected to be where I am right now, but just because I didn't see it coming, that doesn't mean it won't be the right choice."

"That's the point," she said. "*Choice.* This isn't a choice for me. It isn't something I didn't see coming but still got to pick. I don't want to marry him — I don't want to marry *anyone*. I want to live my life the way I want, on my own terms, and I can't do that bound to some man who only wants me because of my last name and my parents and what he thinks that will buy him."

I struggled to keep my mouth shut, to not blurt out everything I wanted to say — that she wouldn't have to go through that, that I had a plan, that she was almost free.

She didn't know me, had no reason to trust me.

Instead, I caught her gaze and held it for a minute. "You're stronger than you think — we all are. We don't think we're capable of something, don't think we're strong enough, but when it comes right down to it, we come out the other side on top."

Kenz furrowed her eyebrows, a look of confusion there, as if trying to place something familiar. I realized my words mirrored something our mother used to say. "I was wondering…"

"Yes?" I asked when she stalled out.

"I don't really have friends because of moving around so much, and I don't have any family to ask." Kenz took a deep breath, then said the next words as if she had to shove them out before she lost her nerve. "I don't have anyone to stand next to me up there. I know it's a lot to ask, but would you maybe be my maid of honor?"

The question took me off guard, making me go still. The more I ended up wrapped up with Kenz, the more it risked her figuring out the truth. Then again, there wouldn't be a wedding, so what did saying yes matter? At least it would make her feel better in the moment.

"Yeah, of course I will," I said, surprised by the way my voice wavered, by the way the question hit me. Before I risked her thinking too much about anything, I changed the topic. "I like this dress, but we finally got you out of the house, so we can't stop at just the one."

Kenz paused before a smile spread across her lips. "Yeah, you're right. Let's try on every damn one and stay out all day."

I nodded, then took my seat and lifted the glass of champagne they'd poured for me. "Sounds like a plan."

* * * *

Bray

"She is such a fucking liar." Dane paced across the small living room of the apartment we'd broken into, his focus almost entirely on Nem instead of the job we were supposed to be doing.

"We can talk about that later." Even as I told him that, I knew nothing I said would change his attitude or behavior. Talking to Dane was like talking to a closed door. The only thing to be gained would be a sore throat for me.

"You *know* she was lying," Dane threw back.

"Of course she was lying. Only an idiot would miss that."

"And you just don't care?"

"I just think the man tied up and bleeding on the floor might be a more pressing issue right now." I nudged said man in the side with the tip of my shoe to prove my point.

The man—Brenton Braid—was a thirty-six-year-old information broker looking to move up in the world.

Then again, it seemed everyone was.

Well, not me. I liked my place, liked knowing where I fit in, what my plan was. At least, I had liked that until

Nem had decided to overturn the table I had placed all my neatly laid plans on.

Hadn't she always done that, though? Since the first time I'd met her, since she had been a kid, she'd managed to throw my world into chaos time and time again. As much as the other men might forgive her for it, I was less inclined to.

Dane peered down at Brenton as though he'd entirely forgotten our whole reason for being there. In fact, the look he offered the bound man almost made me pity him.

Dane wasn't the sort to torture people, but he read them well enough he could reach inside and tear apart their own thoughts, which dug deeper than any blade could reach.

Assuming the man left the apartment alive, which was an exceedingly low possibility.

Dane crouched beside Brenton so he could look directly into his eyes. Brenton was on his back, his hands bound behind him, his feet tied at the ankle. He wasn't gagged, because gagged men couldn't talk, and we wanted him to talk.

"Who came looking for information about Mackenzie Williams?"

Brenton's eyes widened, and he shook his head in an immediate denial. I didn't need Dane's skill to see that for the lie it was. When someone was accused of something they really hadn't done, they tended toward confusion first, then anger. For Brenton to deny it so fast meant he'd expected it. If he expected it, it meant he'd most likely done it.

Annoyance crawled through me at the idea that this fool had thought he could sell Mackenzie out and get away with it, that he hadn't expected us to find out, let alone come after him.

Was our reputation slipping? Were people not fearing us as they should?

Nothing a few grisly murders can't fix.

Fixing one's reputation was easy when we dealt in fear. Fear didn't take a lot to instill, and even less to continue.

That was a problem for another day, though. For today, it was about figuring out who was trying to track down Mackenzie, who Brenton had sold that information to, who he'd gotten it from, then making it clear all the way through that chain why it had been a bad fucking idea. The whole thing was uncovered when a contact of mine had approached us to say Brenton had put out a call to sell information on Mackenzie's schedule and security.

"I would never," Brenton rushed out. "I know better than to betray Mr. Williams."

"Cut the shit," Dane said. "We already know you did. We also narrowed down the moles in Mr. Williams' team down to three people, one of which made a call from Mackenzie's home to your cell phone. All we need from you is who told you, what they told you and who you may have sold that to."

Brenton again shook his head, as though if he did that enough, someone might buy that he had nothing to do with this. Then again, that was like a trapped animal throwing itself at the bars of its cage. They knew they couldn't get out, but they had no other options. Sometimes trying the impossible was the only plan a person had.

"I did get information," he admitted. "But I never sold it to anyone."

I'd watched enough interrogations to know Dane's plan, to recognize the pieces. Knowing in the moment how best to get a suspect to crack was the hard part, but seeing those tricks as they were used, that I could do. Brenton had just decided that the best sort of lie was the one with some truth to it. If he couldn't convince us he'd done nothing at all, maybe he could tell us a partial truth.

He could tell us he'd gotten information from a mole but was too loyal to sell it. We would be angry with the mole, but we'd let him live.

The idiot has no idea how much trouble he's in, does he?

Still, letting people hang themselves require the least amount of effort from us, and the first step a person took down the path, the easier it was to take a second.

Give him a little slack, and he'll do our job for us.

"Who's the mole?" Dane asked.

Rune took a seat beside Brenton, his massive body the terrifying sight it was meant to be. Rune didn't need to say anything to look scary—he just had to be there. Well, Brenton's black eye and busted lip had made the point as well.

Against the wall, Colton leaned, his arms crossed and his eyes locked on Brenton. While Rune was an amazing visual reminder of pain, Colton was terrifying in an entirely different way. The more Rune did, the more he moved, the more he spoke, the scarier he looked.

For Colton, however, it was his silence that drove home the point. As he stood there, Brenton would think about his reputation, about all the bodies attributed to the silent man, all the lives he'd ended and how easily he'd done it.

It was the different between seeing a bear in the middle of the woods, knowing it could eat a person, and catching the glowing eyes of a wolf in the darkness, unable to keep it in sight, not knowing when or how it might pounce.

In the end, they were both just different types of pressure applied to Brenton.

And they worked, just like they always did.

Brenton cracked. "Gary Rochester. He's a driver for Mr. Williams, who took over driving for Mackenzie, and he called me to give me the information. Told me where the mansion was, when the wedding was planned, what the schedules were."

"How much did he want for it?"

"Twenty grand."

"You paid twenty grand for information you didn't plan on selling? That sounds like bad business," I said.

Brenton darted his gaze to me, dismissing me quickly. They always did that, though. He had no idea that I was the one who had found the call records, that I'd been the one to hear the whispers about someone targeting Mackenzie. I might not be the one who would pull the trigger, but there was no doubt I was the reason he'd die tonight. "It was a small price to pay to stay on Mr. Williams' good side."

"If you weren't going to do anything with that information, why not tell Mr. Williams about the mole? That would have gotten you even more good will." Dane lifted an eyebrow as he asked, as if pointing out it didn't make sense.

"You know how information is. There's always a leak, always someone who's willing to sell what others have. I figured if I kept buying, he wouldn't sell to anyone else. If he was plugged, another leak would happen, and maybe that one went to someone else, someone less loyal."

Loyal. I almost laughed at the lie. Brenton was loyal to nothing but money and his concern had been not wanting his source of information to dry up.

"Who did you sell that information to?" Dane asked.

"No one."

"Who?"

Brenton denied it again, the strength in his tone making me think he was trying to convince himself as well. In fact, I'd bet he was going back through his whole damned life in these seconds, trying to work through all the bad choices he'd made, trying to rewrite them in his head as if he could change where he was now.

He couldn't, though. Fuck knew I'd tried that before, tried to fix the things I'd done, tried to change the places where I'd failed or made bad choices. It never worked.

Life didn't give people second chances.

Rune leaned down, placing a knife against Brenton's throat but said nothing. His actions did the talking for him.

Well, and Dane did.

"Playing this game isn't going to get you anything. You've been at information brokering for a few years — you know exactly who we are. We don't show up unless we're already sure. Rune here can make you talk. He can carve out the information we need. He's done it before — he has no problem doing it again."

A thin, terrified whine left Brenton.

Dane kept speaking. "I don't like that method, though. See, it causes a mess, and information can end up wrong, and it really just isn't how I like to do business. I much prefer the simple way. You tell me what I need to know, and we all walk away from here."

It wasn't a lie, not exactly. Brenton would walk away all right—to a holding cell until we were sure his information was good. When it was, well, he wouldn't live beyond his usefulness, and I had a feeling that wouldn't go all that far.

Any resistance Brenton had disappeared at the first drop of blood that escaped when Rune slid the blade across his throat—not hard enough or deep enough for any real damage, just enough to make his point.

"I haven't sold it yet, I swear, but I have a meeting set up for Tuesday. The client is just another broker. If you want to know why he wanted it, you'll have to take that up with him. I told you what I know—can I go now?"

Rune exchanged a look with Dane before they nodded, and Rune removed the blade. He didn't release him, though. Instead, he pulled a piece of cloth from his jacket pocket and slid it into Brenton's mouth, then tied it behind his head. We'd take Brenton elsewhere while we dealt with the security leak and the broker who'd been stupid enough to try and get information on Kenz.

"Why would she lie to us?" Dane resumed his pacing, and it took me a moment to realize he was right back on the Nem track.

"Because she's untrustworthy," I pointed out, already exhausted by the obvious answer.

"You can't tell me you don't want to know what she's up to."

"And we'll figure it out."

"Before or after she screws everything up and gets herself killed?" Dane asked.

Which was a fair question…

"What are we going to do about her?" Colton asked from his spot against the wall.

"What's there to 'do'?" Rune asked.

"You know what I'm asking." Colton nailed Rune with a hard look, the sort that said he didn't care for the whole playing dumb game.

Not that Rune was playing…

He might have been closer than blood to me, but even I could admit he wasn't the smartest man I'd ever met. Not that I'd ever say it out loud…

I wouldn't want to hurt him like that, and he was easily capable of knocking my teeth in if he wanted to.

"To be fair," Dane pitched in, "it wasn't a dumb answer. We've got a distinct lack of options here."

"There are options," I said. When they all looked my way, I went on. "We could force her to tell us the truth. It isn't like we haven't gotten information out of people before." I gestured toward where Brenton squirmed on the ground for emphasis. "We could take her and lock her up wherever we want until we're sure she isn't up to anything that would get her or us into trouble." I paused before offering up the last one, the one I knew they'd balk at the most. "We could cut her off entirely, realize that this little infatuation is a bad fucking idea and headed for nothing good for any of us."

Even though I said it, I knew that was a bullshit option. Even saying it was difficult, as if my mind rebelled at the very thought. Walking away from Nem? Not seeing her again?

Impossible.

"Really?" Dane asked, his mocking tone calling me out.

I dropped my gaze, unable to defend it. Dane would know damn well I was lying.

"Let me make this clear," Dane said. "None of us are willing to walk away. Even before we knew who she really was, we couldn't have left her."

"*Kelsey*," Colton muttered softly, as if he couldn't quite believe it, shaking his head.

And I'd felt that many times. How the fuck could it be Kelsey? How could she have come back into our lives like this? After so long?

I'd mourned her, fallen into a deep pit just as the others had.

I still remembered Rune picking fights, Dane high as fuck, Colton taking every dangerous contract he could find, and me? I fell right into Theresa's trap because I'd been so desperate to pretend I wasn't broken.

Seeing her again hadn't felt like coming back to life, like an injury healing. Instead, it had been like an old bone that had healed wrong being rebroken. It had hurt, down to my fucking core, and I still couldn't shake that.

"It has to mean something," Rune said.

"Life doesn't have meanings," Dane snapped. "I know you want to see some big picture, but there isn't one. None of this means anything except for that fact that she came back with new hair and a lot of new fucking attitude."

I struggled to agree. Sure, her coming back made sense in terms of purpose. If Kyler had done to me what he'd done to her, I was sure I'd seek revenge.

I sure as hell wouldn't have waited ten years to do it, but then again, I wasn't a teenager who'd needed that time to learn.

It wasn't just her coming back into our life that was the issue, but how we felt the same about her. Time hadn't dulled it, hadn't made it disappear. If anything, it had grown. Hell, we'd felt it before we'd even known it was her. It was like there was a pull between us that not even ten years or thinking she was dead could break.

"Whether it means something or not doesn't matter," Colton said. "The question is the same. What now? She's here, we clearly aren't walking away, so what now?"

No one spoke.

Finally, I did it, took the plunge to voice what I was pretty sure we all thought at some level. That wasn't normally my place, but fuck it, no one else seemed to have any sort of idea of how to proceed. "Obviously, we're not letting her go, and I don't plan to lose her by walking away or by her getting herself killed. That means we're going to need to figure out what the hell she is really after and help her."

"And if helping her means we topple the whole damned family? Are we ready for that sort of heat?" Colton asked.

I nodded, the question an easy one to answer. "Yeah. Let 'em come. Nem is more than worth it."

Chapter Seven

Nem

It's time. The feeling ran over my skin like electricity, an excitement that always happened when it was time to finally act.

We were six dresses and a few bottles of champagne in. I hadn't indulged in more than a few sips of the alcohol, choosing instead to pour the glasses into a plant when no one was looking. It was the guards who drank most of it, along with Kenz. By this point, the two guards in the actual shop both had a distinct wandering of their gaze that said the alcohol was doing its job.

Which meant it was time.

I rose. "I'm going to see if she needs help with the laces," I said when Kenz hadn't come out in a while.

The guard by the hallway nodded as I passed him to head for the dressing room. A few paths spread out, but since the shop had been closed for our visit, they were empty. More guards stood watching at all entries and exits of the shop, and the rest of the men sat in the cars outside.

None were in the hallway, or the dressing room, since there wasn't a point. They'd chosen a dressing room without windows, which meant it had no other way for anyone to come in or leave.

At least, that was what they thought.

Little did they know Jarrod was far better at what he did than they realized.

I knocked on the door, and a call from the saleswoman had me entering.

Large mirrors hung on the walls of the room, and Kenz stood in the center on a platform raised up about half a foot.

The saleswoman stood beside her, wearing a black dress probably to help Kenz stand out more. Women were strange, especially ones who were getting married. It seemed there were a million different tiny social expectations to remember, but I didn't know any of them. If was a time when I had to remember just how disconnected from the lives of regular people I was.

"What do you think?" The saleswoman fluffed out the train of the dress.

"I think this one is too old," Kenz answered, her lips twisted into a grimace. "This looks like something my grandmother would have worn."

I had to agree...it was pretty, I supposed, but it mostly resembled a woman on a cake topper. While I didn't know Kenz that well, I sure as hell couldn't see her dressed like this by choice.

"Yeah, this doesn't quite seem your style."

The saleswoman nodded, though a tightness in her cheeks said she might not appreciate the honesty. It made me wonder if she'd picked that sort of monstrosity for her own wedding. "I'll be right back. I'm going to pick a few others from the stockroom."

When she left, Kenz turned back toward me, though with the mirrors, it seemed as though there were six of her in the room. "I can't believe Dad let me come here. I'm sure you had something to do with that."

I offered her a conspiratorial smile. "Maybe. I just figured you deserved a day out."

She smoothed her hands over the dress as if that might make it better.

It didn't.

A creak by the wall echoed in my ears, but I kept Kenz's attention on me. One wrong scream, and the whole plan was over. A smart person never showed their hand until the last minute.

The mirror in the center of the wall moved away from the wall. Jarrod appeared, and relief came over me. Knowing that he'd managed his part of the plan without issue eased me.

Break in before any of the men were in place, but after the initial check days before, and create an opening in the wall. This dressing room's wall backed up against the next store over — an office building for a law firm. Drywall wasn't difficult to cut through, and the mirror created the perfect hiding place to keep it secret from security. The layout of the shop had made it easy to guess exactly which dressing room would get used, which was best protected.

Kenz's guards might have the shop fully secured, but the same couldn't be said for the next business over.

"I think I like the first one," Kenz said with a decisive nod. "I like trying on things and being out of the house, but that one was the most...me. Dad will hate it, and probably Torrance, too, but..." She paused, some of that confidence fleeing. After a moment, she lifted her shoulders in a shrug. "Well, that's too bad, right?"

"Right," I answered.

It was too bad because it wouldn't matter.

Jarrod would grab Kenz, they'd disappear through the wall into the next room, then I'd be found in the room, passed out and a little worse for wear. Kyler would want to speak to me, of course, and when he did that? When I had him alone and Kenz was safe?

I'd put just as many bullets as my gun held into him.

Jarrod didn't know that part of the plan, of course. He thought I'd kill Kyler and slip out through a window or some other getaway plan.

I knew better, though.

Killing Kyler would never let me be free. I'd be on the run for the rest of my life, and that wasn't a life worth living. Not to mention, me being gone as well was the safest choice for Kenz.

Jarrod would explain it all to her, had all the evidence of who I was, of what Kyler had done, and he could help her start over. He'd done that for me—he'd do it for her.

It wasn't much, but it was freedom and a future and that had to be enough. I didn't have anything else to give her.

Jarrod neared Kenz, his steps silent, his black outfit looking far too much like the saleswoman, as if he'd dressed to also let Kenz and her ridiculous dress take center stage.

At the last moment, just when Kenz froze, as though some part of her used to checking for predators sensed Jarrod, he sprang forward.

He wrapped his hand around her mouth, his body larger than hers, able to easily overcome her fight.

"Quiet," he whispered into her ear. "I don't want to hurt you, so I suggest you calm down."

She didn't, of course. I wasn't sure if ever, in the history of kidnappings, anyone calmed down when being told to. I still remembered how Dane had told me when I'd first met him that if anyone tried to abduct me, to fight like hell.

The odds of surviving if I was taken to a second location went down dramatically, and it was better to get shot than suffer whatever the person abducting me had in mind.

It seemed they'd taught Kenz the same lesson, because she bucked wildly. She might have been more successful if she wasn't dressed up in all that tulle and lace.

The door opened, the saleswoman walking in, a single dress over her arm. "I found this one and wanted to bring it in—" She froze when she brought her gaze up to find the scene.

Fuck. Plans rushed through my head, choices, options. Jarrod's eyes held the same things, the same reviewing and discarding ideas at breakneck speed. The hand not wrapped around Kenz's mouth twitched, and I shook my head.

We were not putting bullets into the saleswoman, no matter how horrible her taste was. Part of the reason was that if Kyler believed the person behind this was willing to kill so easily, he'd wonder why they hadn't done the same to me, and I really didn't want another bullet hole to go with the others I expected to collect.

He narrowed his eyes, the familiar color steady and unhappy.

New plan, new plan…

"Let her go," I said, out of options. It was something Jarrod had taught me that the Quad never had. While Dane had focused on keeping me safe, Jarrod had taught me how to win, how to change a plan midway through if I had to.

This was a 'had to' time. This was when I had to move quickly and adjust.

The odds of getting Kenz out were still good, but I needed a witness to make me not responsible for it.

Jarrod's expression didn't change, but I could see the moment he caught on. "No one needs to die here," he said.

The saleswoman started to cry, not bothering to speak or make any sense. I didn't spare her a glance, annoyed by the hysterics. Even Kenz hadn't broken down, and she was the one currently held by a man she didn't know.

It reminded me that some people were stronger than others, that some people were forced to be stronger. Kenz might have been hidden away, might have been protected to the point of being trapped, but that hadn't turned her into a fragile person.

"She's just a kid," I said, walking closer to Jarrod, my hands up. "Just let her go, and you can walk out of here. You don't have to do this."

"You don't understand," he said, holding Kenz tightly despite her flailing. "Do you have any idea the things her father has done?"

Good. Give them a reason this happened.

"Yes, I do," I answered. "And if you know, then you know he isn't the sort of man who's going to simply accept this. It isn't worth the risk."

Jarrod spoke directly to Kenz, and despite the cover, despite the way we were selling a story best we could, his words were true. "You can't possibly *want* to go back to him. You've been nothing but a prisoner."

Kenz met my eyes, and I saw it there—fear.

It was the reason women stayed with men who beat them, why people went back to the things they hated. The devil a person knows can feel so much safer than the devil they don't.

Kenz might not like what Kyler did, but she had no idea what a life without him would look like.

Then again, if Kyler hadn't tried to kill me, would I have believed him capable of it? Would I have walked out a door, especially at gunpoint, and trusted that whatever was on the other side was any better?

Probably not.

I glanced at Jarrod, trying to make him understand.

Kenz stopped struggling, but when someone who was afraid goes still, it was a bad sign.

Sure enough, she lifted her hand and hit the hand Jarrod had placed over her mouth.

He cursed and yanked backward, Kenz stumbling forward. It took a moment to realize what happened.

A pin stuck out of Jarrod's hand, the kind used to tighten the sample dress Kenz wore. She'd fished it out of the fabric, then buried it entirely in the side of his hand.

Which I would have been proud of it if hadn't just fucked us over.

She let out a scream before anyone could move, before Jarrod could grab her again, and there was no way the guards wouldn't have heard that.

Which started a clock for us.

My brain worked, searching for options. Jarrod could get control of Kenz again, drag her out through the exit, but with the guards coming, they'd surround the place in no time. Hauling her would slow him down too much.

Which made the plan a bust. There was no way to get Kenz out, not without risking Jarrod.

I wasn't willing to do that.

Jarrod met my gaze, his lips tightening as if he realized exactly what I had. He reached for Kenz again, no doubt determined to follow through no matter the risk to him. That was so him, too willing to dig in and make things work. The only thing I could think about was the many times we'd argued about him wearing body armor, how he'd tell me he needed speed and maneuverability more than bullet proof vests. That sounded great, until he ended up in a situation where people could shoot at him. There was no way I was going to let him put himself in danger like this, however.

I went forward, shoving Kenz out of the way, putting myself between Jarrod and Kenz. The funniest part was that to anyone else it would seem I was risking myself for her when in reality I was standing in front of Jarrod, defending him from a plan that might kill him.

I tilted my head, my eyebrow lifted, and he knew damn well what needed to happen.

Innocent people never walk out unharmed. The best way to sell innocence is to pay for it in blood.

He pressed his lips together, anger flashing in his eyes.

It was one of those times when he had to do something he needed to, that was best, but he didn't want to. Jarrod was a piece of work, vicious as they came, but it seemed harming me was a line he didn't want to cross.

Still, I could almost see the same lessons that had run through my head, the ones he'd taught me, go through his. He made an angry sound before lifting his hand and swinging it toward me. It connected to my cheek, searing pain through the side of my face. He hadn't pulled the hit—he couldn't, not if it was to be believed.

I let the momentum take me to the ground, and through the peripheral of my vision, I watched Jarrod escape through the wall, pulling the mirror back into place behind him, a snap telling me he'd created some sort of lock so no one could follow him.

A second later, security came into the room, and I forced myself upright on the floor, my face aching and my head spinning.

Well, that had really all gone to hell, hadn't it?

* * * *

It was almost six hours before I could get away from the noise and chaos. After Kyler had been made aware of the incident, he'd told security to take Kenz to the mansion immediately, putting a stop to the rest of the shopping trip.

She seemed nervous, but had held it all together better than I would have expected. It went to show just how tough Kenz really was, that after the frightening event, she still managed to move forward without breaking down.

It meant that when I arrived back at the Quad's, ready to take a breath and try to recuperate from the massive failure, a town car parked on the street made me groan.

I already would have to deal with the Quad once I actually went into their house, but there was only one person who could be inside the other vehicle.

Kyler.

The door to the town car opened, and I gave up hiding. I was pretty sure it didn't matter how long I sat there, he wasn't going away.

I took a deep breath, then left the safety of the limo that was dropping me off. I went over to the town car and slid into the back seat, finding Kyler already there. He nodded at the door, so I pulled it closed.

He reached for me, drawing a flinch from me. The idea I'd flinch from him annoyed me, but it was a reaction I couldn't help.

Kyler didn't stop, didn't seem to care that it had startled me. Instead, his fingers closed on my chin and tilted my head, making the light fall on the side of my face where Jarrod had struck me. He let out a soft *tsk.* "You keep getting hurt."

"You told me it was dangerous being around you."

"It isn't normally this dangerous."

Because I'm the one causing it all…

He let out a soft sigh, then released my chin. "You gave a description of the man who did this, didn't you?"

I nodded. "Dark hair, light eyes, tall. He was…in his sixties?"

"Sixties? I understood he looked younger."

"I'm not good at guessing ages," I lied. "I just know you're in your forties and he seemed a lot older."

A softening of Kyler's features said the compliment worked as intended, to get him to let down his guard. Kyler actually looked every day of his fifty years, and

Jarrod looked younger despite being around the same age.

"Well, I've found out that we had a mole in Mackenzie's security detail, so I know how you were followed and found. The Quad found an information broker who filled us all in."

"Who was it?"

"Her driver."

I frowned as I considered the trip back, and how it had been a different man to drive the limo home. "What happened to him?"

Kyler's hard gaze answered even if his words didn't. Though, it wasn't as if I didn't know damn well that someone who had done that wouldn't live long. A sound I'd heard when getting into Kyler's car came back to me.

Right. That was the driver in the trunk, wasn't it?

I didn't feel bad about that. Sure, *this* attack wasn't due to the driver, but if he was selling information on Kenz, he deserved whatever he got.

I'd have done the same thing if I'd found out about him, if I'd gotten a hold of him first.

"He won't be a threat again," Kyler said. Was he trying to protect me from the truth?

It made me want to chuckle at how horribly he'd misread me.

Still, I was glad to know I didn't have to worry about someone else fucking up my plans. Kenz and a saleswoman had managed it all on their own.

"Mackenzie is scared," I said. Kyler not calling Kenz directly, not even checking in on her, picked at me.

It wasn't like Kyler had ever been an overly caring father or anything, but I guess I'd had higher hopes that he'd give a damn at all. Maybe it was something stupid inside me that still wanted to see Kyler as loving his children in some way. Why, though? What did it matter?

It wouldn't make me feel better, and I doubt it would mean anything to Kenz by the time everything was over.

"She's fine," he answered, wiping away any hope I'd had that he cared at all. "Mackenzie has lived her life knowing the dangers. She reacted well from what I heard, and she is safe and unharmed. She has no reason to be scared."

"Reason doesn't always matter," I reminded him. "I know I don't have a reason to be afraid, but I still am."

"What are you afraid of?"

"You pointed out that I've gotten hurt a few times. Wouldn't anyone be afraid?"

He nodded, sitting back. "I keep telling you that I can keep you safe, and I keep failing that. In fact, you seem to be the one who continues saving the situation. You pushed me out of the way, you stayed alive and evaded attackers until help could arrive, and now you've put yourself between my daughter and danger. It seems you don't need to be afraid of much."

"I guess I'm lucky," I said with a soft laugh, hoping he didn't start looking too closely at just how lucky I'd been.

"I've lived long enough to not believe in coincidences or luck. They're just ways for people to sleep well at night, and I never sleep well. There are too many coincidences for this to not be personal."

"No one would come after you. It would be foolish."

"Yes, it would, but I've found that the biggest threat is always someone with nothing to lose." He put his hand on the door of the limo, tapping his fingers against the buttons there. "About eight years ago, I had a man obsessed with me. He blamed me for killing his wife."

"Did you?"

Kyler tilted his head, no remorse on his face. "Of course." He went on, as if that didn't matter. "No matter what I did, no matter who I hired, he kept managing to slip closer and closer. I ended up in the same room as him eventually, and it was then I realized something important. The biggest deterrent is always threat. The reason people don't do things is fear of the consequences. The bigger the risk, the less likely they'll do it. Most security measures have to do with creating a large enough risk that people won't try. If people believe they won't survive, it isn't so tempting."

His words were the sort that made sense on the surface, but when put together confused me. "I don't understand," I admitted.

He offered me a condescending smile. "Security cameras don't stop crime—they just increase the chances of getting caught afterward. Armed guards rarely stop a gunman before they get what they want—they simply make it more likely a gunman will be killed, and that is often enough for someone to decide it isn't worth it. Well, that man, when I stared into his face, I realized the reason he kept getting closer. He didn't have anything to lose. He didn't care what happened to him after he did what he'd come to do. Cameras, armed guards—none of those things meant anything to him because he never planned to walk out of there."

"What happened?"

Kyler set his palm on his left shoulder. "He fired, but he didn't hit anything important. Colton got there in time and put him down. The thing is, all these coincidences that have happened recently, they aren't random."

No, they aren't. They all have to do with you trying to have your wife and daughter killed ten years ago.

"They aren't?"

He shook his head. "No. One of the first things I learned when I really started gaining power was to bury a body deeper down than you think you need to, because if it isn't deep enough, they have a way of coming back. Someone is pulling the strings right now, and I don't know what they want, but what's happened? It reeks of someone with nothing to lose."

"Have you talk to the Quad about it?"

"They serve their purpose, but I can't rule them out. Who do you think figured out about the mole?"

"Doesn't that make them on your side?"

"No one is on my side. It means they're closer to this than I'd like, and their loyalty is a fickle thing. That's my warning to you, Nem, and it's one I suggest you take to heart. People don't survive in our world without understanding something important. *Everyone* has an ulterior motive, and it's only when you figure that out, that you can predict what they're going to do."

"And how do you figure that out?"

"Look at what they've done. I want you to be careful because the Quad have never been more loyal to anything than themselves, than each other, and while they're useful, they'll turn on whoever they need to. Don't make a mistake and forget that, even for a minute, or you'll end up on their wrong side and find out personally why no one trusts them."

I wanted to argue with Kyler about that, but something inside me couldn't. The Quad were enigmas, laws unto themselves, and I couldn't help but wonder where exactly they rested with this all.

I wanted to trust them, but it seemed I was too jaded to manage it, especially with Kyler's words slithering in my head.

Look at their actions.

Chapter Eight

Colton

Seeing Nem didn't help any of my anger drain away. In fact, the sight of her face already darkening drove my temper higher.

Not that anyone would be able to tell by looking at me. I was a master at keeping my expression blank, at keeping everything hidden.

Rune could terrify anyone by losing his temper but me? I was best served by silence. It let people think whatever they wanted, and people's minds were more twisted than any reality.

"You've got to be fucking kidding me." Rune stood there, his gaze on Nem.

She moved her gaze over each of us, hiding whatever she thought with skills that matched my own.

Well, almost. The tension inside her showed in the lines beside her eyes.

"I'm sure you heard I'm fine." She didn't stop when she walked toward the back hallway, past each of us.

Did she really think we'd let her just walk on by? That she was attacked—and I was damn sure she had a part in whatever had gone down—and we'd let her scurry off?

Not a fucking chance.

I wasn't the only one to think that, since Dane caught her arm before she could pass. "We need to talk," he said without a hint of space for her to wiggle out of it.

And wiggle out of it she'd try to do if she could. Nem was slippery, constantly twisting and turning so she wouldn't get caught. Not by Kyler, not by Kenz and not by us.

That last one was the one that mattered the most to me, since all I cared about was making sure she didn't end up in the grave I'd thought she'd spent the last decade in.

"If you just wanted rough sex, all you had to do was ask say so," she said.

Dane let out an unhappy sound that said he didn't appreciate her humor before gesturing at the couch.

Nem took the seat indicated, probably because she knew pressing her luck now was a bad idea. If she was as smart as I suspected she was, she'd wait for a chance, a weakness, something she could exploit.

We were on our game, though, ready for whatever she had up her sleeve. Plus it was four against one, which meant we had a chance.

"Explain," Rune snapped.

"Explain what? Someone tried to abduct Kenz, and I stopped it."

I snorted. When she peered my way, I lifted my eyebrow. "You know we aren't going to accept that lie."

"It isn't a lie."

"A lie of omission is still a lie. You got Kyler to agree to let Kenz go and you went with her. You picked the place, and you're going to try and tell me you had nothing to do with this?"

"Why would I want any harm to come to Kenz?"

That one stopped me for a moment. It was a fair question, and one I couldn't answer. Nem loved her sister. It was one of the few things about her that I knew for sure. It was one reason I hadn't objected to Nem inserting herself into Kenz's life. She probably wanted to reconnect with her sister. I had no reason to think she would ever do anything that might jeopardize Kenz's safety.

But the idea that this attack was random, that Nem didn't have anything to do with it made no sense, either.

"You said, *'It's been fun,'* when you left," Bray pointed out as he sat at the kitchen table, his gaze locked on her. "That isn't the sort of thing someone says when they think they're coming back."

Nem showed no signs of discomfort. She didn't squirm, didn't bite her lip, didn't run her hands through her hair. All those little things people did to ease anxiety, she lacked.

It meant she was either an expert at hiding them, or she really wasn't bothered by our questions.

It was the sign of either someone sure they were safe or a sociopath.

I wouldn't rule either of those things out when it came to her.

"Make your accusations if you want," she said. "I'm tired. I'd like to shower and lie down. It's been a long day."

I came closer and sat on the coffee table just in front of her. While Dane did most interrogations, he'd already made it clear he couldn't read her worth shit, and I was tired of standing on the edges, of watching as she twisted the others until they couldn't see straight. "You're going nowhere until we get answers."

"Then we're in for a very long night, because I don't have the answers you want."

"Bullshit." I leaned forward, setting my elbows on my knees. "You set up that attack. Why?" She didn't answer, so I went on. "You killed everyone on your little list, save for Kyler. I understand those, but what was the point in this? Did you want to use Kenz against Kyler? Use her for bait? I never figured you'd turn on your sister—"

Nem sat up straight, a fire in her eyes matching her hair. "I would *never* betray Kenz."

Bingo. To get someone to make mistakes, to get them to talk, I needed a reason, a weak spot. For Nem, that seemed to be her sister. Maybe it was wrong of me, but I didn't mind exploiting it to get what I needed—what we all needed.

The truth.

"Well, it sure as hell looks that way. Maybe you realized that killing Kyler was hard, that getting out of there wasn't like the little jobs you did before. Maybe you figured having Kenz as a bargaining chip might just buy you a ride out of there afterward? Hell, maybe you wanted to sell her off to the highest bidder afterward to recoup your loss, as a final 'fuck you' to Kyler?"

She pulled her hand into a fist, and I waited for it to fly toward me. She wasn't the type to slap—no, not Nem—so I was ready to really feel it when she nailed me in the jaw as hard as she could for what I'd said. Hell, I wanted her to do it. I wanted her so riled up that she stopped holding back, that she stopped trying to scheme and plan. If that took a broken nose, well, I'd bear that shit with a smile.

Plus, the thought of fucking her afterward had my cock on board. Something about violence and sex went so well together, and Nem was made of both those things.

She didn't hit me, though. It seemed she still balanced there, on the edge of her control. "I would never do anything to risk her."

"She *was* at risk today because of you."

"She's been at risk! Do you really think I'm okay with just leaving her with *him*? That I wasn't going to get her out of there?"

And there it was. Her eyes widened after she said it, as if she'd just realized what a bad idea it was to say it.

"You came back to get Kenz out of this life?" Dane asked, as if he needed her to directly admit it.

Nem let out a long sigh, that tension inside her sliding away. Maybe by letting it out, she didn't have to hold herself so tightly. "Of course I did."

"So it's not about revenge?"

"Oh, no, it's about that, too. That just happens to go along with my other goal."

"Why do think you need to get Kenz out? Kyler has had the chance to hurt her for a long time, and he hasn't."

"He hasn't yet because he hasn't seen a reason to, but Kenz is still absolutely a prisoner. She can't do anything, can't decide anything in her own life."

"That's how it is for a lot of people. It doesn't mean she isn't happy in the life she has. You can't make that choice for her."

"She doesn't have a choice—don't you get that? She doesn't know anything else, doesn't know there are other choices."

The frustration in her voice made me ask, "Is that why your little plan didn't work?"

She huffed an unhappy sound. "Kenz doesn't know she has options, that she could live a different life. Kyler has brainwashed her into thinking she's stuck."

"She also didn't have a clue whoever that man was—and don't think we aren't going to be talking about *him*. Of course, she wouldn't go willingly. For all she knew, he was some pervert."

"You don't get it. I grew up in the world Kyler creates, and it is stifling. I was trapped, and terrified of the outside world, and didn't know anything else was possible. The only reason I got out was because he shoved me out, because I didn't have a home anymore. Kenz will stay there because she's been taught since birth that she has nothing else."

"You can't make her choices for her," I said. "You didn't want this life, and that's fair, but she might. Maybe she wants the power that she could have from her name, maybe she wants the safety, the money. Caroline reveled in her position, so not everyone hates it. If you make that choice for her without asking her, how are you any better than Kyler?"

That seemed to stick, because Nem frowned, dropping her gaze. It made the darkening skin on her face stand out.

"Now," I added, softening my voice to coax her to answer and to hide my rage. "About the side of your face and this man who hit you…"

She made an almost amused sound. "You don't need to yell at me about that because he will, I'm sure."

"And who is *he*?"

She shifted in her seat, showing the first real sign of discomfort. It made me even more curious about whoever he was.

"Come on, Nem, haven't you figured out that we'll find the truth eventually? It'll be better for us all if you just come clean, now."

Her slow exhalation said I'd won. "He's my father. My *real* father."

And that brought it all together, the pieces of her story that hadn't made sense before. I tried to think back, to reevaluate all I knew based on the new information.

And fuck…it all fit.

Nem had always had these eyes that were nearly silver, ones that didn't match Caroline's dark brown or Kyler's blue. I hadn't thought much about it before, but now?

Everything slid into place, like the final bit of a puzzle I'd needed to understand the full picture.

"Who is your father, Nem?" Dane asked, since apparently, I was taking too long coming to terms with it all.

She blew out a slow breath, as if she really didn't want to say it out loud. Why? Afraid of our reaction? Protecting him?

He had to be someone in our world to have known Caroline, someone skilled enough to aid her not only in training but also in the plan to kidnap Mackenzie.

Did I know him?

"His name is Jarrod."

The name meant nothing to me, not even ringing the slightest bell.

Her shoulders dropped more, as if she were finally surrendering fully. "He's sometimes called The Fox."

Well fuck. That was a name I would never forget.

The Fox was a renowned fixer, the sort of shadow people knew about but never actually saw. I'd never faced off against him, but I'd seen his work enough times.

In fact, a not-so-small part of me felt some amount of jealousy. Him being her father gave me the only reprieve, that it wasn't a competition of any sort.

"You're kidding, right?" Bray asked.

"Nope," Nem answered, her gaze still on the floor.

"How would he have even known Caroline?"

"He was with my mother before Kyler. They split up, but I'm not sure why. He didn't know she was pregnant at the time."

The other part of the story was all too obvious. "And that's why she married Kyler so quickly, because she needed to hide the pregnancy and pass it off as his. Even with her legacy, a child out of wedlock wouldn't have gone well. Did Kyler know?"

"He never said anything."

"That doesn't mean he didn't know. He's always been secretive, and him knowing would explain what he did to you a lot more. Kyler's always been obsessed with his family line. He could get rid of Caroline and you in one swoop, leaving only his blood alive."

Nem frowned, creases in her forehead making me regret having said that. Hurting her wasn't ever my intent, but the world wasn't the sort of place that allowed me to protect her from it all, either.

"How did Jarrod find out about you?" Dane asked, probably trying to throw her off that topic and to a less upsetting one.

She took in a deep breath, that strength inside her still astounding. "He figured out about me when I was around six. He was at a party — he had no idea Caroline would be there — and he saw me." She pointed at her eyes. "I got these from him. The second he saw them, when he saw me with my mother and he did the math, he knew."

"And he just left you?"

"He thought like you did about Kenz, that uprooting my life wasn't right, that I could have things with Kyler I couldn't with him. He lives in the shadows, is always a target. He figured that was no life for a child."

"But he didn't just walk away, did he?"

She shook her head. "He kept an eye on me, had contacts listening for anything about me, and when he got word of the attack, he rushed to the house. It was already in flames, and he found me out back." She lifted her gaze to meet my eyes finally. "I died there. I wasn't kidding when I said I died — my heart stopped. He did CPR, brought me back, took me to the hospital, found a nurse to care for me after surgery, kept me secret and taught me anything I wanted to learn."

"And he helped you try to abduct your sister?"

Nem let out a soft laugh. "He also was the one to set up Geoffrey to try to kill Kyler."

Rune snorted, drawing my focus, along with everyone else's, to him. He shrugged. "Despite everything I've heard about this Fox character, a teenager with a sewing pin managed to outsmart him. I think we've been giving him far too much credit."

The words were met with silence at first, but it was Dane who broke first with a quiet chuckle. That amusement helped to ease the tension.

After a minute, Nem even smiled. "Kenz is a force to be reckoned with. I don't think he was expecting her to be quite so difficult."

"He should have. Both of Caroline's daughters got that damn Hester spirit," Bray said.

Which was a point no one could really argue against. While Mackenzie was still young and less 'in your face' with her attitude than Nem, there was no doubt she had the same backbone they'd both gotten from their mother. The reminder did what it always did and made me think about Caroline. I had loved her—not in a sexual or romantic way. Instead, I'd respected her, the strength she had, the determination. It had felt like we had a bond, some sort of pull between us. Sometimes, in the years since, I'd wondered if that draw hadn't been due to Nem, as if fate had made sure we were where we needed to be. I knew that the world was a worse place without her.

"How did you even plan the whole thing with Mackenzie?" I asked after a moment. "We've been watching you this whole time."

"You're not as good as you think," she answered. "I've met with him a few times."

Rune made a disgruntled snort. "You're not going to the bathroom alone anymore."

"I met him one time in my room *here*."

I nailed her with a hard look at the triumph in her voice. "You think that's a win? All that means is you aren't sleeping in a bed alone, either. If I have to be on your ass every second, I don't have any problem with that at all."

She pulled in a quick breath, the sort that said she didn't mind that idea at all.

Neither do I.

She was entirely untrustworthy, and I had no doubt that even if she told me everything right now, give her a day and she'd have new secrets, new things she decided to keep to herself, and I wasn't looking forward to the idea of bailing her out of anything else after the fact.

If life with her meant being on her ass every second, well, that was a price I didn't mind paying at all.

"So now that your little plan didn't work," Dane said. "What's next?"

She pressed her tempting lips into a thin line.

Reluctant to answer? It didn't shock me.

"Nem," I said, trying to keep my voice gentle. "Did you ever stop to think that if you asked for help, you might get further?"

"How do I know I can trust you?"

Ouch.

I understood the question, but fuck I didn't like it.

Bray answered. "We've been honest from the start — unlike you. We haven't betrayed you, haven't turned you into Kyler, have only helped and protected you."

"But you don't want to help with Kenz."

I refused to lie to her. "I'm willing to consider it. If you're honest, if you let us help, I'm willing to consider a plan that gives her a choice, so long as you give her that choice at the end and listen to what she says."

"And Kyler?"

"Are you asking if I have a problem putting that asshole down? Because you should know me better than that. He betrayed you and Caroline. He deserves to die for that, and I have no problem putting a bullet in his head for it. Hell, I'll happily go tonight and end it."

"He's mine," she answered as she narrowed her eyes. "I get to kill him. I've earned that much."

I leaned in toward her. "We'll see who gets the shot, Nem, but trust me, I've been at this longer than you have."

"To the winner goes the spoils, then."

And that sounded like a great idea to me.

* * * *

Nem

Working on wedding details was strange and entirely unwelcome. I had no desire to pick out flower arrangements or live bands or any other pointless details.

Pointless both because the wedding would never happen and because, even if a wedding did occur, they just didn't matter.

Did anyone really care the exact shade of red for the tablecloths?

"I like this one." Katy, the wedding planner, pointed to one of the two pictures which were so nearly identical I couldn't tell them apart.

Kenz tilted her head at the image, as if doing that might clear it up. At least I wasn't the only one lost by it all.

"I thought having a planner meant I wouldn't have to make all these choices," Kenz said.

Katy sighed, giving her the sort of annoyed look only a celebrity in their business could get away with. "I'm here to help you plan it, but if I picked out everything, it would be *my* wedding, not yours."

I didn't need to even hear Kenz respond to know what she would say — "*It isn't my wedding.*"

Thankfully, an interruption meant she couldn't voice the complaint. A new member of security walked in, one of the countless who now patrolled the large home.

The failed abduction of Kenz had made Kyler increase security in all measures, erasing the backdoors we had built into the cameras, bringing in more guards.

In short?

We were fucked.

I had no clear picture how to get to Kenz now. It wasn't just more difficult — it seemed impossible.

"Kyler is here," the man said. "He's brought Torrance Narst with him."

I turned my gaze to Kenz, to the way the color drained from her face.

I'd never met the man myself, but I didn't need to. The fear on Kenz's face told me all I wanted to know about him.

Sure, any full-grown man willing to marry a teenage girl just because her father had decided it would happen was a piece of shit. We weren't talking about another teenager, about someone as pushed into it by his parents as Kenz was.

This man should know better.

The only thing that kept my temper in check was that the wedding would never happen, and if I disliked

Torrance any more than I already did, I'd just kill him as well.

That made me feel better as we waited for Kyler and Torrance to arrive, with the planner reviewing seating charts and guest lists.

"Have you seen him since this was arranged?" I asked when I couldn't handle the tension anymore.

Kenz shook her head. "I haven't seen or talked to Torrance for probably four years. The last time was just a hello at a party my dad threw."

He hadn't even called her? Hadn't spoken to her directly?

I exhaled slowly, then offered what was meant as a supportive smile.

A few minutes later, the door opened again, and Kyler walked in with the other man.

Yep. I'm going to kill him.

I'd already thought that was a possibility, but now I was sure. Knowing he was older was one thing, but seeing him was something else entirely. The man was older than Kyler by a good decade and a half. He wore a tailored suit meant to disguise the way frailty had started to take over, and the hard set of his eyes implied a man who rarely smiled.

The thought of Kenz being saddled with *this* man turned my stomach.

She rose, as if out of instinct. I didn't, my gaze moving between them, remaining silent to gather all the information I could.

"Mackenzie," Kyler said, then gestured behind him. "It's been a while, but you have met before. This is Torrance Narst."

Torrance came forward and held his hand out until Mackenzie put hers in his palm. He pulled it to his lips and pressed a kiss, an old-world gesture that made me hold back an eyeroll.

I wanted his lecherous lips nowhere near my sister.

"You've grown into a very beautiful woman," he said.

She's still a kid, you pervert.

Kenz showed no signs of being won over, reminding me again that she wasn't a damsel who was going to crumble at the first sign of a problem.

She nodded then withdrew her hand—not hard enough to be rude but firmly enough to show she didn't appreciate the liberties.

Kyler's smile disappeared, lines beside his eyes showing stress. "Torrance wanted to see you after the issue dress shopping."

"I wanted to check on my future bride after such a terrifying event," Torrance said, a haughtiness in his tone that made clear he was as into dominance games as Kyler was.

Good, let them dick measure all they want while I manipulate them both.

"I'm sorry you were frightened," Torrance continued, focusing on Kenz. "I had assumed Kyler could handle your security, but clearly I overestimated him."

"The issue has already been handled." Kyler stood straighter, his chin held high. "The plans for the wedding have gone on, and everything is in order for the event."

Torrance ignored Kyler's words. "The increased security isn't just Kyler's. After the *incident*, he agreed to allow some of my men to join as well. I want you to feel safe here, to know I can take care of you."

He was staring at Kenz as though talking to her, but it was then I noticed he hadn't actually asked her anything. He wasn't talking *to* her, but *at* her.

Kenz turned her gaze to Kyler. "Dad, I don't want more security, especially people I don't know."

Kyler sighed. "I know you don't, but after that attack, I can't really deny him."

"They're going to be people you know soon," Torrance pointed out. "Soon, you'll be my wife, and all your security will be taken over by my people. It's best for you to get used to them now."

Kenz spared him a quick glance before refocusing on Kyler. "Don't I get any say in this?"

Kyler's whole 'we can figure this out' attitude went away, or better said, his façade slipped. He nodded toward one of the exit doors. "Excuse us, please. I need to have a word in private with my daughter."

Kenz pressed her lips together but followed the order. Even after so many years, I remembered one of the biggest rules when it came to life in such a closely watched family.

Never argue in public. Airing personal problems only made people look weak, made it seem like there were cracks that others could exploit. It didn't matter if Caroline and Kyler had screamed for hours before a big party, they would don their nicest clothes and fakest smiles and pretend as if nothing were wrong at all when the first guest arrived.

Kenz had learned that as well, because she followed in silence although I was sure they'd argue once out of earshot.

It left the planner, Torrance and me alone.

At least, until the planner answered what I was pretty sure was a fake call before she excused herself as well.

Torrance's staring was heavy. It wasn't unnerving, like when Dane or Kyler did it. Those people seemed able to peek beneath my defenses to get a look at things I didn't want them to see.

When Torrance did it, if felt amateur. It was a man who would pick up nothing useful, and my annoyance had more to do with him even thinking he could.

"I've heard quite a bit about you," he said, finally, as if he had realized his whole intimidation thing hadn't worked. "It is strange how involved you've become so quickly."

I shrugged. "I hadn't expected to be helping to plan the wedding of a person I didn't know a month ago."

"In my world, it's suspicious when someone shows up out of the blue like this."

"In your world, everything is suspicious," I countered.

He let out a soft laugh, then nodded. "Fair enough. I mentioned my concerns to Kyler, but he doesn't listen to anyone. I could be wrong, but I just wanted to make sure you understand that I'm watching you *very* closely."

At that point, I let some of my mask slip. "And you? You're agreeing to marry a girl you know nothing about. That's at least as suspicious, isn't it?"

"I know everything I need to know, and it all comes down to one word—Hester."

"She's a Williams," I said.

"Not to the people who matter. She's a spitting image of her mother, has the Hester dark hair, the eyes.

The right name can buy a kingdom for someone who knows how to use it."

"And you do?"

His smile lacked warmth. "Of course. With Mackenzie as my wife, quite a few people who were hesitant about working with me will come around."

I leaned forward, setting my arms on the table. "You aren't even going to try and pretend that this is about love?"

"Why? She doesn't think that, either. No one marries in our world without knowing it comes down to power, not love. Mackenzie knows what it's all about. I'm not promising her love—I'm promising her security and a good life."

"Marrying a man in his sixties who doesn't love her is considered a good life?"

Maybe I was pushing the boundaries of what was smart. I should have kept my mouth shut and played my game.

However, I doubted anyone would think twice about me not being a fan of Kenz marrying Torrance. I'd agreed to do as Kyler had bidden, but I hadn't been silent with my disapproval.

Torrance laughed, louder than before but not warmer. "You do have bite, you know that? Most people would recognize that as a very dangerous question to ask." He stared at me, as if expecting me to apologize. When I didn't, he snorted softly. "Yes, marrying a man my age is a good life for her. Women end up with a lot worse, you know, men who beat them, who rape them. With me, she'll have the ability to pursue things she wants—within reason—and she'll have security. I am a man with no shortage of power, meaning she'll be safe, which is the best most women can hope for. In fact, if you really want to help her, you should focus on getting her to accept her place in the world. People who struggle against it don't free themselves—they just suffer more until they're crushed. From what I heard, her mother struggled with that, and it didn't go very well for her."

If he was aiming for a nerve, he sure as fuck just hit one. I leaned closer and smiled, trying to match the same level of threat he had. "I've heard some about her mother, and since we're exchanging advice, I'll give some of my own. I'd be very careful, if I were you. Men have a habit of underestimating women, and if she's anything like her mother? I'm not sure you really want to go toe-to-toe."

With that, I stood, knowing I'd pushed this just as far as I could while still hoping to keep myself out of trouble.

Well, out of *real* trouble at least.

"It was...nice talking to you," Torrance replied, his gaze thoughtful as he stared at me, as if he wasn't sure exactly how to categorize me.

I didn't tell him the same—we both would have known it was a lie.

Instead, I nodded in return and walked out.

Arguing with him wouldn't do anything. What I needed was to make sure he never got his filthy hands on my sister.

And probably plot how to kill him just for considering it in the first place.

Chapter Nine

Nem

I never expected to feel this worn out. I'd trained with Jarrod for years, had learned to keep my body fit and had driven it to the breaking point many times.

However, something about dealing with Kyler, about watching Kenz and feeling helpless, had made my nights short and my days impossibly long.

It had started this damn tension inside me that refused to go away. It simmered, growing in strength until I was afraid it would bubble over. Nothing I did quelled it.

I'd run on the treadmill, I'd tried to lose myself in books—nothing helped. I was as wound up now as I had been when I'd woken, and because it was Saturday, I'd no tasks to fill my day with.

It was almost four in the afternoon now, and I had nothing but a long night of restlessness to look forward to.

Laughter from the living room made me pause when I stood outside Rune's office. While I was sick of reading, I hadn't come up with any better plan to pass the time.

"You're lying," Rune said.

"You only wish I was lying," Dane countered, humor lacing his words.

Rune didn't seem nearly as amused, however. "You never beat my time on the mile run. The only thing you ever run is your mouth."

Dane made a sound, as if he'd sucked in a sharp breath. "You wound me! And to think after all we've been through…"

Before I even realized it, I was walking toward the conversation, as if drawn by the familiarity and ease of it all. Everything in the last ten years of my life had been a struggle, had been an inability to trust anyone, and the way the Quad talked to each other made my chest ache.

I reached the living room before I had a chance to remember it was a bad idea. These men had a habit of turning my world upside down and seeing right through all my bullshit.

And yet, that felt like exactly what I wanted. I wanted to sit there with them, to laugh and recount old stories we all already knew, to feel like I belonged, like they saw me for who I was.

Not Jarrod's daughter. Not a Williams. Not a Hester. Just *me*.

I paused at the edge of the couch, reality hitting me. *What am I doing?* I felt trapped between two lives, two people. Kelsey, the girl who had known them, who had died, and Nem, the one who came back.

The conversation drifted off and all their gazes settled on me, as if they were waiting to see what I'd do. Would I flee? Would I take a seat and accept the company for just a little while at least?

I should go.

Still, even as I thought it, my feet wouldn't budge. I dropped my gaze to the table to find that beside their beers was a single glass of dark liquid — whiskey.

They'd poured me a drink, and not just any drink, but my favorite. It was as if they knew I'd show up — or at least hoped I would — and had made a place for me.

The gesture was dangerous and showed just how far I'd let myself fall into this trap, but it only served to draw me deeper. I took the seat that was open, between Colton and Dane, and picked up my drink.

No one mentioned it. Instead, Dane turned his gaze back to Rune, a pleased smirk on his lips. "I'm telling you, I could have *lapped* you on the mile run!"

I soaked up the conversation, letting myself think for a moment that I really did belong, that this was a life I could have.

It was a nice fantasy…

Hours later, after Colton had ordered food and the men had talked until long after the sun had gone down, I'd found a sense of home I hadn't felt in a long time.

It was funny how quickly the men could make me comfortable. Sure, they were killers, the lot of them, and they'd done horrible things. These were the sort of men who people did not want to find on their doorsteps, the ones others had nightmares about, yet I didn't see them that way.

I saw Rune's prickly ego, easily bruised when he felt he wasn't as smart or didn't contribute as much as the others. I saw Bray's quiet observance, how he rarely spoke but when he did, he made it clear he'd been listening the entire time. I saw Colton's quiet amusement, how he let out soft chuckles at the antics of the others, despite never seeming to feel as if he belonged to the group. I saw Dane's attempts to use humor and lies to hide anything he really felt, but I also saw how that wall came down around the others.

"You tired?" Colton asked, rousing me from my observations.

"No," I said, the word taking two tries to get out. It seemed I really hadn't spoken much during the hours with them, given how my voice cracked.

"You look tired," he added, his dark eyebrow lifted as if to call me out on the lie.

It wasn't a lie, though. At least, I didn't think it was. "I'm really not."

Colton dropped his gaze to where I leaned against Dane, the first time I realized I'd done it. Heat threatened my cheeks, but I absolutely *refused* to blush. I was not some teenaged girl anymore.

"She isn't tired," Bray said from his spot, his beer dangling loosely from his fingers by the bottleneck.

"She looks like it," Colton countered.

Bray shook his head. "She's comfortable. Probably the first time in how many years you've been able to let your guard down?" He pinned me with a look that said he knew the answer but wanted me to admit it.

I couldn't, though. The moment he said it, my head rebelled against the very idea. Despite how I'd just been thinking almost the same exact thing, the words coming from him felt like a threat.

"Hardly." I sat up, losing the warmth of Dane's side where I'd just been curled against. The loss hit hard, but

Jayce Carter

that only made me tenser, made Bray's words all the more dangerous. "It's the whiskey."

"I've seen you drink far more whiskey than that," Dane said. "You aren't drunk, Nem. Is it really *that* terrible that you might actually like us? That you could be comfortable here?"

"Yes." I lifted my lip, as if the idea disgusted me.

It did. Getting comfortable was what got people killed.

"Why?" Rune asked, his eyebrows furrowed.

"This isn't some reunion." I got to my feet when the anxiety inside me refused to let me keep sitting. I needed distance, to breathe without catching the minty smell of Dane's body wash or whatever heavenly scent it was that Colton had—something dark and dangerous. "I didn't come back to fall into some stupid relationship with you all."

"So why did you come back?" Dane asked. "Sure, for Kyler, for Kenz, but you know damn well you haven't spent all this time with us because of that."

"I didn't have a choice," I reminded them. "Kyler assigned you to me."

"He didn't *assign* you to fuck us—again and again."

If he expected to embarrass me, that I'd act like some woman ashamed of my actions, he still didn't know me well. "As you've all pointed out, I was pretty wound up. You were convenient—that's it."

Bray snorted softly, the sound calling me a liar.

I cast him a withering look, one that would have normally sent people running.

Not him, though. Not these men who I couldn't scare away no matter how hard I tried.

"And what is it you're thinking this is?" I asked. "How exactly do you think this is going to work out?

Because last I checked, you four have fucked your way through damn near every of-age woman who steps foot in that club. You aren't the settling-down types, so why the hell do you care whether or not I am? Is this just a game to you? Do you get off on trying to prove I'm some desperate little girl who wants you all just so you can let me down easily later?"

"If you think that, you haven't been paying attention," Colton said.

"Oh, I pay attention just fine. You think I don't hear things? How many girls at the Diamond's Edge have you all fucked? At every other seedy club and bar in town? Don't sit here and act like I'm special, like we're teenagers falling in love and you have to lie to me to get my pants off. I don't need lies."

"I'm not lying," Dane said, drawing out the words as if to prove a point, as if to make it clear that *him* saying that meant something. "You can't hold what we did when we thought you were dead against us. That doesn't have fuck all to do with now, with you, with *us*."

"There is no *us*. This has been fun, and I've enjoyed the sex, but that's all this is."

"Why? Why can't it be more?" Dane rose and caught my chin. He probably knew I'd back away, that I'd try to avoid the closeness, the way he stared into my eyes. "You can lie all you want, but I know you feel it too, Nem. You know there is something else between us, that this isn't just fucking."

I let out a mocking laugh. "Now you sound like the virgin."

He narrowed his eyes. Did he not like being challenged? Too bad. "We know you too well. You're just scared because you feel it too, because you want this as much as we do. What happens with Kyler, with Kenz, that doesn't change that *this* is real, that we're fucking meant to be, always have been."

"What are you, a romantic now?"

"No, I'm a realist, and the reality is that you came back to us, that you could have done this a million other ways, that you could have just fucking said no to us at any time—but you haven't. You want us, Nem. You *need* us."

"I don't need anyone," I bit out, his words like acid dropped on my skin. Needing people was worse than trusting them.

"Everyone needs somebody. You've just been on your own too long, forgotten what it's like, to have someone at your back."

I set my hands on his chest and shoved until he released his grasp on my cheek. "I know exactly what it's like. You want me to tell you? It's getting shot and bleeding out, it's watching your mother die, it's crawling through the smoke, trying to avoid a fire that's meant to destroy you." I closed my eyes, the rest pouring from my lips when I couldn't keep it in. "I fucking *screamed* for you! When they broke in, when they shot Mom, when they turned the gun on me, I screamed your names, but what did that get me? I trusted you all, put everything I had into believing you could do anything, that I was safe because of you and it didn't do shit for me. And that useless girl? That stupid, love-sick girl died that night, crying for *you*, but you didn't save her. Trusting people and needing people only causes pain. She died there, but I crawled out of those flames, and *I* don't need anyone or anything now, least of all you."

No one spoke for a moment, all four of the men staring at me with the worst thing in their eyes — pity.

How dare they pity me! I was stronger now, smarter, and I knew how to play the game. They should pity the pathetic girl who had died in that house, not the person I'd become, the one who stood toe-to-toe with them now.

Bray spoke first, his voice soft as if trying to calm me down. "I'm sorry we weren't there. What happened, it's unforgivable, and we've punished ourselves every day since it happened. Take it out on us if you need to, but you can't let it make you cut off everyone in your life."

"Why not?" Bitterness filled my words.

"Because there's more to life — and you — than that."

Rune shifted, as if to take a step closer to me, but stilled. Not sure if he would be welcomed? "It's like a car. You might get a scratch on it, and that scratch might suck, but you don't throw the whole damn car away."

"Having my father murder me isn't a scratch."

"Sure it is, just a big scratch. You can't decide the rest of your life is a loss because of that."

Sure I can. It isn't like I have all that much of my life left.

I couldn't say that, though, so instead, I went with something safer, trying to make them understand. "You don't get it. You don't understand."

"So explain it to us," Colton said.

I ran my fingers through my hair, pushing it out of my face, trying to find something to hold onto. "You keep thinking I'm still Kelsey, but I'm not."

"You say that, but I can see her. You *are* her. You've changed, like we all do, but you're her, still," Colton argued.

I shook my head. "I'm not. I have this empty space in my chest. I don't feel *anything*. Not happiness, not sadness, nothing. When I say that Kelsey died that day, I'm not being dramatic. I'm not being poetic. The person she was is gone. When Jarrod did CPR, when he got my heart beating again, I came back twisted. I feel like this husk, this empty creature that pulled itself out of that house, that was born from that blood and that smoke. I'm hollow, now — broken."

"You sure as hell feel something when you're with us," Dane pointed out.

I couldn't argue that point. "I know. When you touch me, it's like this fire inside me wakes up, like there's still some spark there, but I can't control it, and it doesn't last."

"It doesn't have to last," Rune said. "If you stop being stubborn and just *stay* then it doesn't have to last at all, because we can keep making you feel that way. And it's proof there's something between us, something that ties us together."

"No. You were just a connection to Kelsey, just something that made me feel like I could be normal again, and I let it distract me."

"We all know that ain't true."

I needed it to be true. I needed the control of believing that the men weren't special. If they were special, it meant too much, made it too risky. I told myself it wasn't true, that they were just some living echo of an infatuation from Kelsey, that I'd let myself want them because of that, and that any other man who knew how to use his cock could satisfied those needs.

I didn't believe it, but I told myself that anyway. It let me reduce them to what they were — just men. Just cocks connected to people who knew how to use them.

Good sex could cloud any person's mind, would make them believe they had some connection that wasn't really there.

Dane slid his hand behind my neck and stared down into my eyes. "Stop fucking fighting this. Stop fighting *us*. Admit you love us." He closed the distance and kissed me, the sort of kiss with a purpose, as if he were tired of arguing with his words and planned to use his tongue in a far more interesting way to prove his point.

And knowing Dane…it might just work.

Which scared me more than anything else. I had too much riding on my plan, on my shoulders, and I couldn't risk letting it go to hell because of them.

I pushed away even though it was the last thing I truly wanted to do. "It's just sex," I told him, meeting his gaze as I said it. "I don't love you."

I turned to leave, ignoring the way their looks tore at my resolve, the way they made me want nothing more than to lose myself in their certainty. I'd enjoyed the time we'd sat there, the first time I'd truly relaxed in so long. I wanted to say yes and see what else they could awaken in me.

I couldn't, though. In fact, the only thing I could think of was showing that they were wrong and proving myself right.

It was *just* sex. Just oxytocin and biochemical bullshit that made a person think they wanted more. It was a biological directive meant to tell someone they should settle down and pop out kids, to override their good sense.

And if sex was all it took to get that feeling, well…

I knew exactly where I could go to find a willing man to prove my point.

* * * *

Diamond's Edge seemed more sinister than it had before. It hadn't changed. The lights, the music, the drunken people grinding up against each other—that was all the same, but it struck me as less relaxing and more sinister.

Probably because I know I'm here to find some random man to screw.

It wasn't my proudest moment—not because of the anonymous sex, though. The idea of sleeping with anyone I damn well wanted didn't make me pause at all.

Instead, it was knowing I intended to sleep with a stranger not because I wanted to but to prove some point. I was a woman who had prided herself on doing what she wanted, on being my own person, and now here I was like a cliché girl at prom pressured into sex I didn't want.

It wasn't some stupid boy pressuring me, though. It was my own fears.

As soon as I went through with it, everything would be better. I'd realize that the men might have started this fire inside me, might have been the first ones to get me on that path, but that didn't mean I needed them for it.

Any man who could work his equipment could give me the feeling I craved, could let me prove that I didn't need the Quad.

Not that I had much time.

I'd snuck out forty minutes earlier, and I'd bet they'd figure it out within the hour. Normally, I'd say leaving my security behind was a stupid move, but seeing that

I'd fabricated most of the dangers against me, I figured I was pretty safe.

Well, from people who wanted me dead at least. I'd bet the men would be furious when they found me.

A shiver of excitement ran up my spine at that, at the idea of Dane wrapping his hand around my throat, pressing me against the wall and fucking me there when he finally found me. I thought about Colton licking me until I begged him to stop, to let me rest, or Rune grasping my hair in his fist as he pressed his thick cock into my ass. Bray, the one least likely to show his anger, would probably watch, enjoying my whimpers, until I was exhausted and the others had finished. The bastard would then probably fuck me once more, making me come even as I apologized.

I groaned softly at how the thought hit me, how my body responded to it. I'd worn a dress to make the whole thing easier, and the panties I'd put on were drenched.

Which wasn't the best way to start proving that I didn't really need them...

I leaned with my back to the bar, a water in my hand. I wasn't stupid, and I didn't plan to dull my senses, not when I was risking getting exceedingly close to a man I didn't know.

Sorting through the options was easy, almost mindless work. I crossed off some men with ease — the twenty-year-old who was clearly using a fake ID to drink was far too young, the two in the corner with wedding bands on yet were checking out women with more than just a plan, the table in the back with men older than Jarrod. None of those were what I needed.

I needed a man who knew what he was doing, but one who I wouldn't risk falling for.

Not that I expected me to go falling in love after a quickie, but given my reaction to the Quad, I didn't trust myself, either. The best bet was a good fuck with a horrible personality. The sort of man who looked perfect but ruined it when they opened their mouth.

That sounded like a fine option to me, because if they wanted to talk, I'd just put their tongue to use in ways that pleased me more.

"Did Ben proposition you again?" one waitress asked another behind the bar.

"Not tonight, no. I think he's looking for someone new."

"Pity," the first said. "He's almost worth the trouble."

"Almost, as long as you go into it knowing he's a lying asshole."

I shifted so I could see where they were looking, and across the club, seated in one of the rooms that overlooked the stage, was a man I didn't recognize. He was attractive, late thirties, with short, shaggy brown hair. I couldn't see much more through the window, but the women's words stuck with him.

He sounded about perfect…

Chapter Ten

Dane

I had no reason to feel guilty, but that didn't stop the feeling from crawling through me and scratching at my insides. Each ten minutes that ticked by, when I hoped it would dissipate, it just grew.

Nem's words stuck with me, made my chest ache and my stomach uneasy. She didn't just think she wasn't the same girl — she thought she wasn't even *alive* anymore. She saw herself as some sort of walking and talking corpse, not really a person anymore. It mirrored what she'd said before to us, made me realize just how real that was to her.

It fucking burned to know that. Anyone with a brain could take one look at her and know it wasn't true, know that she was passionate and sexy and smart and more fucking alive than most of the people I knew.

Telling her that didn't sink in, though. Nem had gotten this shit twisted in her head a long damned time ago and refused to let it go.

And how was I supposed to deal with that? How was I supposed to get her to figure that out when she refused to listen?

"What about therapy?" Bray's voice broke into my pacing, making me pause and look his way.

I'd been so deep in my own head I'd entirely forgotten the other men who sat out back with me. Nem's room was at the front of the house, which meant we had some privacy to talk without worrying about what she'd do to retaliate if she heard anything she didn't like.

When I looked at Bray, he sighed and clarified. There was a good chance he'd been talking for a while, and I'd just missed it all. "Nem. I'd love to say we could deal with her issues, but I'm thinking they're over our heads. What she needs is some professional help."

I snorted at the idea. "Yeah, because tight-lipped Nem is really going to sit down with a stranger and pour her heart out."

"Maybe not at first, but this is for the long run. It won't fix it all at once, but it could help eventually."

Bray wasn't wrong, but the idea of not being able to fix it annoyed me. I'd already failed her once—wasn't that clear by her outburst? Hell, I hadn't been able to shake the image in my head of her as that teenager from before, bleeding and scared and in pain and calling out for me.

And I hadn't been there. I was supposed to read people, to never let a secret pass, and yet Kyler had fooled me for years. It did more than just annoy me—it fucking broke me. Nem had paid a high price for my failure.

So Nem dealing with something I couldn't swoop in and fix ate away at me.

My pride wasn't more important than her, though, so I nodded. "Maybe that's a good idea."

"I'll look around for someone we can trust, someone who understands the risk of betraying us."

It didn't take my long history with Bray to know what he meant by that. If anyone was dumb enough to even think about using what Nem said against her or us, none of us were above putting said person six feet under.

I'd killed men for a hell of a lot less.

Colton shifted his gaze toward the house, as if he could see past the walls and to the fuming woman inside. "We can't just leave her in there alone."

"She might just castrate anyone who goes in after her," Rune countered.

"That's why we have the numbers," I said. "She can only remove the goods from one of us — two, tops."

Rune offered a glare in my direction. "Then you're going in first."

Bray let out a soft sigh. "What if she can't be fixed?"

"Excuse me?" I didn't bother to hide the threat in my tone. Bray might be more than a brother to me, but I sure as hell would kick his ass for saying shit like that.

He leveled me a serious look. "What if she's right and the damage is done? Have you look into her eyes, really looked into them, and seen? What she went through…the years since that she's spent dwelling on it…what if that damage is too deep? What if she can never really heal all that?"

The answer was an easy one. "Then we love her—sharp, broken bits and all. Fuck knows that girl has accepted us, and we're more fucked up than she could ever be."

A nod from Colton and Rune said they agreed, and despite the hesitation on Bray's face, I knew damn well he was all in. He might think things through more, might pause more, mostly because Bray seemed to feel the things more. He saw the danger coming before any of the rest of us and knew exactly how much it would hurt when we crashed and burned.

Even with that, though, he wouldn't be able to walk away. He might question it, try to make us all prepare for the risks, but he was just as deep as I was, as any of us were.

"Guess we ought to face the music," I said, knowing the longer we waited, the worse it would be. Better to go in there, to try to talk to her stubborn ass, to make her understand that she could hiss all she wanted but we were going exactly nowhere.

Maybe that was what she really needed, proof that she had a place whether she wanted it right then or not, that we weren't going anywhere. The girl had gotten it in her head that she was alone, and it was time to prove her wrong.

I went inside, the others behind me. At Nem's door, I knocked.

Her not answering didn't shock me, so I called through the door. "Nem, open the door." When she didn't speak, I sighed. "I can wait here just as long as you can."

It took thirty seconds for me to realize that wasn't true. It seemed I lacked the patience to just stand there and hope she responded. We needed to deal with this, and that wasn't going to happen unless I was in there, unless we were face-to-face.

I turned to grab something to pop the lock with, but Colton held out a piece of metal. I took it and realized it was a paper clip pulled straight. It seemed he was as unsurprised as I was by Nem's hissy fit.

"You can be as pissed as you want, but this conversation isn't over." I slid the piece of metal into the hole on the outside of the handle, twisting it until I heard that tell-tale click. "You can't just walk away and think this is over — we need to deal with it, put it all out on the table and sort it the fuck out."

I tucked the paperclip into my pocket and opened the door, ready to get a punch to the face for my effort. Well, I was hoping for a punch to the face, because I'd much prefer that to her going after my goods.

I scanned the room as the reality became clear.

It was empty. I had no idea how Nem had managed to get out — that was a problem for later — but clearly the little troublemaker had decided that rather than deal with us, she wanted to run away like a kid pissed at their parents.

I closed my hands into fists at the same time as a chorus of curse words sprang up behind me, when the others must have gotten a look at the empty room.

"That little…" Rune let the insult peter out, probably because even if she was acting horrible, none of us wanted to be the one to actually assign an insult to it.

I turned, pushing through the others.

"What are you doing?" Bray asked, the slow way he tended to do when he knew it might not be an answer he liked.

"We're planning a conversation with her, aren't we?"

"Yeah, but she's not here."

"Exactly. Let's go find her stubborn, frustrating ass and have that conversation now."

Of course, she'd made her bed in this. I'd been more than willing to talk nicely with her, to listen, to be gentle, but then she went and ran off.

Now? Now I'd talk to her, but I wasn't in so understanding a mood.

I'd said I loved her, broken parts and all, and I'd meant it. Sometimes that might mean the sweet shit but right now?

It meant showing her my own sharp edges.

The girl had no idea what she'd done.

* * * *

Nem

Ben's hand felt all wrong. He had it on my thigh as I sat beside him, and I struggled to resist the urge to break it for the audacity.

Which I knew was stupid, since I'd come to his private room, since I'd sat myself down without invitation, since I'd come in here for this very thing. The fact he knew it shouldn't have annoyed me as much as it did.

I couldn't help the reaction, though, the feeling almost instinctual. It was like jerking my hand back after touching a stove — my body was rejecting the very action, and no matter how much I told it to quiet down, it refused to.

"I've seen you around," he said, the cocky arrogance in his voice not that of a man who wasn't used to being turned down but one who didn't give a damn if women *did* turn him down. In our short conversation thus far, I'd come to understand what the waitresses meant.

He might know what he was doing when it came to a woman's body, but he sure as shit didn't have a clue how to talk to one.

"Yeah, I'm here sometimes," I answered. I didn't intend to give him any personal information, anything he could use against me.

This was about a need. This was about proving a point to myself and to the Quad. It wasn't about enjoying it, about liking him at all. Basically, as long he knew where to put it, I'd get what I came for. I would prove the Quad were nothing special.

He slid his hand up my thigh until it was just below the hem of my short dress. "I've seen you with the Quad, too."

That made me pause. "Not many people would want to piss them off."

He shrugged. "I like the idea of taking what they have, of tasting what they did."

Tasting made me want to gag, as if I could throw up the word myself and get it out of my head. Instead, I swallowed it down and gave him a smile I hoped was convincing. "I'm not here to talk."

He shifted, grabbing my hips and pulling me into his lap. It spread my thighs out around his waist, but it still all felt *wrong*. The motions were similar to what I knew, but the reaction all different. It was like bathing in slime instead of hot water—same action, different feelings entirely.

I knew why, even as I tried my hardest to pretend this would work. He wasn't *them*. No matter how much it pissed me off, I didn't feel the flutters in my stomach.

I didn't feel a rush of desire, didn't have the fire roaring through me.

Instead, I felt all the pleasure of an uncomfortable gyno exam performed by an inept resident.

Stop it. You're just telling yourself that.

He pressed his lips to mine, tasting of cheap vodka and cigarette smoke, instantly trying to deepen the kiss. The technique was there, I supposed, but it didn't matter. It was like how I hated sushi. How great the chef was or how perfectly they made it didn't change that I hated it.

And I fucking *hated* his kiss, and his hands on me, and his breath.

Get it together, Nem! Get through this, and you'll have learned your lesson, you'll see what you came to see. You just need to relax.

He slid his hand down and grasped my ass.

I broke the kiss, my hand flat against his chest, all of it too much. "Wait," I said without thinking, as if my body had a mind of its own and every intention to use it.

He moved his other hand to my ass as well, then used the grip to pull me against him, to grind me against his erection. "You came up here because you wanted to get fucked—don't play coy now. What, is this the game you want? A no means yes kind of thing? Because I can sure as fuck work with that."

"This was a mistake."

"Leaving would be the mistake." He ground me against him again, but it didn't feel good. It wasn't like when Rune rubbed his hard cock against my clit—even through layers of clothing and set my body aflame. Instead, this was mildly uncomfortable. "I'm really looking forward to fucking you. The Quad walk around here like they're important, like they're in charge. The idea of fucking their newest plaything behind their back feels like one hell of a win. Even better if you fight it, honestly. Lets me feel like I'm stealing you from them."

I almost laughed at that, at how damned wrong he had it, how his big his ego was and how easily I could bruise it. He really thought he was *anything* compared to them? That he could hold a candle to them in any way?

They heated me up with just a thought, and I was starting to suspect this guy could have every battery-powered sex toy in existence and barely get an eye roll from me.

Before I could laugh, though, a dark voice from behind me made me pause and drew the first taste of that fire I'd craved inside me.

"This was a bad fucking idea, Nem."

I twisted to find Rune standing in the doorway, his arms crossed, his tattoos brighter in the lights of the club, his eyes narrowed, with Colton, Dane and Bray behind him.

I was in *so* much trouble, and I didn't bother to try to hide the shiver of excitement that went through me.

Chapter Eleven

Rune

She was fucked.

Sure, she *would be* fucked soon, in a more literal sense, but at the moment it was metaphorical. Nem sat in Ben's lap—a man who fancied himself a playboy but was, in reality, a two-bit criminal who liked to gather protection money for one of the smaller families. His hands grasped her ass, setting my temper soaring, making me want to fuck her and bloody him.

The only thing that saved either of 'em at the moment was how entirely unsatisfied Nem had looked when I'd walked in. She'd looked about as excited as a woman doing her taxes.

So, what exactly the fuck she thought she was doing, I didn't know.

We'd had a fight—sort of—but that wasn't any fucking reason to run off.

Not that her running off was anywhere near the top of my current list of things pissing me off. At the top was Ben's fucking hands on her ass, or maybe his cock against her, or her in his lap, or the lipstick on his mouth telling me he'd kissed her.

Fuck, guess it's a long list....

Nem didn't even have the good sense to look ashamed.

"Guess we didn't teach you good enough self-preservation," I said as I walked into the room fully.

"Guess not, since I died."

I pressed my lips together, hating the way she said that. She wasn't dead, but how to convince a person of that wasn't so easy.

Dane spoke up as he took a seat on a couch next to the one Ben sat on, putting him perpendicular to them. "What exactly was your plan here, Nem? Escape the house, run out on us, and for what?" He dropped his gaze to Ben, his expression dismissive. "A lousy lay?"

"Lousy?" Ben asked at first, as if his mouth were faster than his brain. Us calling him lousy was about the best way he could get out of this alive. At least he seemed to realize it and shut up.

Nem didn't look nearly as worried, however. "You don't own me."

"That isn't even close to true," Colton said, not having moved from his corner beside the door, as he overlooked the room, though his gaze rarely moved away from Ben. In fact, I knew the man well enough to read the way he considered just putting a bullet in Ben's brain to be done with it.

We'd sure as fuck killed people for a lot less.

He was an asshole trying to steal scraps, and he should have fucking known better.

"Listen," Ben said, his tone that 'let's make a deal' one people used when they finally realized just how screwed they were. "I didn't realize she was spoken for."

Nem turned a glare on him that would have withered most men's cocks to all but nothing. "Coward."

Which told me the last thing I needed to know. Ben had been perfectly aware she was ours, had gone into this knowing the dangerous game he was playing.

Did he realize yet how badly he'd lost?

Bray went to the small bar in the back and poured a shot from the vodka bottle there, grimacing after drinking it. "At least your taste in women is better than your taste in alcohol. This is horrible."

I sat directly across from Ben, in an oversized chair that would give *plenty* of room for whatever I wanted to do.

Though I was pretty damned sure I knew exactly what it was.

Nem crossed her arms, looking like a haughty teenager caught but still sure she was right. "You all fuck your way through this club monthly. Why would I think you cared if I did it, too?"

"Because we *told* you, Nem. We fucking told you that you were different, that *this* was different. You can run from it, you can hide from it, you can fucking fight us tooth and nail over it, but none of that changes that whatever this is between us is real. You want to run away? We'll chase. You want to snap and snarl? I'll take the fucking scars for you. You want to come down here and fuck a stranger because your head is so damned twisted up that you can't see what's right in front of you?" I curled my lip into a smirk. "Well, I don't mind dealing with that, either."

She gulped. It was the best sort of sound, one she didn't think about, one she didn't plan. It was proof of how unsure she was, of how for once, she couldn't predict or plan or scheme at all. Goosebumps over her arms and a sexy flush on her cheeks said it didn't frighten her.

At least, it did things other than *just* frighten her.

Then again, I was pretty sure she knew we wouldn't hurt her. She might not want to believe it, might want to fight it, but somewhere inside her knew it. The way she rested against us, the way she turned toward us instinctually said that somewhere inside that hard head of hers was the knowledge that we cared about her, that we fucking *loved* her.

And she had to love us back, didn't she?

It couldn't be possible that a feeling like this could be unrequited, could be a one-way street. This felt like fate, like something ordained from a power a hell of a lot bigger than any of us.

So I had to believe she felt it too, no matter how she struggled against it.

I leaned forward enough to catch Nem by the hips, and the only reason Ben kept his hands — at least for that moment — was because he pulled them the fuck away from her. I tugged until she slid into my lap, facing away from me.

She didn't fight me, didn't even complain. In fact, she let out one of those porn-star moans when her cunt pressed against my cock. It was shaky, as if the sound surprised even her.

The widening of Ben's eyes said he hadn't drawn such noises from her.

Another point in favor of him surviving the night.

Ben went to rise, but Colton made a sound from the corner. When I turned, I found Colton with his pistol in his hand, gesturing for Ben to sit down and shut up. Ben did one of the few smart things he'd done that night and followed the demand.

"Now, Nem," Dane said from his spot to our left, leaning back on his couch, arm thrown over the back. "You came here to get fucked, didn't you?"

She rolled her hips, rubbing her cunt against my length through my pants and whatever she had on under that short dress.

Dane chuckled. "Yeah, clearly you did. The question is, why here? We were there at the house, more than willing to give you anything you need, so why'd you run off?"

She turned her head toward Dane, then away again. *Don't want to answer, huh? Too bad.*

I shifted down in the chair slightly to give her more room, and she leaned forward, her hands on my knees for balance. Instead of giving her what she wanted, I held her still.

Dane didn't stop, though. I doubted he needed her to speak to work through her motivations. He might not be able to read her face the way he could others, but he knew her well enough to figure out what the hell she'd been thinking. "That means it wasn't just you being horny. It's about something else, something you thought you'd get here that you couldn't get there, with us." He tapped his finger on the back of the couch. "Worse, you were doing something you clearly weren't enjoying, which means, again, it wasn't about getting off, wasn't about just needing to blow off some steam, about wanting sex. So, Nem, what was it you really wanted that you thought sex would get you?"

Nem shuddered, a full-body shake as if the tension inside her couldn't be contained anymore. "Stop asking questions and do what you're here to do."

I held tight to her hips, keeping her from the friction she wanted. "You could have made demands before you ran out on us. Now? Now you get to fucking *listen* for once."

I was glad her face was pointed in the other direction, because I was damn sure she had one hell of a glare on her pretty face.

"You said you didn't want us." Bray came around from the bar. "When you stormed out, that's the last thing you said, that you didn't want us, that you didn't *need* us."

Dane snorted softly and shook his head. "That what this bullshit is? Are you here because you wanted to prove you didn't need us anymore?"

Colton chimed in, despite not having moved from his spot, like a shadow watching over everyone. "We were the first ones you slept with, and you thought maybe you could get that same feeling somewhere else, prove it was just a fluke, just sex, huh?"

She dug her nails into my knees, and I let her. If she needed that release to deal with the conversation, with what we were telling her, I'd happily bear it for her.

"You don't know anything," she bit out.

"Oh, I think we know a lot, and I think you do too, now, don't you?" Dane offered a smile that was part kind and part mocking, as if he couldn't help but poke at her a bit for her stupid plan, but also understood just how fucked up her head was at the moment. "Now, you know damn well we're going to prove to you that what you get from us — *with us* — isn't something you can get anywhere else. That isn't the lesson you want to have, I know, but it's the one you're needing. You need to accept what's between us, realize that whatever this is, it's real, and you can't just fucking run out on it and pretend like it isn't."

She twisted toward Dane, and I could feel the frustration rolling off her. "And I get no say in this at all?"

"You always get a say," Dane answered. "You've always been able to tell us no."

"Running out didn't do that?"

"You ran so you didn't *have* to say no. Not the same thing. You want us to stop? All you've ever had to do is tell us no, tell us to stop. You aren't going to do that, though, are you?" Dane nailed her with a hard look, a challenge there. "Come on, Nem, tell us no. Tell Rune to stop, tell us you don't want us to fuck you here in front of your little friend, to prove to everyone — including you — that you *belong* with us, that you get something from us you can't find anywhere else."

Dane offering the out felt like a kick to my stomach, especially with Nem's cunt pressed so tightly against my dick. Still, it was needed, a reminder that despite what we said, despite what she liked to pretend, it really was her choice. It always had been. She wanted to act as if this was nothing, as if she didn't really want us, like whatever was between us, whatever we did, wasn't her choice.

She needed to recognize that wasn't true.

She needed to have the chance to walk away just so she knew she'd chosen not to go through that door.

Still, the wait sent an uncomfortable tightness through my stomach.

She shook her head, the tiniest jerk.

Dane let out a soft laugh, then nodded. "That's what I thought. You want to be here and you want us, exactly like this."

Ben went to rise, but when his gaze landed on Colton again, he sat back down. "Look, I'm sorry, I fucked up, okay?"

"I've seen you around here a lot," Colton said. "And if you think I haven't noticed you like to sleep with the women we've had right after, you're a fool. You can have leftover scraps, can pretend you're more than you are, and I've never really given a damn. What the fuck do I care if you like sloppy seconds? This time, though? This time instead of taking discarded scraps from the floor, you crawled up to the table and tried to steal what's ours. Do you have any idea what we do to people who try that?"

Ben shook his head, but a fear in his eyes said he had a damn good idea.

"We've got a few options, but I have to say, after you kept a grip on her after she said to stop, I'm not feeling all that giving. I could put a bullet through that fool head of yours and be done with it. We could make your mistake clear in the sort of way that leaves you with broken bones and a one hell of a lesson. Or, everyone could walk away from this alive and unharmed."

"I like that last one," Ben blurted out, even folding his hands in his lap like a fucking kindergarten student.

Which sounded fine by me. I'd much rather focus my attention on the frustrating red-haired demon in my lap than the fucking nobody across the room.

I twisted, meeting Dane's gaze, who nodded back at me.

When I released Nem's waist, she ground against me, a broken cry on her lips as if the waiting had only burned her more, made her impossibly more needy.

Which was fine, I was about to give her all she could take...and more.

She shifted up, letting me get my hand between us. I was still wearing my sweats, which seemed like a blessing right then, because I could easily pull them down, wrap my hand around my cock, and slide into the snug heat of her cunt. She'd worn panties, but a quick tug of her thong to the side got it out of my way.

And when I felt the way her pussy felt wrapped around me, when I heard that beautiful gasp of surprise from her, I was pretty damned sure I was in trouble.

That girl could get me to forgive her for damn near anything.

Nem

Rune's cock stretching me was the perfect sensation it always was. I had no idea how, even after all the times we'd had sex, it could still feel like *this*. My body accommodated him better than it had at first, but the burn as his thickness plunged into me, the surprise as it ignited all the nerve endings in my body, created the perfect storm that shocked me each time I experienced it.

And it made me admit...they were right.

Ben didn't make me feel this way. *No one* else had ever made me feel this way. In fact, no one else had ever made me feel the smallest bit of desire, and yet these men could drown me in it.

I wasn't a woman who liked to pretend things that weren't true, who lived in a fantasy world. I'd prided myself on being practical, on seeing the world for what it was no matter how uncomfortable the truth.

It meant right then I had to accept this, too.

I might not like it, I might not understand it, but these men did something to me no one else could. I had to admit it, because a fact someone refused to believe was a dangerous, unpredictable thing.

I moaned, the sound torn from deep inside me, as I gripped Rune's knees.

Worse? When I opened my eyes, when I saw Ben across from me, a strange shame washed through me. On the tail of it, though, was just more want, as if one led into the other.

"See," Dane said from his spot. "You don't get this from anyone else. You could have let this asshole have you, given him a fucking detailed map and all night, and you wouldn't have felt like this."

It was true. There was no doubt in my mind right then that even if I'd let Ben have sex with me, even if I'd given it my all, it wouldn't have mattered. It would have been as unfulfilling and disappointing as his kiss had been.

Rune grasped my hips and set a hard pace. Rune fucking me while not only *my* men, but while Ben watched me as well confused all my senses.

Excitement mixed with humiliation, turning into something different and potent and hot.

"This cunt is *ours*," Rune growled out from behind me, sending a shiver up my back. "We were the first here, the first to touch you, to taste you, to slide into you, to hear those sounds you make, and we will damn well be the last."

I closed my eyes, but fingers carded through my hair and gripped it tight, forcing my eyes to snap open again. Bray stood beside me, my long hair a leash in his hand. "You're ours, Nem. No matter what happens, no matter how much time passes, you're ours. This is a lesson, for you to get it through your head that no matter what you do, no matter where you run, who you fuck, we aren't going anywhere." His grasp kept my face forward, making me stare at Ben as Rune's cock drove me toward release.

It wasn't just Ben I saw there, though. It was every damned thing I thought would fill the void inside me. It was all the things I'd substituted, the things I'd tried to use to distract me.

It was my revenge, the training, the planning, that coldness inside me that had made me feel safe before. All those things were just to hide from what I really felt, to let me focus on anything else.

Ben had lost that fear he'd worn. He stared at me with a ravenous look, as if he could somehow live vicariously through Rune, as if he could feel the way my cunt would wrap around him. *Is he imagining it all?*

It increased all those conflicting feelings inside me, made me feel desired, wanted, embarrassed.

"You like this, don't you?" Dane said, amusement lacing his words. "You're so damned close to coming because you *love* this. You've spent so long shoving everyone away, baring those teeth of yours and getting to do whatever you want, living in isolation because you don't let anyone close. You fucking love having us show you what you're missing, having us chase your ass down and fuck you until you understand how important you are to us. Hell, you love us proving the point to Ben here, don't you?"

Dane dropped his gaze to Ben's lap, then snorted. "He can watch all he wants, but he can't touch, can't have you. You aren't some girl we waste some time with at the bar, someone to get off with because it's been a long fucking night. You're so much more than that, Nem, and Ben here can make fucking sure *everyone* knows it. Hell, if you try this shit again, if you forget you're ours, maybe I'll drag your sexy ass on that stage, put you on all fours and fuck you there with *everyone* watching. You think that'll make our point?"

The thought should have horrified me, but it didn't. Hell, I thought about the dancers I'd seen up there, the lust on the faces of the patrons who watched, then I pictured it being *me.*

I'd had to live my life in the shadows — *always.* First because I was hidden away, protected from everything by Kyler and my mother. Later, because I had to get stronger, had to recover, had to stay hidden until no one would have expected it was me. Finally, I had to make sure I never brought too much attention to myself, that I didn't ruin my cover.

I'd never gotten to be wanted like this, never showed off, never on display, never the center of attention because of me. When I'd been young, people had wanted me only because of my name, my blood, but never me.

Right now, I was exactly that. Rune fucked me hard, while Dane, Colton and Bray watched, a hunger in their eyes and a promise there for their turn. Ben watched me, but he lacked the promise. Instead, it was impotent desire. It was like looking at a mansion knowing he'd never own one like that.

His pants did nothing to hide his erection, but he knew better than to touch it, than to throw off the balance that kept him alive.

Due to my dress and how Rune had only pulled my thong aside, Ben couldn't actually see anything.

Well, other than whatever was on my face, and I doubted I was hiding anything there. It was too much, too overwhelming to even hope to act stoic.

So I gave in, to them, to the lesson, to the insanity of the moment.

Right then, I would have let them fuck me in front of the entire club, to feel as if I was something they cherished, something they'd kill to keep. They'd chased me just because they wanted me and I found that intoxicating.

I'd *never* been desired like this.

Or maybe I had been by them but never realized it before.

Bray didn't release my hair, didn't give me a chance to look away, to pretend the moment was anything other than what it was. It forced me to stay present.

"You're ours," Rune said again, as if the words were an aphrodisiac all their own. Then again, thinking back, he seemed to get off on the idea of knocking me up, of breeding me, of claiming me in some way that no one else ever could. It was a possessiveness he had that warmed me.

And I submitted fully to him, to the moment. I arched my back to take him deeper, my gaze locked on Ben, wondering just how I'd ever even thought I could feel like this with him.

Rune groaned into my ear. "Fuck, I'm close. I'm going to fill you up, and the closest Ben there is ever going to get to you is if he wants to lick my cum up off the floor."

That sent me over—it was filthy and crass and fucking insane, but it did it for me. I cried out, staring at Ben, as my body fell over that edge into almost painful bliss. I didn't know if it was the tightening of my cunt or his own words, but Rune followed me right down. He used his grasp on my hips to yank me down hard, to force every last inch of his thick cock into me as he came.

The idea of having an orgasm in front of someone I didn't know let alone trust would have never occurred to me before, but the men being there made it possible. It was what they'd been trying to teach me, trying to get me to understand. I trusted them. I knew that I could fall into that abyss because *they* were there. They'd make sure I was safe, make sure I came out the other side okay. They'd watch Ben, make sure nothing could hurt me, so I could just fall into that darkness without fear.

It took a moment for me to breathe again afterward, for me to pull myself together.

In fact, for one foolish second, I thought we were done. I expected Rune to pull out of me, to settle my thong back in place, to say his cum dripping from me would serve as a reminder, and for us to go home.

It was a foolish expectation. The men I knew, the ones I loved, wouldn't have been satisfied by just that.

Rune pulled me off his softening cock, making me stand. I might have fallen, but Bray wrapped his arm around me to hold me against him. He took my lips in a deep, aggressive kiss, and even though I could taste the same cheap vodka on his breath, everything else was different.

People shifted behind me, but I didn't bother to look, to wonder, to care. I was drugged on Bray's taste, on the orgasm that still simmered through my body and on the promise and threat of more.

After a moment, hands on my hips pulled me back again. It wasn't Rune's large, wide body that I felt, though. A dark chuckle against my ear told me who it was — *Dane*.

He slid his hands around my front to cup my breasts, to tease my nipples through the fabric of my dress. They hadn't been touched yet, and even that made me tremble and rub my thighs together.

Wetness on my legs reminded me again of Rune, of the fact that it was a mixture of my desire and his seed. My thong rubbed against my sensitive clit, made me whine softly at the discomfort.

"Poor little girl," Dane said, his tone full of mockery. "You're not even close to done yet, though. You really pissed us off, made us get rather territorial, and now you're going to be a good girl and take every last fucking thing we have to give you, aren't you?"

I nodded.

Fuck me, but I nodded. Even knowing how embarrassing those words were, and any other time, I'd have swung my head back and broken his nose for uttering such a thing, right then I just nodded.

I wanted them to take me and to lose myself in this feeling.

"That's a good fucking answer," Dane said before nipping at my earlobe, the sting making me arch my back. He held his hand out to the side, but I wasn't sure why.

Whatever it was ceased to matter when Bray slipped his hands behind my knees and spread my legs. He didn't just move them apart, though. Instead, he slung them over the arm rests of the chairs, opening me to his gaze, to everything. A breeze blew past, teasing my wet cunt even through the panties.

I dropped my head back to Dane's shoulder and wrapped my arms up and behind him.

Bray dropped to his knees before me, then pressed a kiss to the inside of my leg.

Dane shifted, sliding his arm between our bodies. It seemed strange at first, since he could have just reached around me to stroke my cunt, to rub my hardened, desperate clit.

When his wet fingers touched my ass, however, the reasoning became clear. I tensed, both in surprise and with that immediate 'hell no' that seemed instinctual.

He chuckled, undeterred, and teased my ass with his lubed fingers. How he'd lubed them, I didn't know, but it wasn't like I was paying close attention to anything beyond my body. Why did details matter?

"We've been through this," he whispered to me. "You can fight it all you want, can tense that pretty little asshole to keep me out, but it won't stop me. Unless you tell me no, I'm going to finger your ass, then I'm going to fuck it. You sure as hell will remember who this ass belongs to then, won't you?" He pressed harder, as if proving his point, as if reminding me that while I had the power to make them stop, short of that, he was going to use my body as he damned well pleased.

His finger slid into me, the feeling shocking as all those nerve endings that got so little attention lit up beneath his expert touch.

Bray moved up my thigh with his lips, stopping at each spot of wetness. He licked those areas, cleaning them with his tongue, uncaring if it was my wetness or Rune's cum.

Which drove my need even higher. It was depraved and twisted and Ben watched the whole damned thing with rapt attention. The men didn't touch me like it was shameful, like I was a thing that didn't matter, like I was just some toy to them. They didn't give a fuck what Ben thought, other than laying their claim on me.

Bray kept going up, switching from one leg to the other, until he reached my cunt. He hooked a finger into the crotch of my thong and pulled it aside his head blocking Ben from seeing me directly. It gave me an odd sense of security, as if this was for my men only.

The first swipe of Bray's tongue against my slit threw me over that edge again, had me coming hard on a thin whine, tightening around Dane's finger.

I clutched the back of Dane's neck, trying to hold on against the waves of pleasure that rushed through me. My eyes slid closed, letting me bask in the sensation.

Something pressed against my lips, and I forced my exhausted eyes to open, forced myself to look over and find Colton with his thumb stroking my bottom lip. It wasn't a question, but I still answered as if it were, taking him into my mouth and wrapping my tongue around him.

Dane withdrew his fingers, and after another moment of shifting, when Colton used his other hand on my arm to get me to rise, the thick head of Dane's cock pressed against my ass. A press on my shoulder by Colton had me sinking down, had Dane's cock breaching my ass and delving into me.

I might have been more focused on that overwhelming feeling, but Bray wouldn't allow me to drown in it. Instead, he lapped at my pussy, his tongue burrowing into my folds, swallowing everything he could find. He kept the thong out of the way with that one finger, and used his arms to keep my legs spread open and at his mercy, at all their mercies, and sent another powerful rush of need through me.

Across the room, Ben still sat, enraptured, his gaze pinned on them, on me. Rune was on the couch where Dane had been before, a gun in his hand, watching Ben carefully now that Colton was distracted. That gave me the confidence again, reassured me that he had it well in hand.

Rune turned his gaze for a split second to me and gave me a breath-stealing smile, the kind that could have nearly made me come from the sight of it alone.

Dane didn't take long to feed every inch of his cock into me, and even though the feeling was almost painful, so full and overwhelming and just this side of too much, I relished it. It was the men at their core. They weren't soft men — they weren't men who walked quietly and carefully and pleaded for things.

They were warriors who took what they wanted, and they wanted me.

I shivered when Dane grasped my waist and made me ride him, made me move up and down, dragging his length against the hyper-sensitive walls of my ass.

I'm a warrior, too. It struck me then that they weren't the only ones taking. I was taking them, claiming them. Just like Ben sat there as witness, as they made it clear I was theirs, I curled my fingers in, digging my nails against the back of Dane's neck, claiming him, claiming them all.

They were *mine*. How long I'd have them and where this was all headed didn't matter. None of that changed that they were mine, that they'd always been mine, and fighting that truth was pointless.

"There you go," Dane whispered into my ear, as if he could tell I'd worked it out, that I'd really given in, that I'd heard them.

Colton hooked his thumb behind my teeth to turn my head toward him. He'd undone his pants, his cock there, waiting.

And I didn't have to think at all before I bent slightly and wrapped my full lips around his thick shaft.

I closed Ben out, closed the whole world out, shut my eyes and lost myself in the now. I wasn't someone who practiced mindfulness, who understood the obsession with meditation and living in the moment, but right then, I got it.

Colton slid his hand into my hair and used my mouth like a toy, tilting my head, rubbing his cock against the inside of my cheek, tapping on my chin to get me to tighten my lips. It was controlling and so incredibly hot.

"Fuck," Dane said with a groan. "You ass feels fantastic, but have I ever told you just how good you look choking on a cock? Because your lips spread out, and I can see when he pushes against your cheek. Each time you gag, your ass tightens up."

A rush of pleasure ran up my spine as his praise.

Or maybe it was Bray's talented tongue that hadn't stopped. I'd guess he'd gotten every drop of cum—he sure was thorough—because he'd focused on my clit, now. He didn't tease, didn't go gentle. Instead, he flicked his tongue over it, then ground against it.

Sparks rushed through my vision, playing against my eyelids. Colton slipped his hand into my dress, then closed his fingers around my nipple. He pinched tightly, as if each of them needed to make fucking sure I knew they were there.

My cunt ached from Rune fucking me, Colton gripped my nipple in an impossibly tight hold while he drove his cock into my waiting mouth, Bray sucked on my clit as if the meaning of life were there and Dane fucked my ass with short, hard thrusts that drove me mad. There was no way I could forget any of them, because they each claimed me in their own way.

"Almost there," Dane said, his voice rough. "Open your eyes, Nem."

I didn't want to. I wanted to bask in the darkness, in the sensation.

Bray closed his teeth on my clit in punishment when I ignored the demand, so I popped my eyes open.

Dane yanked me down, grinding himself against me, as if to prove the point of just how deep into my ass he was. "Look over at Ben. I want you to fucking *look* at him when you come one last time, when you fucking fall apart on our cocks and our tongues."

Colton pulled back enough that I could glance to the side to see Ben. The desire burning inside me wasn't because of him. It had never been because of him, never caused by him, never for him. That was what Dane wanted, for me to be faced with that, for me to have to admit it to myself.

Still, Dane didn't stop talking—*does he ever?* "You came here to get fucked by anyone because you were running away, but that isn't going to work for you. Anytime you try it, anytime you think about it, we'll be right fucking here to explain shit to you again and again. Whether you like it or not, I fucking *love* you, and so do they." He placed one hand up, around the front of my throat, reminding me of how he'd done that before. "So I want you looking at him when you come, I want you to fucking *remember* this moment so the next time you decide to doubt us, the next time you want to act like there isn't anything between us, you come back to this goddamned moment."

I had no choice but to obey. The way he spoke, the picture he painted, it was exactly what I wanted — what I'd always wanted.

To matter to someone for who I was — who I *really* was. Even Ben hadn't given a fuck about me, about what I wanted, about the person I was.

The Quad, though, they knew. They knew the ugly parts of me, the cracks beneath the surface, the empty wounds where life had carved away the flesh. They'd seen my scars, had kissed each one, and they were still here to claim me even when I tried so damned hard to shove them away.

So I stared at Ben as Colton came first, his hot cum spilling onto my tongue, forcing me to swallow because I wanted to instead of pushing in deep enough I didn't have a choice.

Not that there was much of a choice. I happily swallowed him down, teasing my tongue against his cock as he pulled free.

Dane came next, an almost feral sound leaving him as he bit down on my shoulder, pulling me flush against him so his cock was fully buried in my ass. He panted, not releasing the bite, like some wild animal driven to hold its mate still while he filled her.

He didn't pull out, though, and the reason became clear when Bray drove three of his fingers into my sore cunt, when he filled me as he tilted his head and latched onto my swollen clit.

This orgasm hit me harder than the others, but I kept my eyes open as Dane had told me to. I stared right at Ben, at the idiot who had thought he could stand in for these men, at the man I'd been dumb enough to think could replace them. I arched, the action dragging Dane's cock against my ass, reminding me how damned full I was, and I didn't hide the sound I made.

There was no way the rest of the club outside the window didn't hear, but I didn't give a damn. Why would I? I was drowning and flying all at once, driven to my limits and shoved right the fuck over them.

By the time I collapsed against Dane, when the tension in my body snapped and I could do nothing but pant and whimper, when I finally shut my eyes, too exhausted to hold them open anymore, I had to admit the truth to myself.

I loved them, and that was even more dangerous than Kyler.

Chapter Twelve

Jarrod

I could kill them.

I didn't think that with arrogance, as if I needed to stroke my ego and assure myself I was better. I felt the need to prove nothing when it came to these four men.

However, rather than doing that, I stayed put and waited as they approached my table in the little Mexican restaurant. I'd known they were looking for me — they weren't as smooth as they thought, and anyone who came looking for me, I saw coming. That was why I'd put out the information they needed — my location — and planted my ass in this spot, waiting for them. It was always better to know when someone was coming than to risk getting caught unaware.

I'd heard about these four plenty even without their connection to Nem. They'd made waves in my world, and that made them worth my notice. I wouldn't call them threats, but they were at least interesting.

The four moved almost as one, the connection between them the real risk they posed. Each one was vicious and capable on their own, but when together, the four created something nearly impossible to counter.

And now the four who had failed to protect my daughter, who held the blame for her suffering, had some twisted affair going on with her.

I wasn't a 'cleaning my shotgun in front of the boyfriend' type of father, but I was a 'put a bullet through their skull at seven-hundred meters because fuck them' sort of father.

"Jarrod," Dane said, his leather jacket making him look like a man who hadn't gotten over not being in high school anymore.

"So you found me." I gestured at the chairs around the table. "Take a seat."

They all did so, the lot of us seeming about as trusting as junkyard dogs. Then again, that was how people acted when they knew everyone at the table was a killer. If nothing else, at least it was honest.

"You knew we were coming," Bray said, the light reflecting off the septum ring that hung in his nose. Would he never outgrow his rebellious stage?

"Of course I did. Why do you think I picked this place?"

Bray pressed his lips into a thin line. *So he doesn't like being outsmarted? Too bad.*

"What do you want? You went through a lot of trouble to find me, so let's get this meet-and-greet over with." I didn't rush because I cared what the hell they wanted, but because sitting out in the open made me edgy. The number of people who ever saw my face, who knew my name and lived, made for a very short list. It was one of the biggest reasons I was still alive, because I was careful.

I'd never planned to add the Quad to that list, yet here we were. Children really were good at fucking their parents' lives over, weren't they?

Dane smiled, but it was a practiced one, a fake one to cover all the plans going on inside his devious head. "We seem to have something in common. I figured we ought to meet."

"We have nothing in common."

"What about Nem?"

I let out one soft laugh and shook my head. "I have a daughter. You all are temporary distractions who have fucked up her life more than once, so like I said, we've got nothing in common."

The aggression in the room ramped up, but they could fuck off if they thought I cared about their feelings. The truth was the truth, and they'd screwed Nem over more than once. Her being blind to it didn't change that it was true.

"Exactly what is it about us that pisses you off so much?" Colton asked. He was older than the others, or at least his face looked older—he had the years that came from killing. People made jokes about bathing in the blood of their enemies to stay young, but I'd drowned in more than enough to know it just leached the life out of a person. Maybe that was why Colton pissed me off less than the others, because I saw myself in him.

"You were supposed to protect Caroline, and you failed. You were supposed to protect Nem, and you failed. If that wasn't enough, you make her question herself, make her doubt herself. Nothing gets a person dead faster than hesitation, and you fucking make her hesitate."

No one spoke, and the four men at least had the decency to drop their gazes, to look ashamed for what had happened with Caroline. Not that guilt did a fucking thing to bring a person back.

For a moment I remembered Caroline, as if saying her name broke the chains I'd placed on such thoughts. Her laugh was what hit me, playing through my brain like a music box I hadn't heard in years but that was familiar all the same. I saw her long dark hair, full of waves, and those impossibly deep brown eyes. I remembered the way she smiled — a real smile — one she rarely gave to anyone else.

Pain lanced through my chest, that same old pain, the reason I locked those thoughts away even if I wanted to dive into them and stay until I drowned. I shoved it aside, forced myself to keep my mind on the task at hand.

That was how a person kept going, how they kept moving forward even after such loss. It was what I'd taught Nem and it was what I lived by.

Plans. Steps. Goals. Nothing could smother pain like a good plan. One step after another, one task after another, and eventually a person could outrun whatever threatened to bury them in sorrow.

Or so I told myself. All these years, all my plans, and I hadn't outrun shit.

Which means I just need to run faster.

"I won't make excuses for what happened to Caroline and Nem. We fucked up — never saw Kyler for what he was." Rune was the one to talk that time. He was usually quiet, from what I'd learned, but maybe he wasn't as stupid as people thought. "But we're here trying to fix it."

Or maybe he was just as stupid.

"Can you bring Caroline back? Can you save Nem from what happened? No? Then you can't fix shit."

"Whether you like it or not," Bray said, his tone full of no-nonsense fact. He sounded like a parent who was explaining options to a toddler, ready to tell them how the world worked whether it made them happy or not. "We are part of her life, and we've got no plans on going anywhere."

"I could make you go somewhere." I didn't need to give them some clever one-liner to drive that point home.

"You could try," Colton countered.

I met his dark, serious eyes, and after a moment, I almost laughed. They'd grown a bit since the last time I'd actually seen them. Hell, I'd almost risk saying they seemed like actual men, now.

At least, I might say it if I didn't still fucking hate them with everything I had.

"So why are you here, really? I have a feeling even if Nem puts up with you all, we aren't going to be having family dinners, so what's the point? If you're looking for information on her, you can fuck off. I wouldn't give you shit you could use against her."

"Stop being a dick," Dane said, "because you know damn well we have no plans on doing anything to hurt her."

"You know, I rarely ask the same question more than once, yet here I am, on time three. What. Do. You. Want?" I punctuated each word by tapping my finger against the table. I wasn't going to waste my whole damned day while the men who were fucking my daughter got to their point.

Dane let out a long sigh, as if I were annoying him. *Too fucking bad.* "You probably know her better than anyone—I'm just looking to understand her. I'm not asking for secrets here, for anything that can hurt her. I'm just trying to figure her out."

"So talk to her."

"You think I haven't? She's tight-lipped."

That did make me smile. "That's my girl. At least I know she keeps some of her brains working when it comes to you all."

If looks could wound, I'd be missing skin with the way Dane glared at me.

Colton set his arm on the table and leaned in. "She's in our lives, and I won't to lose her again. She went off without a damn thought, drunk as hell, to Carlos' house. She could have caught a stray bullet and been gone. She went to Diamond's Edge to fuck some stranger because of the shit crawling around in her head. You know the sort of people there, all the ways that could have gone bad. She's running headfirst, and I'm fucking terrified she's going to slam into something she can't handle."

I wanted to snap back that they didn't know shit, that they were wrong. I didn't care for people telling me about Nem, as if I didn't know her, as if I hadn't spent the last ten years looking after her, taking care of her, teaching her every fucking thing I knew.

Still, I'd known about her not-even-half-thought-out attack on Carlos' house. It wasn't the sort of thing that happened without me taking notice, and as soon I'd heard, as soon as I'd known it was Carlos, I'd known Nem had been the one to do it.

What I hadn't known was that she'd been drunk...

I tapped my finger against the table, trying to sort through my thoughts. I didn't love the idea of telling these assholes anything, of giving them something that could get them deeper into Nem's life, but I also didn't want to see that girl destroy herself.

Sometimes life was just picking something, even if it sucked, because it was better than nothing.

"I picked that girl up, bleeding and barely alive and crying out *your* names, from that backyard. Do you have any idea what that's like? Even half-dead, after her heart had stopped, after I got it going again, she fought me, clawed at me. She's tough—always has been."

"You put her back together—we get it," Rune said.

"You don't get it. I didn't put shit back together. *She* did that. She pulled every bloody, ragged piece of herself and taped that shit up all on her own. I gave her guidance, offered some direction, that's it. My point is that she did that on her own. Didn't matter how much I wanted to help, she refused. She felt like she needed to do it on her own."

I went back, remembered those horrible weeks that went into months, when she was sick, when she was weak, when I wasn't sure if she'd even make it. I still remembered finding her late into the night doing her physical therapy hours after she should have stopped, without anyone there to help her because she was so driven.

"There's been one thing that's kept her going no matter what, that's pushed her forward even when it was hard—and trust me, there were a lot of fucking days when it was hard. Her plan."

"You mean her revenge?"

I shrugged. "I don't know. Hell, I don't know if she knows. Maybe it's revenge, maybe it's about Kenz, maybe it's facing her own damned past, but whatever it is, it's kept her going. It's what dragged her out of that house, it's what brought her back after her heart stopped, what kept her going during recovery."

"Everyone needs something to keep 'em going," Rune said, his tone telling me that he was saying it based on personal experience.

Not that I planned on digging into his past. It wasn't my job to untangle the knots in his brain.

Still, he didn't get what I was saying, so I shook my head. "Something to keep a person going in the low times after loss, when you're getting over it, that's good. Sometimes it's all we've got. The question is whether or not you find something else, whether you dig in and find a reason to care beyond whatever that goal is. Nem..." I let out a sigh, admitting something I'd never said out loud before. "Nem's been driven since that day to finish this, hasn't focused on anything else."

"That's why we're here," Dane said. "We want to help her."

"You can help her all you want—won't fix the problem."

"And what's the problem?"

"I don't think she cares what happens when she gets whatever it is she's after. She's twisted her entire life around this plan, about getting to the end point, and I don't think she gives a damn beyond it."

Dane frowned, but the crease in his cheek told me he got where I was going with that. "She'll be fine," he said softly. Was he convincing me or himself? "She'll get her revenge, get Kenz out of there and she'll be fine."

"We aren't the sort of men who pretend about shit." I sat back in the seat, forcing myself to say what haunted me, what kept me up at night when even the memory of Caroline was locked too tight to escape. "I don't think Nem plans to live through this, and I think she's fine with that—in fact, I think she's looking forward to it. I think every move she makes is to reach her end point, and that she's planning to never live a day past that."

The tension shot up again, when none of the men could try to pretend I meant anything other than exactly what I did. Too bad, though. They could deal with their own hang-ups, their own issues with the truth.

"I hate every last one of you, and if I had my way, I'd bury the lot of you in shallow graves so the animals could get to you. Lucky for you, my daughter means more to me than your worthless lives."

"So what do we do?" Bray asked, ignoring my statement as if my threats didn't matter at all.

"If I had an answer to that, I'd have fixed this already. Nem needs something to care about, needs to realize there's more to life than her plan. She needs to believe there is a life worth something at the end of the tunnel. You need to figure out a way to give her something else."

"And if we can't?" Colton asked.

"If you can't, then I'm pretty sure Nem will end up in the dying again, and I don't think she's got another miracle in her."

* * * *

Nem

I sighed as I let the warm water of the bath soak into me. My hair was piled high on my head to keep it dry, and the deep tub let me sink all the way into the water.

All four of the Quad had left a few hours before, only after I swore I wouldn't leave the house. I had no idea what task they had to complete and honestly? I didn't care.

Being alone was nice. It gave me time to relax, to spend on myself without needing to keep up any appearances. I'd first exercised, then made myself lunch out of sandwich supplies in the fridge, then finally decided to take a long, hot bath.

"Go figure — we leave and you get naked."

I opened my eyes to find Dane standing there, a grin as he stared at me, despite how the bubbles hid anything from him. "You know, you could have knocked."

"Sure, but I like catching you off guard."

I couldn't feel the annoyance I wanted. I wasn't sure why, since I could feel that often enough with them. Maybe it was his smirk, maybe it was how the hot water had eased away most of my tension, but I found I was, if anything, glad to see him.

"So where have you been?" I asked.

"Errands. You know how it is." Dane came further into the room and sat on the closed toilet lid. "Then I had to make sure you hadn't drowned in here. What sort of protection would I be if I didn't watch over you?"

That made me pause, brought to the surface something I'd always wondered but never knew.

Dane frowned. "What's going on in our head all of a sudden?"

"How did you end up honor-bound to my mom?"

Dane didn't smile again, instead leaning forward to place his elbows on his knees. His gaze rested on a spot in the tub, on bubbles there, but I had a feeling he wasn't actually seeing that. "That's pretty old history, Nem. You sure you want to dig that up?"

Did I? My time back here was all just more digging, all pulling apart the past to see what hid beneath the rocks. Still, an unease made me hesitate before answering. I was able to see the Quad in a specific way, and I couldn't shake my fear that something could change that.

However, the question still beating at me meant I knew my answer. I hadn't run from the truth in a long time—I wouldn't now. "Yeah, I want to know. I want to understand why you were a part of my life, why you're bound the way you are."

Dane nodded, but it took him a few long moments before he answered, before his soft voice filled the quiet room. "You know better than you used to the sort of men we are, the skills we have and the things we've had to do to hone those skills."

"If you're trying to scare me, you're wasting your time."

"I'm not. I'm just trying to make you understand. You know us as men who have tried to keep you safe, but that isn't what we always were."

I frowned. "You mean you didn't do the same sort of work for someone else before?"

He let out an empty laugh. "No. We weren't security experts or bodyguards before. Instead, we took on more contract work, individual jobs. We started working for your family when we were in our early twenties, so it wasn't like we'd had all that many years to work before then, anyway."

"So how did you go from general fixer to being honor-bound to my mother?"

He turned to give me a smile that lacked his normal humor, one that said the story wasn't one he liked to tell. "We got hired to steal a necklace. The job would pay more because we were supposed to take this asshole with us, let him do the actual theft. No idea why — probably for some stupid idea of credit. We took the job, got the man inside, but while we were working on the safe, a woman walked in."

"My mom?"

Dane nodded. "Caroline came in, and she recognized the man. He was someone who had worked for them, I guess, and he was pissed for fuck only knows what reason, and figured stealing the Hester necklace would make it all better. The thing was, as soon as he saw Caroline, he knew the game was up. He couldn't walk away, couldn't pretend like nothing had happened. The fucker when for his gun, ready to kill her so she couldn't talk."

"And you stopped him?"

"Not right away. I told you, we'd done some bad shit, hadn't worried that much about right or wrong. Anyone who goes into a job knows there's always a chance it'll end up in blood. If you can't stomach that, you shouldn't take a job." Dane's tone said what his words didn't — he was ashamed of the person he'd been. It was strange to think that now, after seeing him so confident for so long, but it seemed he wasn't the same man he'd been back then.

"So what changed? Obviously he didn't shoot my mom that night."

"No, he didn't. Caroline pulled her shoulders back and stood tall, giving him that look — you know the one that could send about anyone running. She didn't beg him for her life, didn't promise him anything, didn't try to run. No, instead Caroline looked right at him and told him to put away his gun before he hurt himself. I'd never seen anything like that, seen someone who didn't show a speck of fear. It was then I heard a kid laughing from the other room—you and Mackenzie were playing—and the man looked that way, a wild look in his eyes. Caroline shifted, moving in front of the door as if to block his way. That's what did it, I think. Caroline could have done a million things differently, but what she did was make it clear he wasn't getting through her."

I tried to think back, to remember that day, but I couldn't. To me it was just another day, another time when I'd had no idea how close to disaster I'd been.

Dane shook his head, though his lips were pulled into a smile. "The man's intentions were obvious to anyone—he wanted to kill your mother, steal her necklace and probably kill your sister and you just to make sure our tracks were covered. I don't know why exactly that day things changed, why Caroline standing against him made a damn bit of different, but it did, and not just for me. I told the man it was over, that we weren't killing unarmed women and children for a fucking necklace. The idiot tried to ignore us, pulled the trigger anyway. Let's just say he wasn't nearly as fast as he thought, and the bullet went into the plaster of the wall."

"If you broke in with him, why did Caroline trust you?"

"I don't know, honestly. The gunfire caused guards to rush in, and Caroline could have told them anything. If it were me, I would have had us killed on the spot. She didn't, though. All four of us were there, on our knees, and Caroline crouched down to meet my gaze.

She stared at me as if she could see right through me, as if she were reading me. I have no idea what she saw in me, in any of us, but when she stood up, she told her guards to release us. She let us go."

"That's how you met, but that doesn't explain how you started working for her."

"We spent the whole fucking night going over what happened, over why. No matter what we did, we couldn't get it out of our heads. She could have killed us but didn't. She gave us a second chance, which was something none of us every got. Fuck, maybe it was deeper than that—she trusted us. Do you know how rare that is? People are afraid of us, they respect us, but they don't trust us. To have Caroline do that, it was this debt we couldn't pay back any other way, and it was a door to a world we never thought we'd get into. So the next day, we visited her again—this time we went through the front door—and swore ourselves to her. Caroline saved us that night, showed us we could be more, that we *were* more. She gave us our lives, and in exchange, we swore our lives to her."

I listened quietly, fitting that together with everything else I knew, surprised by how it managed to color in areas of my life I hadn't understood. The way the Quad had fit into our family, how they had risked so much, that they hadn't left our service even when they could have gone anywhere and done anything. It also made me understand why my mother had trusted them so much, why she'd relied on them the way she had.

"I don't always remember a lot about my mom," I admitted softly. "I should, because I wasn't a little kid when she died, but sometimes I struggle to remember the details."

"Caroline was something else. Tough, smart, vicious." He offered me a tight smile. "That's clearly where you get those things from."

"I just wish I could talk to her now, that I could ask her questions now. When I was a kid, I thought she was stupid, like all kids think about their parents. Now that I'm older, I wish I could have asked her more, could have asked her for advice about what I'm doing, about what's going on."

"I knew Caroline pretty well. We'd sit up talking sometimes when Kyler worked late, and I think she knew how much I hated silence. If you asked her what you should do, I'm pretty sure I know what she'd say."

"What?"

"She'd say to remember exactly who you are, to never forget it, to never let anyone convince you that you're anything other than who you *know* you are. I remember one night when Kyler was being an exceptional asshole. They fought often, because he wanted her to be silent, to listen, to be a good little girl, and Caroline wasn't that person. He wanted to expand operations one way, to use her connections to make it happen, and Caroline didn't agree because it would mean betraying a longtime ally. Kyler never put his hands on her—I think he might have if we weren't around—but he had gotten into her face, yelled that she was nothing but a whore, nothing but a way to create heirs, that she should keep her mouth shut and let him do the thinking. When he spotted Rune at the doorway, he left."

I recalled the bad fights that had happened between my mother and Kyler, the way they'd screamed when others weren't around, the way they'd never really spoken at any other time. Still, Dane recounting the story made my chest ache anyway, as if the reminder that I hadn't grown up in a happy home caused more pain.

"I was ready to reassure Caroline. It was still early in our working for her, so I didn't know her all that well yet, and I expected her to break down." He let out a soft laugh. "That wasn't your mother, though. Instead, she stared at the door Kyler had left from, then walked to the desk as if nothing had happened. She picked up her phone, called the ally in question and warned them about the double-cross. I'm sure Kyler gave her hell after that, and when she hung up, I asked her if she wanted us to get her out of there, to deal with Kyler, to stay there with her that night to make sure Kyler didn't do anything to her when he found out. Caroline shook her head, her eyes without a speck of fear, and I'll never forget what she said. '*I don't run from problems and I don't cower. Kyler can say whatever he wants about me – that's not my problem. He can think whatever he wants, can call me names, but none of that is who I am. Only I get to decide who I am, and I make that decision by what I do.*' Your mother wasn't the perfect person—fuck, none of us are—but she was tough and she did what she felt was right no matter what risks or the dangers or what anyone else thought about it. If you want to know what she'd tell you to do, it isn't that hard to figure out. All you need to do is look into a mirror and decide who you really are. The rest?" Dane shrugged. "Just details."

I tried to think about what he meant, and I could nearly hear my mother's voice in my head telling me the same thing. It felt like her whispering to me from beyond the grave, giving me some important piece of advice that I hadn't gotten before, that there hadn't been time for before.

I cherished it in a way I hadn't expected. I'd written off family and parents so long before that I hadn't given it much thought in so long. Still, hearing that from Dane, it sank into me, soothed me, as if she was telling me I was on the right path.

"You know, I also think she might have said something about always making sure to please your man." Even as he said the obvious lie, he grinned.

"I'm pretty sure she never said *that.*"

"I'm pretty sure she did. It sounds awfully familiar to me, and disobeying your mother would be awfully rude."

"You're right—I really should behave in the way she'd expect me to."

Dane's eyebrow lifted in surprise, as if that were the last thing he expected. His suspicion came a heartbeat too late, though, as if he'd just realized trusting me when I was being nice was a horrible decision.

I reached out of the water, wrapped my fingers in his shirt and yanked. He toppled into the water despite being fully clothed. He sputtered as he tried to right himself, bubbles stuck to his hair, his clothing, more having splashed out of the tub and onto the floor.

"You clearly take after her," he said once he rested against me, over me in the warm water. "Which means I'll need to keep my wits about me when dealing with you."

"You think that's enough to outsmart me?"

His grin spread as he ran his hand up my side to cup my breast. "Maybe not, but keeping a very close eye on you has its advantages."

When his lips brushed mine, I let his touch and his kiss ease me just like the water had. I'd been so excited to have time alone, yet so quickly Dane had shown me just how much I'd missed him.

I couldn't deny any more how much I enjoyed being with these men or how much they meant to me...but that weakness might just take me out in the end...

Chapter Thirteen

Nem

I wasn't a girly girl, but even I had to admit there was something almost magical about sitting in a salon chair and having my hair dyed.

I could dye it myself, but I'd learned it wasn't worth it, especially due to the red. That tended to stain everything, and I had enough money to pay someone else to do it.

Being able to sit, close my eyes for a moment and just enjoy being taken care of was well worth it. Hell, for a moment I almost felt normal.

Rune and Bray were outside, having been driven out by the shop owner, Yazmin. When I watched that, I had liked her even more. She was in her mid-thirties, not even five foot tall and could only reach a hundred pounds if she was holding something heavy. Still, she'd looked right into Rune's face and ordered him out of her business.

It seemed she didn't like feeling people were looming over her while she worked.

It left the two men sitting in their SUV out front, leaving them able to look into the large front windows to ensure I was safe.

"You're brave," I said to Yazmin as she mixed the dye in a bowl, black gloves protecting her hands.

"Not really," she answered, concentrating on her work.

"There aren't a lot of people I know who would take on the Quad even if they had to, let alone ordering them around just so they leave."

"Well, this is my shop. If I can't order people around here, where can I?"

I let out a soft laugh, because I had a feeling she managed that mostly because of her confidence and size. It was like a kitten who snarled and hissed — it didn't startle anyone, but people tended to let the kitten get away with it because it was adorable.

"Besides," she added, "I've been telling those boys what to do for years."

"Oh really?" I lifted an eyebrow as Yazmin took her spot behind me, a comb in her hand and the rest of her things on the small rolling table beside her. "I've never heard that."

"Why do you think they suggested you come here? Because they know this is a safe place."

"And what does safe mean?"

"It means the name on the salon isn't one people usually mess with."

I frowned as I thought back to what it had said. "Gellingham? I've never heard that."

"Because we aren't around anymore really. Think of it like a legacy, a name that used to mean something so people pay it respect because of that."

Boy, that sounded familiar. The Hester name was the same, wasn't it? An old name that wasn't around anymore, one that had passed from current to history. Of course, the Hester name still held power. Another generation or two and that would change, but for now? It still had bite.

"So you grew up around them?"

"Yep. Ran the same streets, and they beat up anyone who looked at me wrong. Well, I mean, they did if I didn't deal with it first."

"You beat people up?"

She smiled into the mirror at me. "Oh, I fight dirty."

Which I believed and made a lot of sense. I'd learned after Kyler that honor didn't mean shit. All that mattered was who won.

No one gave a damn about the honorable folks who still lost, who ended up dead. They turned to dust and their honor did nothing for them.

But the people who fought dirty — especially if no one saw it coming — were the ones to watch out for.

And for a moment, I could almost picture Yazmin running around with the Quad like an annoying little sister.

Though, the fact they'd never mentioned her made me shift. It was a reminder of how one-sided our relationship really was. I knew so little about them, about their history. In fact, I hadn't realized they even had friends.

"You look like you're thinking pretty hard," Yazmin said as she applied the color to my roots.

I opened my mouth as if to tell her, but the words wouldn't come. When was the last time I'd told anyone anything? I never confided in Jarrod, and the Quad were a complicated situation that wasn't made up of honest sharing.

Yazmin let out a laugh. "You're just like them, you know that? Quick to keep things to yourself."

"Loose lips are a fast trip to a short life," I said.

"Sure, normally. I wouldn't suggest you go pour your heart out to random strangers."

"You *are* a stranger."

"No, love, I'm a stylist. This shop is the secular version of a confessional. Whatever you say here never leaves, not even to the men sulking in the car." When I frowned, she lifted her eyebrow. "They've been trying to pry secrets out of me for years, and they haven't managed it yet—I doubt it's going to start now."

The offer tempted me. I hadn't had a friend in so long—maybe ever. Some part of me craved what she dangled in front of me, the idea of having someone I could talk to, someone I wasn't manipulating or being manipulated by.

Not that I planned to tell her the big things, about Kyler, about who I was before, about my plan to kill Kyler or save Kenz. Instead, I opened my mouth, not sure what exactly would come out. "I don't like the coffee Dane buys," I said.

The words were horribly stupid. They were true, of course, because Dane bought a fancy, super dark roast that I found disgusting.

Yazmin laughed, that open, honest humor that could pull anyone in and make them relax. "That's as good a place to start as anywhere else. You want to know the truth? Dane *hates* that coffee, too. When he was twelve, this bad-ass martial artist did a show at his school, and when Dane went to talk to him, the man said that real men drank the darkest coffee available, and ever since? Dane gets that shit even though he has to force himself to choke it down."

I thought about what she said, about Dane being a kid, about him looking up to anyone and about how I'd watched him drink his coffee in the mornings. She was right… He never had seemed to enjoy the cup, to savor it the way I did when it was a good brew.

I didn't bother to hide my smile at the feeling of being able to say something that bothered me without fear it would be used against me. So maybe we weren't talking about deep soul things, about life changing topics or personal traumas, but just tiny complaints. Someone who listened and responded was like a salve on a burn I didn't know I had.

So I relaxed into the chair as she worked, and for what was possibly the first time ever, I talked to someone like a friend.

* * * *

It was two hours later when Yazmin dried my hair, and I had to admit, she was fantastic. The red of my hair was vibrant again, that bright color that I loved. Weeks between dye jobs would allow it to fade, the color leaching out until it had lost its shine.

"This is amazing," I told her, the shade matching the red of my lipstick perfectly.

"Well, I don't get the chance for fun like this often. When I became a stylist, I'd thought it would be awesome, edgy styles and rainbow colors and famous people every day. It turned out to be a lot of perms, bang cuts and those really ugly chunky highlights that were popular in the nineties. It's nice to do something a little wild."

The towel hung around my shoulders to protect my clothing from any stray dye. Not that I needed it, since I'd done this long enough to know to wear black when coming in. Still, Yazmin was meticulous, even as she'd talked the whole time.

Well, not the *whole* time. I'd chimed in plenty, the back and forth easy and surprisingly fun. We'd gone over quirks from the men and more of Yazmin's history. I learned about how Rune had lost his virginity at the age of sixteen in the back of a van while Yazmin had sat outside, since the only way Rune's mom would let him go out was if she went, too. I learned about the time Colton had his wisdom teeth removed and while still high as fuck from sedation had decided he could climb a tree, and how it had taken Rune, Bray and Dane to haul his ass down. She'd told me about Bray and how he had asthma, but was embarrassed about it so never let anyone see his inhaler.

It had made the men feel like people in a way they never had… It reminded me that they had lives, which I'd never been a part of before. They were more than just killers, more than their work, more than the terrifying monsters others saw. It wasn't that I hadn't known that. It was just odd to see, strange to remember that our interaction had always been wrapped around work.

When I was younger, they'd protected me. Now, it was whatever twisted thing we did, but it wasn't as if we went out together to have fun, to talk to each other.

Of course, then I reminded myself none of that really mattered.

The wedding was approaching, the end point for this all, and nothing we had would go beyond that. It didn't matter what they were like when they were able to just be, when they could relax, because we wouldn't ever get there.

A sound in the back of the shop had me turning and frowning. During the two hours I'd been there, no one had come or gone. Yazmin had shut down the shop, putting up the closed sign so it was private.

Yazmin turned as well, but the way she jumped said she expected trouble.

And trouble sure as hell walked in.

"Charlie," Yazmin said, fear in her voice that hadn't been there before.

That man—Charlie—was young, twenty at the most. He had a shaved head and an eyebrow piercing above his bright blue eyes. Tattoos covered his left arm, up that side of his neck, and over his jawline. It wasn't any of that which set off the warning bells in my head, though. I knew damn well people could look terrifying and rough around the edges and be no threat at all, then there were people like me who could look sweet when I wanted to and still take someone's throat.

Instead, it was the piece of metal pipe in his hand that put me on edge. "You got my money, Yaz?"

"My name is Yazmin Gellingham, not Yaz. And no. You just collected last week, and you said you'd collect every other week."

"Yeah, see, I thought about it and realized that I work at protecting you every week—I should get paid every week." He tapped the pipe against one of the shelves, as if to bring her attention to it, to remind her about it.

As if anyone would forget the weapon he brandished about as if it were his dick — far too proud of something that wasn't all that impressive.

"You can't just change the deal and expect me to have it on hand."

"Well, I mean, you could always pay up another way." Charlie's gaze moved down Yazmin's body in a lewd perusal that made me narrow my eyes at his insinuation.

She didn't wilt, pulling her shoulders back as if she were some Amazonian woman instead of the sprite she was. "Not a chance."

He swung the pipe before Yazmin could do anything. He didn't aim for her, however. Instead, he hit a shelf of product, knocking the items to the floor, the bottles and jars skidding across the tile.

I rose from the stool. My purse was across the room, so calling the men wasn't an option. They'd parked themselves where they had a view of the front of the shop, clearly not expecting anyone to break in through the back. It meant we were on our own for the moment.

Though, Yazmin seemed tough enough, and I could hold my own.

Also, Charlie had come in with a pipe, not a gun, so he wasn't as big a threat as he thought. Sure, one hit with that damn pipe could break some bones, but it was slow and he was clumsy.

Charlie turned his gaze toward me, his lip lifting in a smirk I wanted to cut from his face. "Well, well, what do you know? A two for one deal? Hell, a little time with both of you and I might just let Yaz here ride a full month without making a payment."

"What's she paying you for?" I asked.

"Don't worry," Yazmin said, as if trying to draw his attention back to her. "Charlie, she's just a customer. Leave her alone. This is between you and I."

The fact she was trying to take the heat off me, that she wanted to protect me, warmed me in an unfamiliar and slightly unwelcome way, just as our conversation had. It wasn't that I was going to let her take all the danger, to sit out while she handled it, but her keeping his attention had its benefits.

"It *was* between you and me, but then you didn't do what you needed to." Charlie walked quickly, backing Yazmin up until she was pressed against one of the counters where another stylist station was set up. "I explained to you two months ago what happens when you don't listen, didn't I?"

The color drained from her face, telling me however he'd thought to teach that lesson hadn't been a good thing. And how this girl spent so much time around the Quad, but *this* kid could frighten her made me sure he needed to go.

Permanently.

"I can have the money Monday," she said, her back against the mirror as she leaned as far away from him as she could. "I'll have all of it, okay?"

"I saw those men in here again, those four. You weren't thinking about trying to set me up, were you? About getting yourself some help? Because that would be really fucking stupid, wouldn't it?" Charlie grabbed her face, his fingers digging into her cheeks, his palm over her mouth. "You remember what happened the last time you tried to go to someone else, don't you? You went and talked to that nice boy you were seeing, didn't you?"

Yazmin nodded, though she couldn't move much with his hand on her face.

"That's right. He made the most pathetic sounds when he bled out, crying like a little bitch, and all because *you* wanted to be a fucking problem for me."

Tears tracked down her cheeks, such a far cry from the woman I'd spent the last two hours with, proof of how quickly the wrong person could tear down someone.

I reached over to the stylist station beside Yazmin's and grabbed the straight razor from the shaving kit set there, tucking it against my palm.

Her eyes settled on me, and a quick shake of her head tried to warn me off. Not that it shocked me. As far as she knew, I was just a friend of her friends, just some girl, and she didn't want my harm or even death on her conscience.

Too bad.

I had a problem with doing as I was told to.

Charlie leaned closer to her, his fingers digging into her cheeks so hard she'd have bruises later.

I swore they'd be the last ones she'd ever sport from this asshole.

I was so close, almost within range to reach around him and drag the blade across his throat, when he lifted his gaze in the mirror and spotted me.

The blade was still tucked in my palm, hidden, so he wasn't as alarmed as he should have been. He twisted to face me, holding the pipe straight out toward me in warning. "And just what do you think you're doing?"

"Nothing," Yazmin said, a frantic edge to her voice. "She's not doing anything."

"You think you can take me?" Charlie ignored Yazmin entirely, his focus now on me. "You wouldn't be the first whore to think that, but I've proven 'em all wrong." He poked the end of the pipe against my chest, then lifted an eyebrow and tugged the neckline down a bit, like a threat.

Everything I knew, everything I learned, rushed through me. All the self-defense lessons with Rune back when I'd been a kid, everything Jarrod taught me since, all the things I'd taught myself. Those were a part of me, and this idiot only had a piece of pipe against my blade.

I moved fast and knocked my hand against the pipe, forcing it to the side, then opened the straight razor as I swung my other hand, the one holding it, at him.

I was aiming for his throat, but he had better reflexes than I'd expected. Charlie jerked backward, which caused the blade to catch his cheek instead of his throat. Still, the sharp edge was enough to open that cheek wide.

He cursed, stumbling away as Yazmin darted to the side and out of the way. When he lifted his eyes to mine, they were full of hate and so much violence.

And why did that get me going? There was something primal about a fight like this, about the blood and the adrenaline that made me feel alive.

Blood leaked down his face, covering the tattoos on that side of his body. "You fucking bitch," he spat.

"I've been called worse," I answered.

"You got any idea what a bad fucking choice that was? How much worse you just made it on yourself?" He lifted the pipe again, pointing it at me as if to drive home the message.

Which was dumb. Holding a weapon out front like that was the first step to losing the weapon. Never let it get closer to an enemy.

But then again, I didn't exactly take Charlie here for an expert in strategy.

"You know, collecting protection money in this area is stupid. You aren't even a little fish in a big pond—you're a fucking bit of bacteria around here."

"Really? Because I've been collecting for months. No one cares about this block—it's old names and nobodies now. The only people who could do shit have moved on to bigger game, leaving this for me."

He wasn't wrong about that. This was an older area of the city, a place that was popular before but had mostly fallen into disrepair. It lacked the money and reputation of the higher-end areas and shopping centers.

Still, if Kyler knew some newcomer was trying to bully folks, he wouldn't just sit around. Not because he gave a damn about Yazmin or any of the other shops, but because it was technically his territory and so an insult to him.

Not that Kyler would get a chance to deal with Charlie. I'd provide his lesson personally.

"He ever touch you, Yazmin? Other than right now?" I didn't move my gaze from him even as I asked. I knew better than to take my eyes off the threat.

"No," she said. "He broke into my apartment one night, told me he could get to me any time he wanted, but he didn't do anything to me." She pulled in a loud, shaky breath. "But he killed my friend when my friend went to confront him."

I nodded. "Lucky you," I told Charlie.

"What? You going to say you'll let me live since I didn't touch her? That if I leave right now, run away with my tail tucked between my legs, you'll let me go?"

He asked the question with so much mockery, as if it was the stupidest thing he'd ever heard.

"Nope," I answered. "You aren't walking out of here at all. If you'd set one disgusting hand of yours on her, I'd make sure it was really fucking slow. Since you didn't, I guess I'll make it quick."

He snorted. "You? Some fucking upstart bitch?"

"Yeah, me." I gave him a smile that would have made any person with half a brain take a moment to reconsider.

There was arrogance and there was confidence. There were people overcompensating, and there was someone standing in their place, entirely sure they could do exactly what they'd said. I'd run into a few folks like that, the ones who stood their ground, whose expression made it clear they could follow through, and there were few things more dangerous than that.

Charlie should have seen that in me, should have realized that he was out of his league, that I wasn't some petty criminal who threatened innocent women for a few bucks.

I wasn't shocked when he didn't see it, though, when he was too stupid to read the situation, to realize just how fucked he was.

He came forward in a rush, unbalanced and too fast and too large to be able to correct. I took a step to the left, changing his target zone, and when he tried to shift as well, he lacked the time.

Charlie swung that pole, and whether he was an idiot or not, one good hit would really fuck up my chances. Thankfully, I doubted he'd played baseball at any point, because when I leaned backward, the pole swung inches from my face. I caught his arm when it passed me, twisting and using his momentum, along with setting my foot behind his, to trip him. It landed him on the ground hard, the pipe sliding away from him when he lost his grip.

He had a split second in those blue eyes of his where he figured it out, just the briefest flash of realization that he'd really fucked up, that he hadn't had a clue what a real threat was.

It wouldn't save him. Mercy was one of the few lessons no one had ever taught me.

I ran the blade across his throat.

* * * *

Bray

Three hours? It had taken three damned hours for Nem's hair? After hour one in the SUV, Rune and I had decided to sit in the restaurant across the street, the one with a good view of the front door. I would have preferred to have been able to see inside the shop, but the posters on the windows made it impossible.

It would have been an unacceptable choice if the shop had been run by anyone other than Yazmin. I trusted that girl with my life, one of the few people in the world I could say that about.

She was as close to a sister as I had, and I had no doubts Nem was as safe as could be with her. Besides, we could see the entry way and the back door was securely locked.

However, after three hours, I was done. The idea that anyone could spend that much time on their *hair* was so foreign a thought to me that it didn't make a damn bit of sense.

Especially for Nem, who didn't strike me as high-maintenance.

Well, she's almost gotten killed a few times, and I've had to deal with a number of corpses she's left behind.

Maybe she was high-maintenance, but in a very odd way.

"If she's not done, she's not going to be happy about us rushing her," Rune said as we crossed the street.

"Too bad—I've reached my limit."

Rune huffed. "Having Yaz or Nem mad at me isn't something I want to deal with. It's on your head if we manage to piss them both off."

"Deal," I said as I grabbed the handle to the salon door and pulled.

Nem was in the seat, her hair looking amazing. For a moment I was stopped in my tracks. How did Nem do that? She managed to make my brain crash, as if I suddenly couldn't formulate a thought, as if she made the entire world grind to a halt.

Her hair was bright red again, making me realize it had faded over the weeks. It wasn't wet, so they'd dried it fully, and the waves in it made it look impossibly fuller.

Even better, she smiled. Seeing Nem happy was such a rare thing, only the briefest glimpses before she'd smother it beneath a mask. She hid nothing, though, turned in the chair toward Yazmin, her bright red lips pulled into a wide and honest smile. Then, I damn near tripped when she *laughed.*

"He didn't," Nem said, the words between what was almost a giggle.

Yazmin sat in another chair, leaning forward, her black hair braided back. "Oh, he did. Everyone else was busy, so I had to bring Dane something to wear."

My eyes widened as I realized Yazmin was spilling secrets, and this time was about when Dane had decided to sleep with that crazy waitress who had left him in the bar afterward naked since she'd stolen all his clothes.

And Yazmin, the loudmouth, didn't stop there. "Of course, I don't have things in his size or style, so he had to wear a pair of pink sweatpants that said *bitch* on the ass."

Nem leaned over, her hand on her side as she laughed.

Sure, I wasn't in love with Yazmin telling everything to Nem—I had plenty of stories I didn't need repeated…—but that laugh from Nem might have just been worth it.

"What the fuck?" Rune asked.

I turned, because while I agreed about being annoyed with Yazmin, his reaction seemed over the top.

Except, he wasn't looking at the women—his gaze was on the other side of the shop. I followed his line of sight to where the body of a man lay unmoving, blood pooling around him, his throat cut and a metal pipe on the ground beside him. In addition, bottles and product were spread on the floor, a shelf destroyed as if someone had struck it.

What the fuck?

It seemed I had the same reaction as Rune.

Nem turned her gaze to the body, not seeming shaken in the least that they'd been laughing and joking with a corpse a few feet away. She twisted to look at Rune. "All done. You were right—Yazmin is fantastic."

I opened my mouth, closed it then opened it again. The cycle repeated more times than I wanted to admit when I just couldn't seem to jump on a specific line of thought.

Finally, I managed *something*. "Why the hell is there a dead body on the floor?"

"He slipped and fell."

"His throat is slit."

"He slipped and fell on a shaving razor. Good thing I had your protection, because as it turns out, salons can be very dangerous."

When it was clear Nem would say nothing more, I turned a hard look on Yazmin. "What happened?"

She didn't wilt at all, probably because she'd dealt with my bad moods since we had been kids. It was hard to intimidate someone who knew me when my voice was still cracking... "Slippery floors," she said, nodding. "It's a real problem."

I rubbed my fingers against the corners of my eyes, behind my glasses, trying so hard not to lose my temper. Afterward, I pointed at Nem. "You are *never* coming back here. You two are bad influences."

"On who?" Yazmin asked, an innocent smile on her face that fooled exactly no one in that shop.

"On each other," I pushed through gritted teeth.

A laugh from behind me had me turning on Rune, who had the nerve to look *amused* by the incident.

"What are you laughing at?" I asked him.

Rune shook his head, as if there wasn't even a reason to try and explain it to me. "I'll call Colton and wait here. Looks like we've got another body to deal with."

Yazmin looked toward Nem with a grin. "Another?"

"What's a few corpses between friends?"

Friends. The word hit me hard, like an olive branch, like an admittance that there was something there, that Nem was a part of our lives, no matter how small.

Maybe it was that, or maybe it was the absurdness of the situation, or the absolute no-fucks-given attitude of both of the women in the shop, but suddenly Rune's laughter made sense. Suddenly I was in on the joke.

I let out a soft laugh before giving in to it, because if there was one thing I'd learned with Nem, it was that there wasn't any reason to fight her.

She always seemed to win.

Chapter Fourteen

Nem

Five days.

The words kept repeating in my head every few minutes like a countdown to doomsday I couldn't escape.

Five days until the wedding.

Five days until I had to do something.

Five days until I could get everything I'd ever wanted.

Five days until I risked losing everything that mattered to me.

Five days until, one way or another, it was over.

"You good?" Rune's voice woke me up as he put the car in park in front of the large mansion. He turned his head to look at me, as if he didn't trust my answer and wanted figure out the truth from my expression.

I didn't bother lying. "Not really."

He reached out and set a hand on my thigh, squeezing it tightly, almost to the point of pain as if to shake me free of worries. "We've got this."

"Got what?" I tore my gaze from him and settled it on the huge house. "From where I'm sitting, we've got nothing. Because of Torrance coming in, I don't have access to the security anymore, there are too many guards for a frontal assault, no holes in the defenses I can see to use, no chance of Kyler letting her out. So, please tell me, what exactly it is you think we have?"

He didn't respond right away, and when he did, his voice was soft. "Do you remember when you were fifteen and you snuck out?"

"Which time?"

His eyes darkened, as if he didn't care for a reminder that I'd done it more than once—and that I'd done it when he hadn't known. Still, he pressed past that to answer. "When you went to that party to meet up with that punk with the purple hair."

I almost smiled at the memory of Ignite, the idiot who had picked a dumb name for himself. He'd been someone I'd met through a friend, and we'd talked a few times in the moments between arriving somewhere and when one of the Quad would scare him off. He'd been that sort of sweet-tough that happened when a boy was honestly nice but thought bad boys got all the chicks. He tried to be a rebel but always had to explain himself so it didn't come off as insulting.

"Yeah, I remember that night."

"Well, you'd wanted to go to that party so damned bad, and your mother said no. She had us change up our patrol times, add locks to your windows, even put a tracker in your purse just in case. Any other fifteen-year-old would have thrown her hands up and called it a lost cause. What did you do?"

I blew out a slow breath, remembering back. "I waited until the shift change, went out through my mom's window, which wasn't locked, and tossed my purse in the back of a taxi."

He let out a soft laugh, as though enough time had passed for him to find it funny. "Yeah, you had us chasing that fucking taxi for two hours before we figured out your plan. Anyone looking at that would have figured you were screwed — that you had no options. Instead, you managed to outsmart the four of us for *hours* and went to your little party. I can't imagine you've lost that tenacity over the years."

I knew his plan was a pep talk, a chance to tell me we could do it, but I struggled to believe him. "I was a kid trying to sneak out, not someone trying to abduct the daughter of one mob boss and the fiancée of another. That's a different sort of matter."

"It really isn't. It's about looking at it calmly, figuring out what you need and how to get it. You've been doing that your whole fucking life, Nem. Stop doubting yourself, stop leaning in so close that you're missing things." He pointed at the door handle and pulled at it. "If you wanted out of the car, and the lock is on, and you focus right here on the handle, nothing'll happen. You won't get shit. If you pull back, if take a breath and look at it from back here though" — he leaned away from the door, then pointed at the lock — "you see that you can unlatch it, that you can roll down the window, fuck, you see that you can kick the damn window out. You've buried yourself in so tight that you can't see the whole picture anymore."

The advice sounded good, like most advice did. I wanted to write him off — Rune wasn't the brightest of the bunch anyway — but he wasn't wrong.

Or, at least, I didn't have any better ideas.

I took a deep breath, then nodded. "Okay. Let's go in and figure out a plan."

Because this was my last trip to the mansion until the wedding, so if I didn't have a plan worked out by the time we left...

We were all fucked.

* * * *

Kenz smiled as I met her gaze, though my reaction was more reserved when I spotted Kyler and Torrance behind her, speaking farther into the room.

The house already looked different. Much of the furniture had been cleared away to make room for items more suited for a party. There were areas for gifts near the front, bar height tables with chairs for mingling, and new decor to make the place seem open and airy.

Despite there still being a few days until it was time for the actual event, a place this size needed more work than was reasonable to complete in a day.

"What do you think?" I asked as Kenz ran up.

Her steps faltered as she glanced around, her smile dropping. "It's fine," she said.

"It looks good," Rune offered.

Kenz peered past me to him, her smile returning. "You don't have any style sense, so you thinking it looks good worries me."

"You're such a brat," he countered.

To the left and right, I couldn't help but spot the increased guard presence. They were a reminder of what I was up against, of how many things had to be considered, how many different avenues had to be worked out.

Rune and Kenz spoke, and I tuned them out, casting my gaze around the house instead.

"Nem," Kyler called, drawing my attention away from the task at hand. He waved me over, so I followed his unspoken order. I reach him just as Torrance passed me, neither of us acknowledging the other.

"What do you think?" Kyler asked.

"It's coming along. The planner is good at what she does."

"She is," Kyler agreed. "Mackenzie wanted the actual ceremony outside, but I think there's too many risks there. The fence line is better than it was, but I'm hesitant to allow her out in the open like that."

That gave me my in, however. I wasn't sure of all the details, but anything Kyler felt wasn't a good idea was probably the best for me. "The tree line is rather far," I said. "We can put patrols to make sure it's safe."

"A sniper could set up still."

"What about a tent? We can create privacy with the fabric, ensure no lines of sight during the ceremony." More of it came together, then. "In fact, I know we've set up a lot in the house, but what if we did it outside entirely?"

"Outside is more challenging to secure."

That's right... "Not really. Outside is hard to secure in the woods or at places with a lot of hiding places. Here, though? By setting up two large tented areas, we can reduce the amount of guards needed by not stretching them so far. The open space in the back means placing guards at each of the corners ensures no one comes in or out. There's no way to access anything a person doesn't come in with, no need to watch guests in all the corridors and rooms inside the house."

Kyler ran his thumb across his jawline as he thought. "So we escort the guests directly to the backyard, into the areas already created for the ceremony and later the reception?" He nodded slowly. "It would make keeping eyes on her easier, ensure she's never outside the sight of the guards. After the last attack, I'm hesitant to allow her anywhere someone could potentially have hidden away."

"A tent is a lot easier to secure than a mansion."

And far easier to plan around for me...

After a long pause, Kyler nodded. "That's a good idea, Nem."

"As a bonus, we can sell it as giving Mackenzie what she wants, which should buy you some goodwill," I said.

Kyler let out a soft laugh. "Goodwill is hard to come by. Very well, I'll call the planner and have her get the tents set up."

Finally, things were looking up.

* * * *

Colton

Seeing Nem in her environment was sexier than it should have been. Still, with the map of the mansion spread out on the table, her bent over in front of it, dragging her pointed red nails across the image as she spoke, I had to admit—she wasn't the same girl she used to be.

She'd said that, over and over again, but it was hard to believe it. I still sometimes saw her as the kid, as the teenager who was still figuring herself out, the one I'd known and watched grow up.

Boy, had that changed.

Nem was a grown-ass woman, now. She was tough, smart and more than capable of doing whatever she set her mind to. Right now, that was taking down Kyler and getting Kenz out of there in one swoop.

Bray sat at the kitchen counter, his laptop out, his fingers moving as he listened. It put him in position to look up anything we needed to know as we went.

Rune stood to Nem's left, Dane across the table and Jarrod to her right. She hadn't looked all that surprised when Jarrod had walked in—or when it became clear we'd all already met.

Maybe she'd known better than to expect any of wouldn't have spoken, that we wouldn't have gone behind her back to figure out what the other people in her life wanted.

"This is resting on a lot of maybes," Jarrod said, a look of unhappy concentration there.

"You've done things that are more dangerous," Nem pointed out.

"Yeah, but not with you."

She shook her head, then jammed her finger against the outline of one of the tents. "All the guests will be in here already. Kenz will be brought from the house once everyone is secure and seated for the ceremony. There will be guards placed outside the tent, at each entrance, and another four inside." She ran her nail along the back wall. "But none right here."

"Because there isn't an entrance there," Rune said.

"It's cloth. Making an exit in cloth isn't that hard." Nem tapped the spot. "This has to be the plan. Inside the house, there's too many cameras, too much security, too many things to get in the way. Outside, Kyler feels safe, doesn't think there's any chance anyone else can move in. Jarrod and Colton can take out the guards here and here, at the back corners. Bray knocks the power out. Rune uses the smoke grenade to give us some cover. I slice the back of the tent, and Kenz comes with me."

"And my part of this plan?" Dane asked.

"You're in charge of getting her out of there. I'll hand Kenz off because she knows and trusts you, and you'll have a four-wheeler just outside the fence line here. It's a short run, and without any lights, the two of you will be all but invisible until you reach your ride."

"Two?" Dane crossed his arms. "You mean the three of us, don't you?"

The expression on Nem's face said what we'd already figured out. She didn't mean the three of them.

"Nem..." I said, my voice low.

"I still have to deal with Kyler, and that is the time to do it. He'll be up at the front, since he had to walk her up the aisle. If I don't strike then, I'll never get the chance. With Kenz gone, Kyler will make it all but impossible to reach him."

"It's suicide. There isn't a chance we're going along with this if your plan has you sacrificing yourself. Getting Kenz out is one thing—she's essentially a hostage and a human shield. No one wants to hit her with a stray bullet. The second she's out of there, though, what's to keep the guards from filling you with lead?"

She shook her head. "You don't get it. I'm not planning on sacrificing myself here. I'll be quick, and the smoke will make it too hard for anyone else to be able to get a shot in. Hell, they won't know where to shoot. I'll have one knife hidden to cut the tent, then I'll bury it in Kyler's throat."

It sounded good, except those shadows in her eyes remained. They still said what Jarrod had claimed, still screamed that while she might not be planning to die, she didn't care if it happened.

"Fuck that." Jarrod shook his head and pointed his finger at her. "I told you before we started this that I wouldn't be a part of anything so dangerous."

"You're going to be set up far away from anything," Nem argued, staring at Jarrod like he was a fool. "You will be perfectly safe."

"I don't mean dangerous to me!" His raised voice silenced Nem, and I got the feeling he'd never done that before. He paused, drawing in a deep breath then letting it go slowly. "I didn't save you that night just to watch Kyler get you this time. This is a horrible plan."

"I'm not letting my sister get married off to that man like property."

"And I'm not going to be a part of something that's going to get you killed."

"Then don't," Nem snapped. "I never said you had to be a part of any of this. I never asked you for help."

Jarrod went still, his lips drawn into a thin, unhappy line. After a long and tense moment, he shook his head. "I can't stop you from stepping in front of a firing squad, Nem, but I sure as hell won't be one of the people holding the gun." He turned and walked out of the room.

Nem didn't look away, staring as if trapped somewhere between disbelief that he'd walked away and expectation, as though it surprised her and validated her beliefs at the same time.

Though it was the pain beneath that that hit me.

I wanted to pull her against my chest and tell her it was okay, but I knew better. Besides, Jarrod wasn't wrong…

"This isn't a good plan," Dane said, his tone soft.

"It's the only one I have," Nem said, her gaze still locked on the door Jarrod had left from. "I've been over this again and again, and *this* is it. This is my only play. If you have anything better, I'm all ears, but from where I'm standing, this is what we have."

I wanted to offer up something else, but I didn't have anything. I didn't have any idea of something with better odds, something safer.

That didn't make her idea good, though.

Drinking salt water wasn't a good plan just because there wasn't any fresh water. Usually, doing something stupid was worse than doing nothing at all.

Not that Nem would accept the doing nothing option.

And…I couldn't blame her either.

If it were Nem we were talking about, could I have sat by and watched her married off to some old man? Could I have stood there, knowing what would happen next?

Not a fucking chance. The only reason I managed it with Kenz was that the girl was still young, and she hadn't asked for help. Kenz could be like Caroline, a woman willing to marry a man she didn't want because it was part of the life she expected for herself. Fuck knew that Caroline hadn't been some wilting flower in

Kyler's shadow, and I had no doubt Kenz could have twisted Torrance to her whim in time.

However, what I felt for Nem was different than Kenz. Kenz was like a little sister, but Nem was *mine*. Even if Nem wanted to marry someone, I was pretty damn sure I'd not let it go without complaint.

Or a lot of bloodshed.

"Are you going to back out now, too?" she asked, facing Dane as if ready to fight with him. No doubt she preferred fighting to anything else. Fighting was easy — it was a distraction.

For a woman like Nem, as secretive and distrustful as she was, fighting would be safer than anything real.

"Not planning on it, no," Dane said. "Just trying to figure out how to remove as much risk as possible."

"You know as well as I do that risk is part of life."

"Sure, but we don't take *unneeded* risk. We don't go in half-cocked. Even Rune, who once tried to challenge a bull because he was drunk, doesn't rush into a situation like this. He takes his time and thinks it through, tries to see it from all sides."

"And when he realizes there's nothing else to do, he goes through with it," Nem said. Her frustration was obvious when no one seemed willing to give her the fight she wanted.

I caught her chin and lifted her face toward mine. "Yeah, that's how it works. So right now, we're in the 'are there ways to minimize the danger' stage."

"The mission matters more than anything else."

I pulled in a slow breath as I narrowed my eyes and grappled with my anger at how that she didn't seem to give a damn about surviving.

How could I make her see that she mattered? That she could have a life? That she was more than just this damned mission?

She'd come into this to kill Kyler, to save Kenz, and she thought that was all she was. She thought she that was as far as her life could go. She'd decided that she wasn't worth anything else.

"You matter," I said.

She shook her head, her red hair falling forward, over her shoulder. "I don't."

"Yeah, you do, and if you don't want to listen to words, I've got no fucking problem explaining it to you in whatever way you need."

Her eyes widened, and I swore I could already taste the way her cunt grew wet just from my words.

She never listened worth shit anyway, so we'd explain it to her the only way that seemed to work for her.

Chapter Fifteen

Nem

When Colton's lips found mine, everything we'd been arguing about stopped mattering. How he could shut my brain off so perfectly, I had no idea.

Moments before, I'd been caught up by our argument, by the plan, by Jarrod leaving. All of that had seemed so important, then he had kissed me, and it all drifted away.

It wasn't that it didn't matter, but it was as if he had paused us between moments, when I could let that go and bask in the way his lips moved against mine. He kept his grasp on my chin, then tilted his head to deepen the kiss. He ran his tongue against my bottom lip, then delved into the warmth of my mouth.

I moaned at his taste, at how taken over I felt, and I went with it. They'd taught me fighting was useless when it came to them, that there wasn't a point in trying to resist them. My body gave in every time.

Hands slid up my sides, and it took a moment to realize it they weren't Colton's. Lips pressed to the side of my throat, and the roughness of a beard told me it was Rune. He reached beneath my shirt, then pulled the hem up above my chest and cupped my breasts. The lack of a bra meant his rough palms touched my bare skin, and he groaned against my neck as he stroked my breasts.

"You fucking matter," Rune said. "I lost you once, Nem, and I got no intention of losing you a second time."

I tried to block out his words, tried to ignore them, to focus only on the feeling. Things felt so simple, so easy when I could just feel them. Questions about what would happen, what could happen, what it meant, none of that mattered. Instead, it was all about how I felt in the moment, how they made me feel.

If I could have this all the time, hell, maybe it would have been worth sticking around...

Rune pulled away, then took my shirt off entirely after Colton broke his kiss.

Colton glanced down my front. "You're a fucking sight," he said in that rough way that made me almost believe it. It didn't set off the annoyance I got when others leered at me, when they did that slow perusal, when they clearly liked what they saw.

I didn't react by wanting to knock Colton's teeth out. Hell, I *liked* it. I felt wanted, felt as if I mattered to him.

Which was the exact thing he was trying to tell me, wasn't it?

The men started to strip, and I was reminded just how good they looked like that.

Rune's wide chest and his tattoos against his pale skin, the way Colton's dark hair ran down from his navel in a perfect trail, the lean build of Bray and Dane's devastatingly sexy smirk. How was it that four men could be so damned different from one another yet so perfect for me?

They each fit me in a different way, each molded to a different aspect I had. Rune was sweet in a way no one would have expected, a safe place for me to rest against. Dane could make me laugh even when I didn't want to, even when everything felt as if it were falling apart. Colton made me feel like I was okay, as if who and what I was wasn't so bad. And Bray? I knew he'd never lie to me. Even when things were hard, even when I wouldn't like what he had to say, I knew he'd offer me honesty no matter what.

Maybe that was the real issue, that other people tried to find everything they wanted and needed in a partner in a single person, and I was far too broken for that. Instead, it took no less than these four men to be everything, to connect to each facet of my personality.

I wasn't one to be passive, so I hooked my thumbs into the waist of my pants and slid them down my legs, taking my thong with them. I wanted to be bare, to not have anything between us, anything to keep any part of them from me.

Soon, not a stitch of clothing remained on any of us, and I was rewarded with the view of the four men I loved.

No more fighting it. The wedding was tomorrow, and I didn't think I'd live past that. What was the point of fighting any of this now? Why resist it? What good would that do?

Instead, I wanted to drown in the feeling. I planned to embrace it all, to curl my fingers into this feeling and cling to it, let it wrap around me and live there — at least for the night.

I'd never really understood love before, never figured it was something I was capable of — giving or receiving. Now, in what was likely my last night, I damn well was going to sink into it as if it were forever, as if it wouldn't ever end.

I went to Rune first, his intense green eyes locked on me. I reached up, able to slide my fingers into his hair and pull him down to my lips only because he bent forward as well. I kissed him as if I couldn't breathe without it, rough and without finesse. He grabbed my ass and stood straight, holding me against him, letting me wrap my legs around his waist.

I had no fear of falling, of him dropping me. I knew damned well he never would.

We might both fall — some things couldn't be helped — but if I went down, he would, too.

That was a powerful feeling, to know that even if something happened, I wouldn't be alone. It hit me even harder after Jarrod had walked out, as every other person in my life had abandoned me.

I closed my teeth on his bottom lip, wanting to drive him harder, wanting to make him take me roughly, the make this as angry as I knew it could be.

He broke the kiss and shook his head. "Not doing it, Nem." He must have read the confusion on my face, because he pressed his forehead to mine. "I don't want angry — I don't want to just fuck you like you don't mean a thing to me anymore. I'm fucking tired of that."

I wanted to complain, but he set my legs down instead. I peered around to find myself in the bedroom they'd given me.

As quickly as it happened, Bray came forward and kissed me, more forward than he usually was, as if he couldn't wait another moment. He walked me backward until we hit the bed.

Bray laid me back, then followed me as I scooted up on the mattress, coming to rest over me. It felt strange and far too personal having him so close, being in a bed. Sex was always angry and spur of the moment, yet suddenly it seemed like more.

Even if I'd decided to embrace this night, anxiety hit me at his closeness.

"Stop shutting me out," Bray whispered when I closed my eyes, when my hands rested on his chest but before I actually pushed him away.

"I don't know how to do this," I admitted in a small voice.

"How to do what? Last I checked, you're not a virgin anymore."

I kept my eyes closed, the darkness giving me a sense of privacy, letting the words slide freely from my lips. "This is different. You want something from me now, want me to be someone I don't think I can be."

"Do you really believe that? Because if anyone knows you, it's us." He pressed a kiss to my jaw, then another, speaking between the gentle touches. "You think you're dead, have some dumb idea that you're not really alive, not a person anymore, but you couldn't be farther from the truth."

I opened my mouth to argue, but he took that moment to press his cock against my pussy and sink deep. It wasn't rough, not like most of the times we'd had sex, but that didn't change how it took my breath away.

He whispered, his voice low and sweet, which wasn't something I'd have ever expected from him. "You *want* to think you're different because it's easier. It's safer to think you're dead, because then you tell yourself got nothing to lose."

I shook my head. "You just see what you want. You weren't there—"

He set a hand over the scar on my chest. "I wasn't and I'm never going to forgive myself for it. I'm never going to stop trying to make up for it, trying to make it right. I fucked up—we all did—and you paid the price. The thing is, you don't have to *keep* paying that price. You don't have to keep living like you're still dead, like everything stopped that day."

When he rolled his hips, when he sank deeper into me, I gasped. It was so hard to think or argue when I felt him that deep inside of me, when I savored the way his length teased all my senses, when he kept me off balance with his lips, his words and the way his fingers idly stroked over my scar.

Fingers stroked through my hair, and it took a moment for me to realize it wasn't Bray. Even as he took me with deep, measured thrusts, as his lips played across my throat, it was Dane who toyed with my hair.

I lifted my gaze to Dane, my entire body drunk off the lust they had lit inside me.

"My poor Nem," he said softly, his touch downright romantic. "Always running, always looking for something to give you purpose. You've got to be exhausted, don't you?"

I am. The answer came to mind so fast, I knew it was the truth. Exhaustion ran right down to my bones, weariness from planning, from fighting, from watching everything in the world like it was a beast waiting to take a bite out of me hung heavily on me.

I nodded without thought.

"Good girl," he said. "You don't have to be tired anymore, though. You aren't alone anymore. I get it. I know you were alone in the house that day, that you crawled out of it, pulled yourself out, because it was just you. You feel like it's all on you to do what needs to be done, but that isn't true. Stop fighting for just tonight—lean on us. Fuck knows we can hold you that long."

The temptation wasn't fair. It was more than any person could be expected to refuse. Dane's gentle words were coaxing, but they lacked his normal level of manipulation. I didn't hear the way he talked people into what he wanted, the way he tricked them.

Instead, he sounded honest, like the words meant something to him.

Another game?

Maybe, but I didn't care. The desire to do as they said was too strong. All the fear I had, the years of loneliness, of waiting, of planning, of sacrifice all wore on me until it proved far too heavy to take another step with. Someone coming up and offering to hold it, even for the night, offered more than I could refuse.

Bray caught my thigh and pulled it up, angling my hips so he could take me deeper. He pulled back enough to stare at me, to capture my gaze with his, for me to lose myself in his dark eyes. He'd removed his glasses, which made him seem open and vulnerable. He was handsome in a way he never understood, with the sharp lines of his face, the way his piercing helped offset how young he appeared.

His thrusts increased, taking me harder, deeper. I lifted my hips in time with him, then slid my hand behind his neck. I couldn't tell him I'd changed my mind, that I agreed, so I said nothing.

I didn't want to waste tonight arguing.

He didn't look away, even as tension seemed to fill his body, as his thrusts lost their rhythm, as they turned more desperate and erratic. He didn't lean closer, didn't bury his face in my neck, didn't hide. "I fucking *need* you," he whispered before he plunged in and stilled. He rocked forward another few times, a tremble running through his body, down his arms, even to the hand that still grasped my thigh.

Before I could respond, he leaned in and kissed me, deep, as if that said something he couldn't on his own.

When he pulled away, I whimpered at the emptiness of my pussy, as I missed the way he fed the fire inside me.

Thankfully, I didn't have to wait long. A moment later, Dane took his place, moving from where he'd sat at the top of the bed to over me.

He was heavier, but he didn't sink into me right away. Instead, he caught my chin and ran his finger across my bottom lip.

"Nothing to say?" I asked, wishing my voice sounded stronger and less nervous.

"You don't listen worth a damn anyway."

I can't exactly deny that…

"Figured I'd say this in a way you might just understand," he said.

"And how's that?"

He grasped my hip, then turned me over. He didn't pull my hips back, didn't put me on all fours like I would have expected. Instead, his weight settled over me, his body lifted so there was a small amount of space between us.

I squirmed, but he didn't take notice. He kept my thighs together, his knees outside of my legs, and ran his hand down my back in a touch so soft, it made me shiver. His fingers found my cunt, and to my own embarrassment, I tried to lift my hips to get more.

He let out a soft chuckle before he pressed his cock against me, before he plunged into me in an unyielding slide that stretched and tormented me. This angle meant he didn't sink nearly as deep as Bray had, but that didn't matter. The tightness of my thighs together made him feel so much thicker, offered me an entirely taken over feeling.

He fucked me similar to how Bray had—not gently, but sweet in a way that made it feel different. Despite the fact that I'd slept with them each a few times, despite all the twisted things we'd done, despite how tame this was compared to everything else, it felt so much scarier.

He wrapped his hand around my throat, and I let out a moan at the touch. Was this it? Would he tighten his grasp and take us back to what I was used to?

The warmth of his lips sank into me when he kissed the side of my neck, next to where his fingers held me. "You think I'm going to choke you? Threaten you?"

"That's almost a love language for us," I said, trying for funny but knowing I'd missed it by miles.

He huffed, his breath blowing strands of my hair around. "I don't do it as a threat," he said.

"No? What else would it be called?"

"I always feel like you're running, like you're headed for the door, like you're a few seconds away from being gone entirely."

"So?" I asked as he sank in deep, as I arched against the feeling.

"So, I find this is the only way to reassure myself that you're still here, at least as long as I can keep a hold of you." He scraped his teeth along my shoulder, then kissed the spot. "I don't want you to run, Nem. I don't want you to hide, to think you've got to go anywhere else, that you need to escape me. I can't promise you a lot—we won't ever be normal, won't ever have some fantasy life—but I can swear I'll always be behind you." As if to make his point, he grasped my hip and sank in even deeper, taking me with a hard thrust.

Leave it to Dane to make a stupid joke at a time like this...

"I don't think you mind it as much as you pretend," he whispered. At my snort, I could feel his lips spread into a smile against my shoulder. "You tilt your head. Did you know that? You lean into me and expose your throat sometimes, like you're thinking about it, like you want me to hold on to you."

He was right. There wasn't a point in me pretending that wasn't true. There was something about the way he held me, the way he would wrap his large, strong hand around my throat that made me feel oddly...important. Even if there was a threat behind it, there was a safety in it, as well.

Like I mattered, like he wanted to make sure he never lost me.

I shifted as much as I could, angling my hips, pleading with him to give me what we both wanted.

He laughed softly. "Fuck, you're needy. You want to come? You want to break apart right here on my cock?"

Easy answer. "Yes," I whispered, throwing my pride away. I wanted that so badly, to let my mind go blank beneath him, to just feel for a moment when I felt like everything was normal.

He nipped me again, the sting soothed again by his kiss. "Too bad. I want you wound up. I want you so worked up that you can't think straight. Later, we're going to ask you a question, and only if you answer it right will you get off."

"Why?" I asked, the frustration bleeding through.

"Because I want you honest. You lie like you breathe, Nem, and this is way too important. So we're each going to show you how fucking much we love you, how damned important you are, and you'll feel it all. We can keep it up just as long as we need to."

I shook my head. Just knowing that he planned to deny me, that I'd have to get through Rune and Colton taking me before I got any release of my own, put me even more on edge. I was sure the bastard knew that, expected it, had planned on his words causing this reaction in me. Dane knew *exactly* how to play me.

I cried out when he delved into me again, when he sped up, when the strength of his fingers around the front of my throat all melted together.

Hell, I was close enough, I felt like I could have possibly managed to get myself off all on my own. Just a quick stroke, just one touch and it would have probably been enough.

I shifted my hips, trying to get any sort of friction to my needy clit. Dane's dark chuckle in my ear stopped me. "Won't work. We can keep you on this edge just as long as we want, and all the begging and pleading won't do a thing to get you what you want, so be a good girl and just take my cock, huh? Let me love you for a little while like this. Let me have you for a bit without the fight."

It wasn't really a question that needed an answer, yet I nodded.

He groaned, the sound deep and masculine against my ear, just before he seemed to give in. His thrusts stopped being measured, and, a few moments later, he took my earlobe between his lips and bit down on it as he shuddered. His cock, buried deep inside me, twitched, something I felt due to how turned on I was, how close to my own release I teetered.

His breath spilled over my cheek as he released my ear, and when he pulled out of me, wetness on my thighs made my face heat. I could just imagine how I looked, already fucked by two of the men, a mess of their cum and my own desire on my thighs.

Dane kissed down my back, over my spine, then delivered one more nip to the left cheek of my ass. It stung, drawing a gasp followed by a moan from me. He laughed again, the sound so much freer than I was used to from him.

They gave me no break, though. Not that I expected one. The Quad weren't the sort of men who would let a good advantage go, who would back off until their point was made. Besides, they knew I was tough enough to take whatever they dished out.

It meant that when a new set of hands grasped my hips, I had no idea who it was at first. Still, I trusted them, no matter how much my experience warned me not to.

I was rolled to my side, and the roughness of a beard told me it was either Rune or Colton who'd taken a spot behind me.

The answer was made clear when a hand slid around me and cupped my breast, the dark hair on the arm obviously Colton's.

My back pressed to his front, and he closed his fingers around my nipple. I arched into the touch, and despite the pain, despite the roughness, it was still different, still sweet.

"You make the best sounds," he told me. "Feels like the only time you're entirely honest, when I know where I stand with you. Are you going to spread your thighs, now? Are you going to let me have you?"

It was a stupid question. Of course I was. I would give him everything, just as I had the others.

I slid my foot along his calf, then hooked it behind his knee to offer myself up.

He made a noise in his throat, one I couldn't quite understand. "You're more than I ever thought I'd get, and a hell of a lot more than I deserve," he admitted softly as he released my breast so he could grasp himself and line himself up. He paused when the head of his cock nestled against my drenched cunt. "Close your eyes, Nem. Don't think about anything but me, about how this feels, about what you want."

I frowned at the request, but followed it still. It was funny, since Bray hadn't wanted me to close my eyes, hadn't wanted me to have any distance, yet Colton wanted the opposite. The men were impossible to keep up with.

Yet, in that darkness, I didn't feel distant. When he sank into me, when he used his thick shaft to take me, I couldn't put up any walls. All I could do was feel him, give in to him.

Once he'd bottomed out, he wrapped that arm around me, setting his hand on my hip to hold me still as he withdrew and filled me again. I arched my back to push against him.

His chuckle was strained. "See what happens when you stop fighting? When you stop thinking? When you give in and just feel? This is what I want, Nem, to have all of you. You aren't ever defenseless, but I want you to let me in, let me have you."

What did he think this was? I was letting him have whatever he wanted.

"I won't ever hurt you," he swore, his voice so low I almost missed his promise.

It didn't sound empty, like the sort of thing people said when they planned to do whatever the hell they wanted. Instead, it sounded like an oath, like he was telling me something that he'd never break, like it was a vow more important than any he'd ever made before.

And I believe him.

Our world was dangerous, so telling me that he'd never let anything happen to me, would have been foolish. Instead, he promised me what he could, that he'd never hurt me, and no matter how stupid it was to believe him, I did.

I reached down, wanting to stroke my clit, wanting to feel the same bliss I knew he was approaching.

Except, he let go of my hip to catch my wrist. A sound of pure frustration left me at the way my cunt squeezed around him uselessly, the way my body screamed for just a little more, just enough to get what I needed.

Still, he refused. He brought my wrist up, between my breasts, and pinned it there. "Not yet," he said in a gentle voice. "You don't get to come just yet. You'll need to take me, let me fill you, be a good girl and you'll get your chance afterward."

"You sadistic asshole," I snapped.

Jayce Carter

He didn't laugh, but amusement filled his words when he responded. "Maybe. You do look pretty, covered in sweat and cum and straining for something. And, yeah, I like that only we can give that something to you. You spent ten years on your own, ten years out there thinking you didn't need another damned person, so I admit it, I love how your body just begs me." He kissed my shoulder, and over the bite mark Dane had left. "Not that it'll get you what you want. Press your thighs together for me—tighter—fuck, yes, that's good. I'm not going to last much longer, not when your pussy feels this good."

Jealousy swamped me that he would get to experience what I wanted. Yet, another part of was thrilled. I *wanted* to feel him come, feel him lose that perfect control of his, all because of me. I couldn't imagine he reacted this way with anyone else, that any other woman had ever done this to him, made him crave something so badly, that anyone else could shatter his calm exterior like this.

Sure enough, he held my wrist tighter—probably a good thing since I would reach for my clit the second he let me go—and fucked me hard. It was wild, the sort of sex that would leave me sore come tomorrow.

For a split second, tomorrow threatened me. I thought about what was coming, about what would happen. His voice pulled me back. "Stop it, Nem. Don't go anywhere else—stay here, with me."

I cried out when he thrust in especially deep, when my body rebelled against the unmet needs inside me, and his words chased the thoughts away.

He made a deep sound that rumbled from his chest as he came, but unlike the last two, he didn't freeze. He continued to fuck me, his hands tightening almost painfully on my wrist, as if terrified I'd get away, that he'd lose me.

It took him a long moment to come down, as his thrusts slowed to almost nothing, as each movement of his cock drew a broken sound from me.

He kissed the nape of my neck before he released me, before he pulled away and withdrew from my desperate cunt.

I knew who would go last without having to look. Sure enough, Rune grasped my thigh easily and rolled me onto my back. I was too tired to fight, too on edge to make a joke or insult. Each nerve in my body sparked wildly, looking for the slightest bit of attention to push me over the edge. My pussy ached already, yet I wanted nothing more than feel Rune sink deep into me.

He spread my legs so wide, a stretch occurred in my hips. It put me entirely on display for him, and his hungry gaze reminded me of a wolf as he stared.

He brought his hand toward me, but the bastard avoided my clit. Instead, he stroked along my inner thighs, against the crease where my legs met my groin, and even brushed my slit. None of it was enough to get me off, though.

"You have the prettiest cunt, you know that? And it's so fucking swollen right now, just pink and puffy and drenched."

He swiped his fingers up the center of my pussy, then lifted those fingers to his mouth. He licked them clean of everything—of the cum, of my own desire, and the expression he gave me said he enjoyed it.

I left my legs as he'd placed them, because the men had pulled me so far beyond thinking. I had moved past arguing with myself over anything. As long as the Quad kept up whatever they were doing, I was happy.

Rune pulled me closer to him, scooting me down on the bed and reminding me of his size, his strength. The tattoos that ran over his chest and arms seemed even scarier in the dim light, the black ink standing out against his pale skin. They made him seem like he was from a different age, as if he really were the Viking he so often resembled.

He took a pillow and slid it beneath my hips, angling me better, then fit his cock against me. He paused, as though distracted by the sight. "You know, I didn't ever have this need inside me before."

That made me draw my eyebrows together, trying to understand what he meant.

He didn't raise his green eyes to mine, but he did keep speaking. "I didn't get it the first time I saw you, why I had this need, this craving. I've never wanted to own anything, yet from that first fucking glimpse of you I got, I *had* to have you. When I finally got my hands on you, this voice inside my head screamed to leave a mark, to do something that would make it clear you were *mine*."

I had no idea what he meant.

"I want to breed you." His words came back to me, the fevered way he had fucked me, the look on his face when he'd pressed their cum back into me. I'd thought it just some kink, but was he saying it wasn't? That it was something to do with me alone?

I couldn't ask because he took that moment to sink into me, to feed every inch of his thick cock into my pussy. After taking the other three, my body struggled. I arched and squirmed, reaching to the sides as if to find some sort of footing.

What I found was warmth. I had managed to grab Dane's thigh on one side and Bray's wrist on the other.

I hadn't even realized they were still that close, and a glance to the side revealed all the desire still on Bray's face.

Rune fucked me harder than the other two, right from the start. He watched as his length disappeared into my cunt as if that soothed him somehow. "I wasn't kidding," he said softly.

I risked a look at his face, and he finally met my gaze head-on. It was strange, since he wasn't right against me. The distance almost made his words more personal, because they had to travel so far, they floated into the empty space between us.

"Took me a while to figure it out. Why the fuck did I need you like this? Why couldn't I get the idea of knocking you up out of my head? Why the fuck did I even care when I never had before?"

His words ignited that fire inside me as they had every time he'd talked like this. Why did I like it? What the hell was wrong with me?

"Finally, I think I get it. I haven't had shit worth keeping, not ever. Never wanted anything, really. You're the only thing I've ever wanted for good, only thing I didn't want to get away, so when I look at you, when I see your sexy fucking body, your sweet cunt, all I can think about it breeding you. I want to fill you up with my cum, with their cum, and make you lie there. I want to see you growing, know that I did that, that you're mine forever, that we've got something between us that ain't never going to break." He grasped my hips, my thighs still spread open for him, and used the grip to hold me still as he took me hard.

It was rough, but it wasn't mean, it wasn't anger. Instead, it felt like desperation.

He panted as he spoke. "I ain't saying I want kids now, or hell, if we'd ever be ready, but fuck if I don't look at you and think for the first time in my life that I want that someday, that I want a future with you, that I fucking want to wake up next to you every damned day and spend every night worshipping every inch of your body."

I imagined what he said, the vulgar words painting a picture that made me moan. Sure, I didn't know if I ever wanted kids either—the very idea seemed impossible—but the fact he wanted me that way, that he was so driven by the need that he couldn't seem to control it, proved more intoxicating than anything else.

He let out an almost pained sound, as if trying to hold off. When I tried to reach for my clit again, Dane and Bray grasped my wrists, kept me from it, denied me.

"Please," I begged. We all knew what it was, knew how desperate I was. I'd have fallen to my knees if it would have gotten me what I needed.

"You want to come?" Colton asked as he stood there, just outside the group as he so often did.

I nodded, my eyes stinging as if tears had started there. I was sure the word *please* escaped my lips again, like some prayer.

"We said we'd have a question for you, didn't we? That you had to answer before we'd let you come." He glanced at Dane. "You think she's ready?"

Dane reached out with his free hand and brushed one of my hardened nipples with a light touch. It ran right to my clit, made me buck as my body went haywire even though it didn't send me over that edge. He offered a kind smile, even though I wanted to hate him for making me wait. "Yeah, she's ready."

Ready for what? For some stupid question? If my brain had been working right, I'd have called them names, have insulted them and their mothers for making me wait, then reminded them I could handle this all on my own, that they were obstacles at the moment.

Except, my brain *wasn't* working. They'd fried it somehow, made it hungry and slow and unable to think about the past or the future.

Rune stared down at me, his green eyes almost glowing, as he went still. His thick cock made my cunt react, made me want to shift around to get more friction. His grasp on my hips held me still, though, forced me to endure. "I want you to be honest," he told me.

I nodded helplessly. I didn't care what the question was. I'd tell them anything they wanted to know.

He leaned in, over me, caging me with his large body, my hands trapped already by the other men. It made me feel vulnerable, trapped, at his mercy, and I love that.

"Do you love us?"

The question hit me like a sucker punch. That was the sort of thing a person shouldn't ask, and certainly shouldn't ask *me*.

Love was something so much larger than whatever I was left. It was for normal people, and I wasn't sure I even understood the concept. Even the times I'd thought it, allowed the idea to form in my head, I'd never considered saying it out loud. That was so much farther.

I trembled, my body reacting from a mixture of the denied orgasms, the way the men touched me, and a question I hadn't expected to ever get asked.

Had I thought about it? Sure. I'd all but accepted it in my head. I fucking loved each one of them, no matter how I told myself not to, no matter how stupid I knew it was, I loved them.

Knowing it and saying it were different, though. Inside my head that was safe. It was private and it was mine. If I said it out loud, if I let it into the world, I had to deal with it. If they knew…

Rune caught my cheeks, forced my gaze to his, trapped me with his eyes. "Do you love us, Nem? It's an easy question."

"You already know," I whispered back, broken.

We *all* knew the answer. They'd known it when I'd been a kid still, when they'd pitied me for the stupid infatuation I'd had with them. They damn well already knew it now, too. They knew I was hopelessly in love with them, had been the entire time I'd known them. Even when I'd hated them, when I'd thought they might have been in on my attack, I'd loved them.

Why did I have to say it?

Rune brushed his lips to mine. "Maybe, but you need to say it."

"Why?"

"Because you think it ain't real if you don't say it. You think if it's trapped in here."—he tapped my temple—"then it doesn't count. You bury it, bury everything you feel, and then think you're dead. The thing is, dead people don't love. Corpses don't love. I want to hear you say it, to admit it, because then maybe you'll realize you ain't dead."

My trembling spread until I shook all over, a battle inside of me between what they wanted from me and what I didn't think I could do.

The room was silent beyond my erratic breathing, and even Rune's body couldn't warm me, couldn't make me feel like I wasn't going to shake out of my own skin.

He made a soft sound, deep in his chest, as if to reassure me.

"You ain't dead," he whispered again. "I don't give a fuck what happened, you ain't dead. You're the most alive girl I have ever fucking known, and I'm sick of you not seeing it. So come on, one answer and you can have what you want. Tell me the truth and we'll give you everything."

My body teetered on that edge, so close I felt as if I could reach out and touch the release I wanted.

The words came to my lips before I could think about it, a reaction from how far they'd pushed me, from how badly I wanted them.

"I love you," I admitted, terrified of what it meant, of the connection it seemed to build between us, as if the words alone bound us together.

What did the admission mean? Where did that leave us?

"Good girl," Rune whispered before pushing up again to his knees, so he didn't have to rest his weight on his arms. He grasped my hip with one hand took me hard, recklessly, as he stroked my clit with the fingers of his other hand.

It only took a heartbeat for me to come, for me to lose myself in the pleasure that overcame me. Rune fucked me through it, prolonging my release, and by the end of it, after he'd come as well, I was breathless and limp, my body feeling as if I'd passed a limit I hadn't known I'd had.

He pulled out of me, but I lacked the energy to make a sound, to complain or move at all.

Another weight settled over me, and I found Bray's face above me. I frowned, confused.

He gave me a rare smile. "You did good."

"So let me sleep," I said.

He shook his head. "Tomorrow's dangerous, and I have no idea what might happen. If you think I'll let a single minute of tonight go to waste, you're a fool. You just admitted you love us, and now we're going to spend the whole fucking night making sure you know that isn't one-sided."

I opened my mouth to tell him he was crazy, but instead, he slid his cock into my drenched and exhausted pussy, taking me without asking, giving me what I needed even when I couldn't ask for it. Even though I was exhausted, even though I wasn't sure I could take anymore, the drag of his cock against my cunt, the words he said, the reminder this might be all we got overcame me.

I'd been terrified of love for so long, but if this was what it was like? If this was what I had to take the risk for?

Maybe sticking around wouldn't be so bad…

* * * *

I slid my hands up my ribcage, cupped my breasts and lifted them slightly. I didn't have a lot there, but I'd worn a bra with plenty of padding to make the illusion of being amply blessed. It being strapless, however, meant some adjustment was needed.

Large, warm hands slid around me and cupped my breasts just as I'd done. Dane's voice came out amused and more than a little turned on when he chuckled.

"What are you doing?" I asked, even though it was obvious.

"I'm helping."

"This isn't helping."

He shifted his hands, the action causing the fabric to rub against my nipples and reminded me that no matter what else was going on, he could distract me. "Of course I am. Your arms looked tired, so I stepped in. I'm always here to carry your burdens."

"Did you just refer to her tits as burdens?" Colton walked in, laughing softly as he buttoned one of the cuffs of his long-sleeve button-up shirt.

And... damn, while he looked good naked, he was positively sinful in a tux. His hair was still dark and wild, but he'd groomed his beard nicely.

"I feel rather burdened by them." Dane pressed against me so his erection rubbed against my back, making his point clear.

I elbowed him — not because his behavior annoyed me, but rather because I knew he could convince me that we had time, that stripping out of the panties I wore and bending over was in our schedule, despite me knowing it wasn't.

I'd done my hair, my makeup, zipped myself into the long black dress. Redoing it all would take far longer than we had.

Though...the idea tempted me. The desire to capture the feelings from the night before, to pretend things were different, was strong.

I turned to find Dane dressed as well, looking every bit as stunning as Colton. I had to stop and consider…had I ever seen them in tuxes? I didn't think so.

Suits were one thing, but this whole black-and-white thing was a whole different level.

From the hallway, Rune and Bray walked in, and as a group, they took my breath away. It was funny how they could look every bit as lethal dressed this way, that the fancy clothing didn't civilize them or take away their edge at all. Sure, they could fit into the classiest of parties, but no one would think they were stockbrokers who spent all day behind a desk. They were still *them*. Still killers, still the Quad others feared, still *mine*.

Rune curling his lip into a smirk woke me up. I couldn't spend all day staring at them. We had a plan, and we needed to get going.

Leave it to Dane to not do things on my schedule, though. He caught my wrist and tugged me against him. At first, I didn't lean against him, afraid to mess up his outfit. His coaxing got what he wanted, though—didn't it always? "Take a deep breath."

I did as he said, because it would be quicker than arguing.

"We've got this."

I went to tell him that we didn't, that he couldn't possibly know that, when a swat to my ass made me turn my head and offer Rune a glare.

Dane spoke again, drawing my attention back. "We've got this, Nem. We've planned out every step, every contingency. You clearly can handle yourself, and this isn't our first dangerous job."

"What if something goes wrong?"

"Then we improvise. By the end of tonight, Kenz will be safe and Kyler will be dead. Let me hear you say that we've got this."

I pulled in a deep breath, held it for a moment then released it slowly. "We've got this."

One way or another, we've got this.

Chapter Sixteen

Nem

Kenz brought me up short as I walked into the large downstairs space where they'd set up a dressing room for her. She sat in a chair in front of the mirror, a woman behind her working on her hair.

She looked like a grown woman, like she could have been sitting there for real, getting ready to marry a man she loved. Her hair was curled, with the popular almost messy style. The stylist had pulled it into an updo, leaving a few long tendrils down around her face. Her makeup was minimal, with a dusting of shimmers on her cheekbones and eyebrows to highlight, her lips pink, a light gold over her eyes.

The dress she'd chosen was sexy, but because of the white, it was unmistakably a wedding dress and gave her an edge of innocence.

It made me wonder for a moment if that was how our mother had looked on her wedding day. I hadn't ever thought about it, since before my mother had died it hadn't mattered, and afterward? I'd focused on revenge and hadn't cared.

Right then though, I wondered. Not just about how she looked, but how she felt, if she'd been excited, scared, upset? Marrying Kyler wasn't a decision I'd ever really understood, but that didn't mean she hadn't cared for him at some point. Had she stood there and wanted to marry him? Had she thought about Jarrod instead?

Kenz lifted her gaze to see me through the mirror and her smile shook me. It was stunning—bright, welcoming, everything I wasn't. It solidified my need to be here, to do this, to make it work.

I wanted her to keep that, to have the things Kyler had stripped from me. Kyler had twisted me, and I had to get Kenz away before he did it to her, too.

The stylist put in one more bobby pin before moving away, leaving Kenz to rise from her seat and turn. She was barefoot, so the dress pooled around her feet, but it didn't stop her from rushing over and hugging me.

I resisted at first, the same feeling I always got when she did this. It felt wrong. I didn't deserve this sort of thing, wasn't the sort of person who got people being happy to see me, didn't understand this sort of easy affection.

Except, however this ended, I doubted I'd see her again. It made me throw caution to the wind and really hug her back, as if I could get back all the hugs I'd missed, all the time stolen from us both, the relationship we could have had — *should* have had.

Too soon, she pulled backward, a slight smear to her eyeliner.

I swiped my thumb beneath her eye, wiping it away along with the tear. "You aren't the crying type," I told her.

She laughed, repeating my action below both of her eyes. "My mom used to say that." As soon as she said it, her smile slid away. "She should be here."

I waved her toward the small couch, taking a seat beside her and the yards of fabric she wore. "She should be. I'm sorry."

"I wonder what she'd say."

I made myself go back, to see our mother's face. She hadn't been a warm woman, one who laughed easily or showed much affection. She'd been tough, willing to bear what she had to for duty and family.

So what would she have thought here?

She probably would have told Kenz about responsibility, about how life often wasn't fair or fun or happy but how we had to keep moving despite it. She'd have told Kenz to keep her chin up and never let anyone see her weaknesses.

Except, those were lessons for me, not for Kenz. I accepted my place in life, but she deserved *more*.

"She would have been proud of you," I said instead of anything else. It wasn't a lie, but kinder than the full truth.

"Maybe," Kenz said, leaning forward. "I don't remember a lot about my mom, to be honest. I get the feeling I'm not a lot like her, though. I've seen videos, and she was bigger than life. She could drive off someone with a sharp look. Rune told me about a time when someone tried to mug her while she was out. He said she pulled her shoulders back and stared him down—sent him running with just that look and a good threat. I'm not much like that, am I?"

"No," I admitted softly. At her flinch, I rushed out the rest of my statement. "You're more than that. You smile, and you *enjoy* life, and you haven't let any of the shit that's happened to you dull your shine at all. Do you have any idea how rare that is?" I should have shut up, but I kept going because this was likely to my only chance to ever tell her these things. Sure, a sister heart-to-heart right now was pointless — and I didn't have the right to it — but I felt like I needed to say something. Her mother was gone, her sister was both gone and would be again soon, and her father was a piece of shit. She hadn't grown up with anyone there to give her advice other than the Quad, and they gave horrible advice.

I dropped my gaze, unable to look into her familiar eyes as I went on. "Your mom, from what I've heard, was jaded by the world. It shaped her and crushed her and made her hard." *And it did that to me, too.* "You, though, you haven't let it do that. Even after what you've lost, even after being so alone, you're still kind. You still see the good things in the world, in people, even if I'm not sure they're really there. That's something rare and amazing."

As I spoke, wetness tracked down my own cheek. I touched below my eye with a strange confusion. *Crying?*

What the fuck? I didn't cry. I hadn't cried since that man had shot me, since I'd dragged myself out of that house. Weeks of recovery, months of physical therapy, and I'd never shed a tear. That softness had been part of that other girl, the one who had died.

I brushed away the evidence, knowing I could fix my own makeup later.

"So, how are you feeling?" I asked, trying to put us back on topic.

"As ready as I'll ever be." Her shrug was full of unhappiness but acceptance.

"Can I ask you something?"

"Anything."

I waited, making sure I phrased it right. "If you had a way to not go through with this, would you take it?"

"I learned a long time ago that when my dad makes up his mind, there aren't other options."

"But if there was, even if it was dangerous or risky, would you do it?"

Her answer didn't matter in terms of my plan. I wasn't going to allow this to happen even if she felt resigned, because I knew that would only be because she was afraid, because she didn't know she had choices.

After a long moment, she nodded. "I've always wanted to stand up to my dad, to tell him I want to live my own life."

"So why haven't you?"

"Because I always lose. I tried, when I was younger. It never worked. I told Dad I didn't want to cut the Quad out of my life after Mom's death, and I tried to call them after even when he told me not to. When he found out, he shipped me off to a different boarding school across the country, took away the only things I had—a relationship with him and one with the Quad. No matter what I ever did, it never helped, so I realized trying only hurt me. Don't get me wrong—I'm not happy with where my life is, with where it's going. If I saw a door, a chance, I'd run through it in a heartbeat. I've just lived in this long enough to know better than to hope. This is my life. I don't have to like it, I don't have to be happy about it, but there isn't any changing it."

Oh, yes there is.

I tried to give her a smile, one to reassure her without letting her in on anything. "Life changes, Kenz. You never know what might happen, what tomorrow looks like."

Kenz set her hand on mine, the touch strange, holding me between wanting to enjoy the contact and wanting to pull away. "You're not as bad as you think."

"What?" I frowned as I lifted my gaze to hers, going back over what I'd said, wondering for a moment if I'd been so worked up, I'd made no sense at all.

"You're always telling me how great I am, but I can hear what you're not saying. I don't know why you're so mad at yourself, what you think you've done that's so terrible, but you don't give yourself enough credit."

"This isn't about me."

"Everything is really about us, in the end." She smiled, a sad one that tore at me. "I have a friend who told me that everything we see and think is filtered through us, through not just our experience but how we see ourselves."

"Smart person," I said, even if I wasn't sure I believed it.

"Dane sure thinks he is." She paired the statement with a soft laugh. "You haven't told me much about yourself, and I respect that. We've all got things in our pasts we'd rather not talk about. But, Nem, you need to let go of whatever it is that you're punishing yourself for."

Last talks and all made me honest. "What if it's unforgivable? What if whatever I am isn't worth anything more?"

She squeezed my hand, leaning down slightly so I kept my eyes locked to hers. "It is. You're a better person than you think, and you don't give yourself enough credit."

I mirrored her smile even if I didn't feel it. I wasn't a person, and certainly not a good one. I was a mission, a name, a set of steps, nothing more.

However, she wouldn't know that, wouldn't ever really understand it. When it was all over, the men would tell her who I was, but they'd pretty it up.

Not to help me, but to save her from the ugliness I'd become, to keep her able to think of me as something else.

I squeezed her hand back. I didn't believe I was the person she said I was, but it was nice, just for a moment, to see myself how she saw me.

As someone worth a damn.

* * * *

The men were putting in their face time before they would go to their designated spots. They needed to play the part that this was like any other day, that nothing strange was happening. Colton would have to handle Jarrod's shot as well, since Jarrod had opted to walk out instead of helping me.

The sting in my chest from that hadn't gone away. I would say it might not ever go away, but since I still doubted I'd live past the end of the night, I guess it wouldn't last all that long.

My fake father had betrayed me, so why my real father abandoning me could still hurt, I didn't know. It did, though, this ache inside me in a spot I'd thought was long dead.

It really seemed unfair to feel it at all. Hadn't I gone through enough that those parts of me should have been numbed?

"Nem." Kyler's voice drew my gaze from the mirror as I fixed my eyeliner. The waterworks with Kenz had smudged it, and I didn't plan on dying without my makeup right. It felt like as much body armor as a bulletproof vest.

Which the men were wearing, but wouldn't fit beneath my dress.

Maybe that was the real reason why women were expected to wear skimpy clothing—men needed the added advantage of access to their weak spots.

I swiped the brush over my lid and to the point I'd set, making sure the lines were strong and the point sharp. "Weddings," I said with a smile, as if I could be excused for the whole crying nonsense due to that.

He leaned against the doorframe of the bathroom I'd ducked into, his tux jacket missing, making him appear more dressed-down than others. "How is she doing?"

"She's nervous, but she's good."

He nodded. "Mackenzie has always liked to fight against the inevitable, but she knows what she needs to do in the end."

I put the eyeliner and lipstick into my small makeup bag, then tucked it beneath my arm and turned. "It looks like everything has worked out." I meant my own plan, of course, but shrouded the meaning in the plans for the wedding.

"Yeah. You did a good job setting it up. I knew you were the right woman for the job."

I turned slightly, shifting my gaze toward the doorway. "I should probably get out there, make sure everything is ready for her big entrance."

"The planner has that handled. I actually needed you for just a moment."

Changed plans are never a good thing…

"What for?" I chastised myself as I asked, the words automatic even though I knew better than to question Kyler.

"It'll only take a moment," he assured me. "I just have something for you, something I think would mean a lot to Mackenzie."

I wanted to get out of whatever he had planned because I had a schedule to keep and being so close to the end point, I didn't want to risk any part of it. However, the set of Kyler's shoulders told me there wouldn't be any polite getting out of it to be had.

"Sure." I tried to feign excitement as I followed him through the mansion, up the stairs, and into an office on the second floor.

As soon as we walked in, I knew it was one he'd claimed for his use while there. It was in the way his cologne hung in the air, in the massive desk I was sure he had moved in there, the one that was more a status symbol than a functional piece of furniture.

The room reeked of him — self-importance and arrogance with little substance.

When I entered fully, he shut the door behind me.

"I have a piece of jewelry for you." He passed me and went to his side of the desk. The drawers opened smoothly, his attention on whatever sat inside.

"I don't need anything," I assured him. I didn't want anything from him, either, and I was certain anything he had would be gaudy and so far from my taste. "You've done more than enough for me."

"It isn't for you, exactly." He pulled out a black box, larger than his palm, then came over to where I was. "I mean, it is, you can keep it, but it's really for Mackenzie."

I didn't understand what he meant until he opened the box and I laid eyes on the necklace inside.

It was an onyx stone with silver wrapping around it in the shape of a tree. I'd grown up seeing that necklace nearly every day on my mother's throat.

She'd gotten it from her father, and it had followed the Hester line. I'd wondered what had happened to it a few times in the years since the attack, after Carlos had torn it from her neck. I'd figured Kyler had destroyed it as if that would rid him of the Hester legacy.

It seemed he'd kept it.

"It was my wife's." Kyler's words reminded me that Nem would have no idea what the necklace was or the importance.

I chided myself for the stupidity of falling to sentimentality. "I can't take this," I said. "It should go to Mackenzie, not me."

"Mackenzie is a Williams, not a Hester. Besides, you've stepped into her life in a way that would have made Caroline proud. I think she would have liked if someone who stood by Mackenzie's side had this on, as if she were there in some form."

My hand trembled as I reached for it, and when I touched the cool metal, the oddest feeling washed through me. It was as if I had reached back through the years, as if I could see my mother touching the necklace, as if I could hear her telling me about it.

How many times has she lectured me on the meaning? About how the onyx represented something precious, and how only the family tree could keep it safe, how everything we did had to be to protect our family, how that was the only defense in our world.

"Let me." Kyler took the box and set it down so he could remove the necklace. It was on a different chain than it had been before, though that shouldn't have shocked me. I recalled how Carlos had grasped the pendant and yanked it from my mother's body, how the chain had snapped.

I turned when Kyler gestured, ignoring how much I didn't like him standing so close to me or—more importantly—behind me.

"Your hair," he said.

I reached behind me and lifted my hair, letting him fasten the chain. On the back of the door was a large mirror, and the sight of me in my mother's necklace was perhaps the most shocking thing of all.

I knew I looked like she did, though the red hair hid it. It hadn't ever really hit me just how much until I saw that, until her necklace rested on my chest. It was like a final shove for me to recognize that she was gone, that I'd grown into a woman in that time, that I was her heir.

"It suits you," Kyler said, forcing my gaze up in the mirror to meet his, further throwing me into the limbo between the past and the present.

I went to tell him thank you, to muster some response despite the turmoil inside me.

What silenced me was the curl of his lips into a smirk, the sort he used when he thought he'd won, when he sprang a trap no one had seen coming. The look set off warnings in my head, but it was his words that made it clear I was in trouble.

"It really is fitting for you to have it. You should be wearing your mother's necklace, Kelsey."

Chapter Seventeen

Colton

I really hated not having eyes on Nem. No matter how much I'd told her she had this handled, that we had a good plan, I knew it wasn't true.

We had a cobbled-together plan when we didn't have any other options, but that didn't make it a good one. I'd gone in with less, of course. I'd taken jobs when the odds were worse, but never when it mattered.

One of the things I'd learned doing the work I did was that cutting my losses and running was sometimes the best thing a person could do. If a situation changed, if I knew that my odds had gone down significantly, if I realized that it was no longer a good idea, I'd pull back.

I could always come back another day, regroup, find an opening later — at least, I could if I wasn't dead.

However, that wasn't the case tonight. We lacked the luxury to just back out of the plan because it became inconvenient. Even if Bray, Rune, Dane and I could do that, Nem never would. She'd hold on tighter no matter what happened, and we couldn't leave her.

Which meant no matter how fucked our situation got, we were committed.

Of course, that offered me a sense of peace as well. Knowing it would end one way or another tonight took away some of the doubt, some of the worry. I didn't have to question if I should pull the trigger—I didn't have a choice.

The tiny, sharp pieces of the guardhouse roof dug into my arm. I glanced down my scope, surveying the large, tented area. Without Jarrod there to take the second shot, I'd had to set up on top of a guard tower along the fence line. Patrols had passed beneath me, but I'd let them be. There wasn't a reason to risk tipping our hand before the right time.

From my position, I had eyes on both the guards at the tent I needed to drop to ensure Kenz's escape. The shots weren't difficult, but they needed to happen in quick succession. The last thing I wanted was for the second to get frightened and run. Moving targets provided a much harder shot.

I checked to the left to find Rune talking with one of Torrance's security team. To the side of the house was Bray, his gaze hard. Normally, that sort of intensity might alert someone, but if Bray ever didn't look stressed, it would be far more suspicious. He was near the door to the basement, where the breaker was located.

The sun had dipped behind the mountains, but there was still enough light to easily see. A glance at my watch said the wedding would start in an hour.

Nem had better be okay…

I shook away the thought. As much as I wanted to worry about her, this wasn't the time. I had to trust that she knew what she was doing, that she'd understood our point before, that she really would be as careful as possible. The idea of finishing this, of being free of Kyler, of having Kenz able to live a real life, of actually avenging Caroline but walking away from it all without Nem?

I couldn't even finish that to the end, as if my brain outright refused to fathom such a thing. It would make it empty, make it feel as if there hadn't been a point to any of it. I didn't need some hallow win — I'd spent the last ten fucking years feeling lost. Losing Nem before had been heartbreaking but now? Now that I'd tasted what life with her could be, now that she'd grown into a woman I was hopelessly in love with, it would shatter me entirely.

Keep your mind on the task.

I tried to scan the windows of the house, but with all the curtains drawn, I couldn't see in. When I returned to where Rune had been, I found the spot empty.

Strange... He was supposed to stay there until it was time to move inside the tent. I judged the distance to the tent.

He could have gone inside, and I'd missed it, but it seemed unlikely. It was too early, and Rune didn't tend to ignore plans. Perhaps something else came up?

Unease crept up my spine as I shifted the scope to the side of the house, toward Bray.

Nothing.

That unease grew, my mind working at grasping the pieces, at turning them into a picture that made sense. I'd done this long enough, been with the others through enough to know when something had gone wrong.

There was this tingle that started in the back of my neck, down at the base of my skull, that would warn me. Even before I could identify what had happened, or just how badly we were all screwed, that same tingle always alerted me.

That feeling was all but stabbing me at the moment.

I twisted to sit up, to grab the phone from my pocket, when the crunch of asphalt behind me told me I wasn't alone.

I'd been so busy thinking about Nem, distracted by my worries about a future with her, that I'd been careless. I hadn't listened well enough, hadn't been ready.

Pain streaked through my head when something struck me hard, before I even got the chance to see who it was. I crumpled, the world fading away.

Worrying about what kind of future I could have with Nem might have just robbed me of the very thing I wanted most...

* * * *

Nem

There comes a moment in every con when a person had to decide whether or not the game was up. They end up faced with someone who knew—or thought they knew—about the truth, when they confront the con artist.

A person would only get a split second to choose where to go from there. Stick with the lie? Try my hardest to sell it, to gaslight the other person into questioning what they knew, or give in? Try to reduce the damage that could be done?

I usually went with selling the lie or telling a bigger lie on top of it. The truth was generally the worst option, since in my world the truth got people killed. The truth was that I was going to betray and kill Kyler, then steal his daughter. That wasn't the sort of thing that would put me on better footing.

So instead of swinging my elbow around into Kyler's face—and boy did I want to do that—I turned and painted on my best 'I have no idea what you're talking about' face. "Who? Kelsey? The daughter you said died?"

He clicked his tongue as if disappointed by my response. "Come now, Kelsey, the game is up."

I pressed my lips together, then shook my head. "You're confused."

He gestured toward the chair, and it was then I realized he held a pistol in his hand. "I wouldn't claim to be the best father in the world, but do you really think I wouldn't recognize my own daughter? Even after all this time?"

The set of his jaw convinced me that he had his mind made up. Lying was out of the door, it seemed. I sat where he'd indicated. "How long have you known?"

"From the moment I first saw you."

"No one else knew."

"Everyone else is a fool, tricked by your pretty face and prettier lies. I watched you grow up for seventeen years, watched you look more and more like your mother. A decade isn't all that long after that. The second I met you, I knew."

"Why didn't you say anything?"

"I never let a good advantage go to waste. I might have known it was you, but I had no idea why you were back, what you wanted or what you might have planned. Besides, you coming back afforded me one hell of an opportunity."

"And a risk."

"The best opportunities are always the biggest risks." He leaned against the desk, his gaze moving over me. "You truly do look like your mother. At seventeen, you were still a child, still looked like a teenager, but now? Now that you've become a woman? You look so much like she did."

"Before you killed her," I said.

He smiled, one that didn't have a hint of regret. "Yes—before I had her killed."

"And why exactly did you do that? I have plenty of guesses, but I want to hear it from you."

"Do we really need to go over history right now?"

"What other time will there be?"

He sighed as if put out by the topic. "You know your mother and I married because of what we could give each other. I needed her name, her connections, and she needed someone to claim you and to help her save face."

Which answered another thing, didn't it?

"So you knew all along I wasn't yours?"

"Of course I knew. I'd already tried to get Caroline's attention before, but she never gave me a second thought. I noticed her getting sick, however, and it wasn't difficult guess as to why. She knew exactly what a child out of wedlock would mean for her—if it even happened. More likely than not, her father would have demanded an abortion, and she'd have been shamed for it. She couldn't exactly get someone else on board to marry her fast enough to pass you off as theirs, which left me as her only true option. Caroline was a lot of things, but she wasn't stupid. We both got what we needed out of it."

"Do you know who my real father is?"

"No, and I never bothered to ask. What did it matter? Some man who donated a bit of DNA then ran off was of no interest to me."

I tried to hide my reaction, his dismissal like fire on my skin. "So you never cared at all?"

"About you?" He tapped the fingers of his free hand on the edge of the desk. "I did, at one time. There were a few times I even thought I might have loved you, when you followed my lead, when you did some especially clever trick or outwitted someone. In fact, as time has passed, I've started to wonder if you're more like me than my own flesh-and-blood daughter is."

"I am nothing like you," I snapped.

"You are. We're all products of our circumstances and environments, all created by what's around us. I told you how I grew up, what I was born into."

"And you were also clear about how you changed."

"Then you misunderstood the point of that story. I didn't change from who I was—that poor, powerless boy created who I am now, the drive I have, the willingness to be ruthless when others aren't. You were created by me—first by what I tried to teach you and later by what I did to you and your mother. You might not be my blood, but you're my daughter nonetheless."

I shook my head, his words a reflection of what I'd feared so many times. "You might have turned me into what I am now, but you'll pay for it."

"I won't." His smile was full of confidence. "No matter how much you want to pretend to be my equal, you aren't. I've been miles ahead of you this whole time, directing you, making sure you went the way I wanted you to. I ensured you had access to nothing important, nothing that could really hurt me. Have you really not figured that out yet?"

"What I've figured out is that you're arrogant, that you think you've won before you have. That's how I survived the last time, because you thought you'd succeeded, thought I was dead when I wasn't."

He let out an unconcerned laugh. "You're smart, but you're still just one little girl. The only risk to me could be the Quad, and they're already in custody—or dead, if they fought."

Fear gripped me, something I wasn't sure I'd felt since that night. It was real, honest fear, one that played havoc with my heart. That wasn't possible, was it? The men always seemed untouchable, beyond Kyler's influence or control, and yet it was the certainty he'd said it with. "That isn't true," I answered, even if I knew my voice wasn't as strong as it should have been.

"Of course it is. Colton was on the roofline of a guard tower, Rune near the back door, Bray around the basement door and Dane near the fence line."

Fuck.

"What did you do to them?" I asked, some of that fear replaced by fury. How *dare* he touch my men.

"If they could be taken alive, nothing yet. I know better than to destroy chess pieces before they can be used properly."

"And how do you plan to use the chess pieces you think you have?"

He smiled wider. "I've been thinking ever since your and Caroline's deaths about what to do with Mackenzie. Every time I look at her, all I see is Hester. She was supposed to be my heir, to be a Williams, to be my legacy, but no one who looks at her sees that."

"Because she's too good to be a Williams," I spat.

He didn't look annoyed at the statement, as if he expected nothing less from me. He didn't even respond to it as he went on. "Even though she has continued to be a thorn in my side, she's been useful, a connection to power I've leveraged many times—just like Caroline. The problem is, every good piece of leverage is a risk as well. Mackenzie has reached the end of her usefulness to me."

"So you'll marry her off and be done with her? Bested by a teenager again?"

He let out a soft laugh. "No. By doing that, I'd be handing that power to someone else. Just like what I got from Caroline, Mackenzie would give that to another family. No smart man ever gives something so potentially useful to someone who could use it against him."

That pit in my stomach grew as his words sank in, and I tried to work through what they meant.

Thankfully, I didn't have to ask. Kyler seemed only too happy to tell me. "The Hester name has given me a lot, but it has stolen a lot from me as well. I've taken it as far as I can, so I need to cut ties fully."

"So why let Torrance marry her?" As soon as I asked, the answer became clear. It was one of those times when my brain caught up, when I was forced to recognize something my mind had refused to see sooner, and when I wondered why the hell it had taken me so long. "She isn't going to marry Torrance, is she?"

"You're finally working it out? You think more like me than you want to admit."

I thought back to what he'd done with Caroline and me, to how he'd used our deaths to his own advantage. He'd pinned the attack on the enemy he'd wanted removed. Why let a good plan go to waste rather than using it a second time? "You're going kill her and blame it on Torrance." I frowned and shook my head. "That doesn't make sense, though. Why would Torrance go through all these wedding plans just to murder Kenz? That wouldn't get him anything, so no one would believe it."

"You're thinking too small, ignoring all the other chess pieces I have at my disposal, all the problems I can rid myself of at the same time."

What else was there?

The men…

He smiled, as though he could see me putting it all together. "I've wanted the Quad out of the way for a long time. Like Mackenzie, like Caroline, they served their purpose, but they've always been loyal to Caroline, then to Mackenzie and you—never to me. With Mackenzie gone, they'll have no connection to me at all, and they know far too much to be allowed to go out and potentially turn against me. It is truly tragic, but see, they had a part in Caroline's death as well, and now? They decided to get rid of Mackenzie, myself and other heads of other families. The wedding gave them the perfect opportunity to get these people together in one spot."

"Nobody will buy that story."

"You underestimate the stupidity of the average person. I mean, I've known who you were from the start, have been able to manipulate you and drive you in the direction I want you to go, and you never once suspected it. I was able to twist you, to get you to doubt the Quad, to figure out every single thing you had up your sleeve, and you're smarter than most people. Even the few times you got the better of me—such as the dress shop incident—I turned it around for my advantage by using it as a reason for the presence of Torrance's men. I've also kept the Quad in the dark for a decade over what really happened. Do you really think that normal people are going to look too closely?"

I pressed my lips into a thin line, furious that I couldn't argue with any of that. "And you think Torrance is going to just go along with that?"

"Of course he will, seeing as he helped to plan it all."

I froze at that. "Torrance was in on it?"

"Having someone else in power to back up my statement will sell the story. Once we've done away with the other families in attendance, we'll split all that territory between us. There won't be anyone who can stop us then, anyone who can stand against us."

"And you think the people who aren't coming will accept that? They'll just believe you?"

"They will because it has the perfect villain."

"The Quad? They're scary, but they've never tried to gain any real power, so why would anything believe they would do all that now?"

"No, not the Quad." He gave me an indulgent look. "The missing Hester heir, Kelsey, who plotted with the Quad to kill her mother and faked her own death. A decade later, when she was ready, she came back to kill her sister, her father and anyone else in the way so she could reclaim the Hester throne and power."

I shook my head, even as something inside me whispered that it could work. "That is insane."

"Is it? The Hester name has always been feared rather than loved, respected because of what those in that line have done. Do you really think anyone will doubt that the last of the Hesters would come back?

Would do this? It's like the boogeyman returning from the shadows."

A tremble started inside me, as if the anxiety and fear had grown to a level where my body could no longer contain it. Try as I might, I couldn't counter what he said, I couldn't figure out a reason why it wouldn't work.

All those little steps that had happened, every conversation, every word he'd spoken, it all rushed past me and moved into place, as I watched his plan fit together. He'd been headed this way from the start, pushing us all toward this outcome, and I'd never seen it at all.

Jarrod's warning to me echoed in my head. The Quad's warnings as well, the way they had all told me to not trust Kyler, that he was more dangerous than I realized. I'd ignored them, dismissed it, thought I was so much smarter than Kyler.

Now we would all pay the price for my own arrogance.

"You can't really believe no one will question this," I said, desperation lacing my words.

"Someone might, but not loudly enough to matter. What do these people care about Mackenzie? About the Quad? About some girl who they all thought died ten years ago? Even if anyone cares, they won't stand up against me—they have their own problems, so they'll mind their own business. You see, Kelsey, that's the lesson you never really took to heart, the one you didn't let sink in. We're all just pieces in this game, locked into our place by who we are. I was always meant to be a king in the game and you? Mackenzie? Caroline? Even your precious Quad? You're all just pawns I can sacrifice for my game. Out in that wedding, there isn't a single person who gives a damn about you. So after I walk Mackenzie down the aisle, as we stand there, the lights will turn off and the men I hired will rush the tent, kill Mackenzie and the guests, and everyone will believe it when Torrance and I say it was the Quad. By the end of the night, everyone in my way will be dead. I'll offer you and the Quad up for public execution for the families of the guests, and that will be the end of it. The people who survive get to make the story whatever we want it to be."

I stared at him, the horror washing over me as I couldn't deny what he said.

He tilted his head, an expression that could have almost been fondness on his face. "You know, I've wondered, if I hadn't had you killed, if I'd really taken you under my wing, what could I have made you into? Maybe you could have become the heir I always wanted. I let Caroline raise you, let the Quad intervene, but if I hadn't?" After a moment, he shrugged. "I guess none of that matters now, does it? Try to relax, because this is all done. I'll be back when it's finished."

"You're not going to just kill me now?"

"What good is a dead villain? No, the best monsters need to be beheaded in front of everyone, so they know they're really dead. That goes for you and your precious Quad."

And as much as it terrified me, as much as I wanted to remain in control to know what needed to be done, to formulate a plan, nothing came together.

For the first time in my entire life, I felt lost. I had no steps, no plans, nothing to hold on to.

I'd done the one thing Jarrod had warned me not to do—I'd underestimated Kyler, thinking him some spoiled idiot I could easily take.

And now I didn't know if I could fix it…

Chapter Eighteen

Nem

My hands bound behind me didn't cause the panic it would most people. I recalled back to Jarrod doing this, to him teaching me to think through the situation, even when that seemed impossible. How many times had he done this to me and forced me to think, to slow down, to figure out what I had to work with and how to use it.

Panic led a person to rushing, to reacting without thought, and that was a quick way to losing.

Not to mention struggling would wear a person out, make it impossible for them to use an advantage when they finally found one.

So I didn't let panic take over, even though I didn't see a path through, didn't see a plan that would get me what I wanted.

I had no idea where the men were. According to Kyler, they were alive but trapped. I doubted anyone could trap them for long, but for now, it meant they couldn't help. I had to trust that they could come out of it, that they could deal with whatever faced them. As hard as it was to trust that, I knew that I was needed elsewhere more.

Mackenzie would get walked down the aisle by Kyler soon—I could hear the music playing, knew the song list by heart after having had to go over it with the planner so many times.

Step one was to escape my bindings. Kyler had used zip ties, hooking my wrists in front of me, then using bungee cords around my chest to hold me to the chair.

It was a rather lazy attempt at restraining me, but I had to accept we were more alike than I had realized, than I'd admitted. It seemed we both underestimated the other.

I took a deep breath, closing my eyes for a moment.

You can do this. I repeated the mantra like a stupid New Age affirmation, as though I were looking into a mirror and trying to positive-think self-hatred away. Still, I used the pep talk to cage up those feelings inside me, the ones I'd thought were gone, the ones I'd craved and feared for so long.

The fear, the anger, the panic of losing what I had finally realized I really wanted. For the first time, I knew clearly what I truly craved.

A life.

It was something I'd never had—I'd been a child under Kyler's thumb and later something mostly dead, seeking nothing more than revenge. I wanted to have more, now. I wanted to go to sleep beside the men I loved, I wanted to know my sister was safe and happy and I wanted it for a long damned time.

I wanted the chance to see what life really could be for me.

After one more deep breath, I opened my eyes. I had everything I needed to come out on top. I recalled the time Jarrod had taught me to break out of a locked trunk, and to what he'd told me.

I'd said I couldn't see anything, that I didn't have anything, and he'd responded that wasn't true. He'd said I didn't need to see how to get out. I didn't need to know the solution. I only needed to take it one step at a time, to keep moving, to keep looking and I'd find a path even if it wasn't immediately obvious.

I lifted my foot until I could bring the heel of my shoe up to my bound hands. After hooking my nail beneath the tiny circle at the bottom, I pulled, releasing the thin blade that was shaped like an icepick. It had a sharp end with a cutting edge near the tip, making it ideal for cutting the tent wall and sinking into Kyler.

I slid the blade through the plastic. There wasn't enough of a sharp edge to slice the zip ties with, which meant breaking was my only option—and boy was I not looking forward to that.

I turned the pick so it rotated and twisted the zip tie. It tightened the plastic around my wrists, and I prepared myself for it to get worse before it got better. To break the ties, I needed to apply pressure by twisting it until they snapped. They'd tighten them around my wrists, however, until they finally gave.

The music changed, to the one Mackenzie had picked to walk down the aisle to. It spurred me on, made me grit my teeth even as the zip ties dug painfully into my skin. None of that mattered—only getting to Mackenzie mattered.

I let out a soft cry as the plastic tightened to the point I feared I wouldn't manage to break it, a tremble in my shoulders as I shoved that worry aside and twisted the piece of metal farther.

The snap of the plastic was loud, even over the music, but I didn't let the relief take hold of me even for a moment. There wasn't time.

I'd made a mistake by underestimating Kyler, by thinking I could easily outsmart him, by not seeing him for the monster he really was. I'd learned my lesson, though.

Just like I'd learned when I'd been bleeding out after being shot, just as I'd learned from Jarrod, from the men, from life, I'd learned from Kyler exactly what he was.

He'd made a mistake, too, leaving me alive.

I opened the window to his office, the overhang low enough I could jump from there.

We'd both made our share of mistakes, but I was done with it.

Now we'd finish it, for good.

* * * *

Rune

I stared across the small basement room at the man who held a weapon and watched over my brothers and me, trying to ease the frustration inside me at our current position.

We were the Quad. We were the ones others feared. How the hell had Kyler managed to get the jump on us like this?

Not just one of us, but all four. I touched blood from a split on my lip with my tongue, a reminder that one of those assholes had gotten the best of me.

Is Nem okay?

The question ate at me, made it even harder to sit still, to plan. Planning wasn't my thing, yet it seemed no one else had a clue in fuck what to do.

Bray's gaze moved around the room, as if trying to find some option. Colton remained silent, his hands opening and closing as if that made his mind continue to work. Dane, however, stared at the man who watched over us, probably trying to read something in him that could help.

And while they all worked through it, Nem was out there alone.

"How could he have fooled us?" Dane asked, frustration eating away at his words.

"We were too close," Colton answered. "We were so sure he didn't know that we missed it."

Hell, it seemed Kyler didn't even think we were important enough to speak to directly. Instead, after getting taken off guard by four men I didn't recognize, I was dragged to the basement where the other three already were. Even without Kyler coming himself, however, I knew damn well who was behind it all.

And the more I considered that, the more it pissed me off. I didn't like losing, and I sure as fuck didn't like losing to *him*. If someone took me out, the thought that it'd be that coward burned.

"Do you think Nem's okay?" Bray asked.

No one answered, because the question wasn't one any of us wanted to think about. Considering it meant accepting that there were two options.

She was okay or she wasn't, and it was that second part that made my brain short out. After everything, after losing her once, I couldn't force myself to think I might lose her again. Especially after the night before, when I'd spent the whole damned night losing myself in her, when she'd been so perfectly open and honest for once.

Dane lifted his gaze to the man who watched us, a sharpness in Dane's eyes saying he wasn't playing around. "So you're the unlucky one assigned to the shit detail, huh?"

The man should have kept his mouth shut, but it seemed no one had told him not to interact with Dane. "They put me here because they knew I could handle you four until after the wedding is over."

"The wedding?" Dane asked. "There won't be a wedding."

The man snorted. "You're right about that. Maybe it's more apt to say after the bloodbath is over."

That got to me. While I knew Kyler was behind this — these were men at his disposal — I had no fucking idea why. Clearly, he suspected us, which meant he had to know about Nem. However, *bloodbath* wasn't a word used on just a couple of people.

Dane no doubt read the same, because a crease beside his eye said he'd zeroed in on that detail. "What you mean is that you got stuck here instead of getting to do the important parts. Don't feel bad — the world needs henchmen."

The man narrowed his eyes. Then again, I could almost feel bad for *him*, since I knew damn well how quickly Dane could get beneath anyone's skin. This guy had no shot at resisting the way Dane could dig through a person's mind. "If I'm so unimportant, then why did he hire *me* to find the guys who are going to take out the guests?" As soon as the man said that, his eyes widened, as if he just realized his mistake.

Not that he looked all that worried, probably too sure that since he had a gun and we didn't, he was safe.

Of course, his words helped me put it together. Even I could figure it out when it was made that clear. Kyler wasn't just concerned about us — he was planning on killing the guests.

"Yep, you make for a good middleman, I'm sure."

That shove made the man take a few steps closer, his expression hard. "I'm no fucking middleman. You think you're something just because you have some nickname, huh? Yeah, well, after tonight, you won't be shit. You or the redheaded bitch or Kyler's little princess."

I froze. As much as I might have hoped this was all some mistake, that Kyler had doubted us for reason, I now knew the truth. It wasn't just about us, about our plan. Kyler's plan included not only our deaths, not only that of the guests, but also Nem and Mackenzie? It was bigger than I'd though, telling me Kyler wasn't playing around.

I peered around the room, at the faces of the others who didn't seem to have any ideas as to how to get out. However, we couldn't just sit here, couldn't wait and see what happened.

We needed to help Nem, to help Mackenzie.

I narrowed my eyes as I stared at the man who held the gun, sizing him up, the distance from us he stood. We had no other options, so when I moved, I did it in a rush to take him by surprise.

The only thing that mattered was taking out that man, the one who stood between us and our goal. He might get a shot off, but that was fine. That didn't matter — I'd take that fucking bullet if it was what it took to get to where we needed to go.

I got to my feet and charged the man with the gun.

* * * *

Nem

I really wished I had a gun. Normal people rarely thought such things — they didn't usually need to. They went along their lives, where moments of danger and violence were rare, and even when such moments happened, they were more than willing to escape rather than fight.

I hadn't been normal in a long damned time, though. So instead, I rushed toward the tent at a dead run, the blade gripped in my palm, having kicked off my shoes because running in heels in grass was a horrible idea. The music from the tent thundered in my ears, like a war cry telling me to hurry.

If I didn't make it in time, if I couldn't save Kenz, then everything I'd gone through, everything I'd suffered, would have been for nothing. The rest of it — my potential life, my revenge — they didn't matter if I wasn't fast enough to save my sister. I remembered how we'd stayed up when we were younger, how we'd talk late into the night in her room, after everyone had gone to sleep, and how I had sworn to always look out for her.

No one looked my way, including the few guards outside the house. Then again, Kyler wouldn't have told many his plan — people talked too much. It was why he'd hired outsiders for the actual attack, so he could take them out and remove anyone who knew the truth. It meant to most of the people I passed, I was just Nem — security, real estate and wedding planning expert. My running barefoot through the backyard was above their paygrade.

Unfortunately, none would likely give me their gun, either.

I neared the tent, my feet wet from the grass. Fear clutched me, but there hadn't been any gunshots yet, which meant I wasn't too late.

The door flaps for the tent were closed to give it a cozy atmosphere. Even though I couldn't see in, I flung myself through the doorway. On the other side, I found myself at the end of the white aisle, with Kenz and Kyler at the front and beside them, Torrance.

Kenz turned to stare at me, confusion on her face. I couldn't blame her, though. I was supposed to be her maid of honor, and here I was, looking like I'd been to hell and back, bare, dirty feet and bloodied hands, interrupting her big moment.

Kyler's eyes widened, a moment of shock that I savored. The ability to surprise him, to outdo him bolstered my confidence, even though I still had no idea what I was supposed to do.

Just stay in the game until you have an option.

"What are you doing?" Kenz asked, her surprise showing Kyler hadn't said anything to her directly about me, yet.

Which was probably the one good thing about the entire situation. I wasn't sure how I'd react to Kenz believing Kyler, to her thinking I could do what he was claiming I'd done.

Kyler set a hand in front of Kenz and pushed her backward, as if trying to shield her. "Stay away from my daughter," he said as though he were some savior.

I pointed my finger at him. "The game is over. Let her go."

"This isn't a game," he responded, then looked around as if rallying support from the guests. "I didn't want to tarnish today, not for my daughter, but Nem isn't who she says she is."

"What are you talking about?" Kenz asked as she tried to push Kyler's arm away from her.

"Nem is a name she uses which is just like everything else about her — fake. It's all been a game to get close to us." He took a deep breath, as if it were hard to say what was coming next. "She's Kelsey, your sister."

Kenz tore her gaze from Kyler, swinging her head my way. The weight of her stare was like a physical blow to my chest, and it made it hard to draw breath. I'd seen that look before, when the men had figured out who I really was, when they'd tried to piece together who I was now with who they'd known before.

It was far more painful when Kenz did it. The men knew the ugly parts of life, lived in them, but Kenz didn't. For her to see me, to know who I was, to realize I'd lied, hurt more than my bloody wrists did.

"Kelsey?" she asked as if it made no sense, as if even the name felt wrong in her mouth.

It was like it had been with Kyler, where I had to decide how to deal with a blown cover. Except, with Kyler I'd only cared about the game, about the plan — with Kenz, I actually cared...

I nodded, because there was no reason to deny it. As quickly as I did, however, I tried to bring myself back on track. "You're not safe, Kenz."

She furrowed her eyebrows. "You called me Kenz. You were lying to me this entire time? How could you sit there and just lie to me like that?" As she spoke, each word was laced with more pain as she put it together, and each one hurt me just as much.

I tried to push that aside. That was something to deal with later, to address once she was safe. "Kyler is lying to you, Kenz."

"You're the one lying about who you are," Kyler interrupted. "I didn't want to have to tell you this, Mackenzie, but your sister is the one who really planned your mother's murder. She faked her own death with the Quad's help. I was suspicious, which is why I pulled them off your security. She's come back now to kill you, too. With you gone, she's the last of the Hester line."

I shook my head. "That isn't true. You *know* me, Kenz, you know that isn't true."

"Oh, now you want her to believe you? After being gone without a word for ten years? After showing back up and lying to her? I've been the one here, the one who has done everything for her! Mackenzie knows which of us to believe."

This was the worst part about Kyler, his ability to twist a few truths into a bundle of lies and make the whole thing look honest. The parts of his story that were real—me not telling her I was alive, me lying to her—made it look as if everything he said was right.

"That isn't true," I countered, desperately trying to make Kenz understand, for her to believe me. "Kyler had our mother killed, and he tried to kill me too. It took a long time for me to heal, and I stayed away because I knew he'd finish the job if he knew about me. I came back to save you, Kenz, to get you away from him before he hurts you, too."

"Then why didn't you tell her any of that? Instead, you worked against her. You tried to have her abducted during dress shopping," Kyler said.

Fuck. The expression on Kenz's face said Kyler was winning, that she was falling for his stories, his lies.

"I knew you wouldn't believe me," I said, a plea in my voice. "I was afraid you'd believe him, and you are too important to risk. Please, Kenz, just listen to me. Kyler set this whole damn wedding up for *this*. He wants to kill you, too. He wants to get done with the Hester line, to get more power, and getting rid of you to do it is a benefit to him."

She looked toward Kyler, as if she didn't want to believe it, but a spark in her eyes showed doubt. It was the same spark I'd had, back before I'd known the truth, when try as I might to ignore it, I'd seen a darkness inside Kyler. Even when I'd thought he was my father, even when I wouldn't have ever thought he'd do something so heinous, there had always been a splinter in my mind that had whispered not to trust him.

Kenz had that same splinter, and it was my only chance.

"She's lying," Kyler said. "She wants the Hester power for herself — she always has. She had the love of my life murdered just to try and get it, to get her out of the way, and when she realized you were coming of age, she came back to finish the job." He turned his gaze on me, a mask of fake sorrow there. "I treated you like you were my own daughter, even though I knew you weren't."

Whispers came up from the guests, and Kenz's face filled with shock.

Still, Kyler played the victim card. "I raised you like my own, and I never suspected you'd sink this low."

He turned his gaze toward the room. "*She* planned this wedding, she picked the venue, all because she wanted the chance to take over. When I realized it, I was able to capture her, or so I thought. My men are looking for the Quad right now. She wanted to kill Mackenzie, me, Torrance and anyone else here she could have. She planned to take over *my* people, everything I built. How could you do this, Kelsey, to your own family? All for greed?"

The fact he used his exact plan against me was the most twisted and brilliant part of it all. It was so easy for him keep it straight, to blame it all on me, since it was exactly what he'd been working toward.

The whispers from the room rose and made my heart sink. They were believing him.

Of course they were. They didn't know anything about me at all. Why would they believe me? To them, I was some new coming who had wormed my way into a position of power in a remarkably short amount of time. To them, I was just a Hester — not even a Williams anymore — and that made me dangerous.

"Hate me all you want," I told Kenz. "I don't care. I'll take that. Just please, move away from Kyler. If I'm lying, you don't lose anything, but if I'm telling you the truth, I could save your life."

"I've taken care of you your entire life," Kyler said to Kenz. "After your mother was killed, I did everything I could to raise you. I may not have always been the perfect father, but you *know* I love you."

The uncertainty from Kenz killed me. I remembered when I had found out the man I'd thought was my father had tried to kill me. It didn't matter if, after it happened, I realized I should have known. There was this horrible sinking feeling, as if my foundation had been shaken, as if one of the few things that should have always been true—that my parents cared about me—suddenly wasn't.

I hadn't wanted Kenz to ever suffer that, even when I knew it would have been inevitable. At least before Kyler changed it all, it could have been that her father was a piece of shit, but he still loved her. Now I had to convince her that he wanted her dead as well.

I knew exactly how that felt, how deep the scars it left behind ran, and I'd never wanted her to suffer those.

Kyler turned his gaze toward the crowd. "I'm searching for the Quad, but until we know everything is settled, everyone needs to stay calm and remain here while I have the property secured and checked."

Of course he was trying to keep them all calm...he still needed to get his men inside the tent to kill all the guests. That would be a far more difficult task if the guests started to panic or flee.

I turned toward the crowd. "You might not know me, but you know *him*. I know damn well that Kyler Williams is a selfish, vicious man. Can any of you say he's actually done a damned thing for you? Can any of you say you trust him at all? I mean, my grandparents, Caroline's parents, were murdered just before Kyler married Caroline, when they disapproved of it, and that never struck you as odd? Or that his wife and daughter are killed and he gets to turn around and slaughter a family he'd wanted to get rid of? And now, after all this time, he's trying to pin another 'tragedy' on someone else. Either Kyler is the unluckiest man to ever live, or the most incompetent, because the people around him keep getting killed, but he keeps benefitting from it."

The people in the seats exchanged looks, as if they couldn't deny the things I said while they couldn't exactly believe them either. Or perhaps it was better to say they agreed it was suspicious but weren't sure it was worth it to pick me over Kyler.

Part of it came down to safety, to risk. Who was safer to believe? The truth didn't matter as much as the outcome in our world. It wasn't about who was right or wrong but, rather, who would prove the better ally.

Kyler was still the safer bet…

"You may not know Nem, but you damn well know me," came a voice that nearly made me cry in relief. I never thought Dane's arrogant, smartass mouth would make me so damned happy, but it did. "Nem is telling the truth—Kyler has been behind all this."

When I turned, it wasn't just Dane who walked in. On his heels came Rune, Bray and Colton—all a little worse for wear. Still, bruises, busted lips…none of those things mattered because they were alive. The rest would heal. Later I could ask how they freed themselves, but it didn't matter that much. The reality was that they were tough, that they could have only been slowed down, but not stopped.

"Oh, we know you," Kyler said. "Everyone knows the Quad and exactly what you've all done. You have a grunt, a hacker, a hitman and a conman. You are not exactly beacons of truth for anyone. Only an idiot would trust you four."

"I trust them," Kenz said, her voice unsure and quiet.

"More than you trust your own father?" Kyler asked.

She didn't respond that time.

Kyler nailed me with a hard look, the very corner of his lip tilted up so slightly, I doubted anyone else could see it. "You see, Kelsey, I told you from the start. This is about who we're all born to be. You may want to be a Hester, or a Williams, or whoever the hell your real father was, but you're not any of those things, and everyone knows it."

A horrible sinking happened inside me, a feeling that I'd lost, that I was watching everything I'd worked toward rushing out of my reach. Even with the men there, we were outnumbered. There was no way so few of us could hope to win against the men Kyler had hired to kill all the guests.

And the men and I, it seemed, since we were in the middle of it all.

I faced the guests once more, growing desperate. "You need to believe me. In a few seconds, there are going to be men coming. If you aren't ready, they'll kill you. Kyler will win, and he'll get exactly what he's always wanted."

"And you expect them to believe some girl?" Kyler asked, voice full of mockery.

"I believe Nem," came a voice from the crowd a moment before someone familiar stood.

Valeria. She was dressed to kill, in a silver gown that made her look like some moon goddess.

"What does some whore's opinion matter? No one cares what you think."

She didn't wilt at the insult, though I'd bet she'd heard worse. Instead, she met Kyler's gaze as an equal. "When one of my girls was attacked three years ago, you didn't do a damn thing. In fact, when I showed you proof that one of your men was behind it, you tossed a hundred at me and told me to get out. Nem, on the other hand, has treated everyone in my club with respect. I don't care what her last name is—I care what she's done, and even in the short amount of time she's been here, it's been more than you've ever done for anyone but yourself."

Kyler went to respond, but someone else stood. This time it was a man I didn't recognize. "You know me and most of you know my son, Carlton. He got caught pick-pocketing Nem a few weeks ago. Instead of killing him—like I'm sure Kyler would have done—she taught him, connected him with someone who could make sure he learned enough not to get himself killed. She did that having no idea who I was, who he was, what we could do to help her in return. I haven't ever met Nem, but I'd trust her miles further then I would Kyler."

I swallowed hard as a spark of hope started inside me, as the murmurs changed amongst the guests.

Another familiar face stood up—Yazmin. "Kyler hasn't given a damn about Old Town getting hit up for protection money. I've told him, explained that random lowlifes were threatening us, but it wasn't important to him. Nem was in my salon, and when someone came in threatening me over it, *she* stood up to him. She didn't have to do that, could have stayed out of it, but she didn't. She risked herself to deal with the situation. I don't care who she was, I don't care what name she uses, but the woman who stands up against someone like that is a woman I trust."

"So she's helped a couple people," Kyler snapped. "What does that matter? She is a nobody!"

Valeria turned to give Kyler a look with so much malice I wouldn't have been shocked if he'd turned to ash on the spot. "You never understood this, Kyler. It isn't about the name a person carries. It never has been. You've been so desperate to prove yourself, so afraid people cared about your last name or the Hester last name, that you never bothered to be worth a damn on your own. I'm not standing up because she's a Hester — I'm standing behind her because she's *her*."

That was the point that tipped it all over. The guests shifted, but they didn't stare at Kyler anymore as if he were in charge. It seemed that after people had spoken out, the risks had shifted. Kyler wasn't the same threat he had been, not when compared to others who no longer backed him.

People were only in power in this world because they could keep it. It wasn't about the truth, but rather about who had the ability to back up what they said. The people who spoke out showed cracks in Kyler's power, in his ability to keep order, which allowed others to question him.

Kyler's face twisted, frustration there. He was smart enough to feel the change, to recognize he was losing support. It was the look of a cornered dog, and nothing good came from a person in that state.

He reached behind him, to the small of his back, and pulled a pistol concealed there. I took a breath of relief when he pointed it at me. "You think that you've won? Because you haven't. In a few minutes, my men will still come in here, kill every one of these people, and Torrance and I can tell whatever story we want when you're all dead. None of this changes a damned thing."

Torrance, meanwhile, cringed back, inching away. The coward was clearly used to other people fighting his battles. At least it meant he wasn't much of a direct threat...

"Dad?" Fear radiated from Kenz's words, as if she'd started to catch up but still didn't fully understand.

Or maybe she did understand, but struggled to accept it, to believe it.

He reached to the side and grabbed Kenz, pulling her in front of him, using her as a shield. It blocked any shot anyone in the room might have had,. Still, he kept his gun trained on me.

"You won't get away," I told him. "I don't care where you go, I'll track you down to find her. You destroyed me — you won't get that chance with her."

The look he gave me, for the first time ever, lacked any of the subterfuge he normally wore. It was disgust, pure and simple. I'd seen threads of the same thing while I'd grown up, when he'd looked at me knowing damn well I wasn't his biological daughter, when he'd hated me for it. At least I understood it now, didn't let it sink into me, refused to let it matter.

"You're not as smart as you think you are," he said. "You've put yourself too high up on a pedestal, and you can't see clearly because of it. I don't need to worry about you coming after me, because I won't make the same mistake twice." His words told me before he moved, before the blast of the gun or the final bit of betrayal hit me.

Sure, he'd hired someone to kill me, but pulling the trigger himself was different. It took far more guts, more resolve to take the shot himself, and I guess I'd still been unsure if he had it in him to go that far.

It seemed I was wrong about that.

Something struck my side, the world shifting as I was thrown to the floor. I hit the ground hard, a weight on top of me, but I didn't take notice of that. Instead, I peered past whatever had hit me to see Kyler hauling

Kenz out of the tent, using the same plan I'd been going for, just as the lights turned off.

It seemed Kyler really had known my plan, and he'd even stolen some of it.

Others poured into the tent, and the sounds of fighting filled the space. Instead of that, however, I finally focused on the person who had hit me.

Jarrod. He rolled off me with a pained grunt. It was then I realized that red stained his white shirt, on the right side of his chest. He'd taken the bullet for me, shoved me out of the way to keep me safe.

When the man who had raised me, the one I'd grown up believing to be my father, had tried to kill me, Jarrod had risked his own life for me.

"I thought you weren't coming," I said as I applied pressure to the bleeding.

He let out a strained laugh. "Seems we have the same temper. I might storm around, but I'm not walking out on you, not again."

I stared down at the wound, a tightness in my chest.

He shifted, then pulled the pistol from his hip and shoved it at me.

"I'm not leaving you," I said, shaking my head, terrified I'd walk out, and he wouldn't still be breathing if I made it back.

"Yeah, you are. You came back for Kenz. You know what Kyler really is, what he'll do, so you need to finish this."

"But you—"

"I'll be fine. If all it took was one bullet to put me in the ground, I'd have been dead a long time ago."

I lifted my gaze from him, to find the room in chaos around us. Kyler's men had breached the tent, but, even with the darkness, they weren't much of a match for the

Quad and a crowd full of pissed-off criminals. The whole 'no weapons' rule must have been a joke because I wasn't sure I saw a single guest who hadn't smuggled in at least a blade or two. Because they'd listened to me, because they'd seen the truth of Kyler, they'd been ready and it seemed they'd refuse to be easy targets.

"Go," Jarrod said as he shoved my hand away and set his own palm over the wound. "It's time to introduce Kyler to who you *really* are."

I nodded, forcing myself to my feet, away from Jarrod, away from the men I loved, having to trust that they could handle this themselves. The only thing I allowed myself time to do was to loose a single, well-placed bullet between Torrance's eyes — no matter what happened, there was no way in hell he would be walking away from this.

I went through the slit in the back of the tent, the pistol gripped in my hand.

Kyler thought he knew me, thought he understood what he'd turned me into, but he had no idea exactly what was after him.

Chapter Nineteen

Nem

As it turned out, hauling a struggling girl in a wedding dress could slow a person down. I was sure Kyler had figured that out when I caught up to him so fast. He'd been toward where the four-wheeler sat for Dane and Kenz's escape. He really had known about every part of the plan I'd come up with, hadn't he?

He'd made it just outside the fence line, but it seemed my sister put up a bigger fight than he'd expected.

I reached them just in time for Kyler to backhand Kenz, sending her to the ground. The hit hurt me, as if I'd taken the blow instead of her. However, when she twisted, when she looked back at him, her expression showed the same backbone that I had.

The same one we'd gotten from our mother, the one Kyler had always hated and resented us for.

Jayce Carter

"You should have just listened!" he yelled at Kenz, once again trying to place the blame for his actions and failures on anyone except himself.

I crept forward the last bit of space. A stick cracked beneath my bare foot, and he twisted toward me.

I held my gun to the side to show I didn't have it aimed at him. "You should have just walked away," I said.

"You wouldn't have let me go. You think I don't know what hatred does to a person? What that desire for revenge does?"

"Are you wanting me to apologize for that? Because you can fuck off. *You* put that hatred inside me when you tried to have me killed! This is all your fault, all because you decided you didn't have enough, because you were greedy and willing to sacrifice anything to get what you thought you deserved."

"Look at you, building your own little alliances. You can hate me all you want, but you're exactly like me."

"Not even close. I didn't give up the people around me for my own petty ambition! You could have lived happily with my mother, with us, but no. You needed more, could never be content. You killed her and tried to kill me because you were afraid her name and popularity would matter more than yours. You were willing to murder your own daughter because you were so fucking afraid she might end up more than you."

"I did what I had to do, just like anyone else."

"You didn't have to do any of this. You *chose* to do it because you're a coward, because deep down, you know you can't stand against any of us on your own."

He moved his gaze between Kenz and me, as if trying to figure out his options.

He didn't have many. He could shoot me, but I'd probably put a bullet in him before he could kill Kenz or escape. Even if he managed to kill both of us — which he wouldn't — he had the Quad who would track him down.

Basically?

He was fucked. That didn't make me relax, though. People who were trapped were the most dangerous.

"I'll let you walk away," I said finally, the words shocking me when I realized I meant them.

He frowned. "What?"

"You heard me. Leave Kenz and run."

"Why? So you all can track me down? So I can live my life looking over my shoulder?"

"I won't come looking for you and neither will the Quad — you have my word. Any of the others here, well, that's on you, but none of us will come looking for you if go now."

He shook his head. "You wouldn't do that — it's nothing but a trick. You came here to kill me. You wouldn't just let me go now, not after all this work."

My gaze shifted to Kenz, who was still on the ground. "Yeah, I want you dead. I want you to pay for every last horrible thing you've done. I've spent the last ten years wanting to put you down for everything that's happened. I want you dead, but I want Kenz safe more. I might not have been sure about what I came back for, but I know it now. I didn't come back to kill you — I came back to save her, to make sure she got the life you stole from me. Filling you with bullets would have been just a happy side effect."

"You could just forget about your revenge? You could let me go?"

Funny, I'd wondered the same thing before. How many times had I questioned it, wondered if I could actually let all that past go? I'd wondered because of how often I'd woken with nightmares, because of how much I hated him for all he'd taken from me, all he'd done.

The strange part was how easily the answer came to me in that moment, how obvious it was. I didn't question it, didn't have to wonder. It was so easy when it came down to actually picking one.

I would let him go without a second thought if it was between him and Kenz. If I pushed this, Kenz or I would end up dead, and for what? For revenge? For an old score? Him dead wouldn't change what happened, wouldn't give me anything back.

"Yeah," I said. "I'd let you go because my sister is more important than you will ever be. Having a future is more important to me than you are. You're not worth it, not worth the risk, not worth anything. Kenz will have her freedom, her chance to live her life however the hell she pleases, and you can go rot in some safe house wherever the hell you want, forgotten and powerless and irrelevant. We will move forward and have lives and you can fade away to nothing."

Something about that pleased me almost more than the idea of him bleeding out. For a man so obsessed with legacy and power, to be entirely forgotten, to be considered unimportant, was a worse fate than death.

Still, I'd bet the coward would take the option, believing somewhere inside him that he could come back, that he could succeed somehow if he made it out of this alive. Hell, he was welcome to tell himself whatever story he wanted afterward, that he was the real winner, that he'd come out on top. I just didn't give a damn. I'd sacrificed too many years of my life to him—no more.

He pressed his lips together, and I didn't bother to hide my smile at the thought of having him trapped, of knowing he had no options, that his *only* choice was to run away because he'd been out maneuvered, because his plans had failed, because after so long of believing himself untouchable, the children he had raised and thought so useless had bested him.

"You know," he said softly, "I really did love your mother. I'm sure you don't believe me, that it's easier to think I never cared about anything, but that's not true. I really did love her at the start. We sat there late at night talking about our future, about everything we were going to do someday."

"You don't kill people you love," I told him.

"Things change. Years went on, and I realized that we'd never really get past her being a Hester, that the name would always hang over us, that you would always be the daughter of another man—one she loved more than she would ever love me—and I realized that if I couldn't have the life we'd talked about, I'd have one I chose, at least. It's funny that after everything, after all of this, you really are a Hester. I was so afraid that the last name would be the end of me, that something would happen because of that damned line, and here you are, proving me right."

"You're wrong," I said. "I'm not a Hester. You said it yourself. I'm not a Hester, not a Williams, not even of my real father's line. I'm not any of those names, none of those families."

"Then what are you? Now that you've had time to figure out what you're planning, to decide who you are, who exactly is that?"

"I'm Nemesis," I said. "I built myself into this person, for better or worse. I took the jagged pieces that everyone else tried to make me into and I formed them into *me*." I turned my gaze to Kenz, who had pulled herself to her feet. "You'll get to decide who you want to be, too, Kenz. You get to pick the future you want—not what he wants, not even what I want, not what some man who wants you to be his trophy wants. You'll get to decide the life you'll live, and I swear I'll do whatever it takes to give you that."

Kyler snorted. "You really think it would be that easy? Even if I'm out of the picture, Mackenzie is a legacy. She's a name, and there's power in names. She'll never be free. The only reason you got that was because of what I did, but Mackenzie? She'll be trapped by it forever."

I shook my head, refusing to let it be true. She'd suffered enough—I'd do anything to give her the life she deserved. "Get out of here," I said, waving my hand to dismiss him. He didn't matter anymore—not to me, not to Kenz, not to our lives.

"You can't just send me away," he shouted. "I'm not some insignificant nobody!" As he spoke, I saw him as the kid he'd said he used to be, the one no one gave a damn about, stomping his feet and swearing up and down that he'd matter someday.

After years of fucking over everyone in his life just so he could tell himself he mattered, he was right back at his roots. He was a man who wasn't important, one whose own children didn't give a damn about him.

The shift happened so quickly, I hadn't predicted it. Cowardice usually won out, but it seemed some wounds were too deep, some couldn't be ignored no matter what.

The sharpness of his gaze said he wouldn't run.

"You have one shot," I warned him. "You had better make sure it lands."

I expected him to pull the trigger, to send that bullet through me. It was how this entire thing was supposed to go, how I'd thought it would end. Even if the idea now pained me, if I realized the things I wanted that I'd lose — time with Kenz, time with the Quad — I'd gone into it ready to pay that price.

He met my gaze head-on, the hardness in his expression causing panic inside me. "Oh, I will."

He turned the gun away from me and toward Kenz just before a shot rang out.

I brought my gun forward and pulled the trigger, but it wasn't fast enough. His body crumpled at the same exact time as Kenz, leaving me the only one standing.

Ten years of planning, of thinking, of heading for this moment with nothing else mattering to me, and now that I was here? I realized the problem with miracles, the problem with prayers were that even when they're answered, it's rarely in the way we want them to be…

* * * *

Colton

My gaze moved to the tear in the tent where Nem had fled, where she'd followed Kyler, everything inside me wanting to give chase. That way held the things that mattered most to me in the entire world, the two women I'd sworn to protect.

But I kept myself in place. I reminded myself that Nem was far from useless. The woman was tough, skilled and more than capable of taking care of herself and her sister. The best thing I could do was hold the line here, was make sure they had a place to come back to.

The tent was still dark, but that didn't slow anyone down as we made short work of Kyler's men, of the ones who had stormed in. How had we all underestimated Kyler so far? How did he get this all set up without any of us realizing it?

Him killing Kenz, trying to kill off so many of the guests — that hadn't even occurred to me as a possibility, yet it was exactly what he'd done.

I unloaded another bullet, taking down yet another guard. Just how many idiots had Kyler managed to convince to be a part of this madness? Muscle was cheap, and too often people didn't give a damn what a job was so long as they were paid enough. On the plus side, it meant dealing with them was easy, because they were a far cry from professionals.

Especially because they'd made the mistake of thinking that 'no weapons' meant a damn thing to people who were already criminals. These were folks who killed people — what did they care about weapons rules? It meant it wasn't just the four of us against what had to have been ten to fifteen enemies, but those enemies against an entire tent full of pissed off bad-guys.

"This is some shit," Rune muttered before slamming into the back of another man, knocking him down and leaving him to other guests.

I nodded. It really was…

The fact Kyler had gotten the jump on me pissed me off beyond reason. I didn't mind losing to someone who was better than me, but to have Kyler of all people outsmart me made me want to put a bullet through him for the insult.

They should have killed us. Don't get me wrong, I was thrilled they hadn't, but it had been one massive mistake to leave us alive. One hired gun against the four of us?

Insulting.

"How many of these fucking assholes are there?" Dane asked before taking a shot at yet another who had just come in, as if he were late to the party. "We have to be getting to the end. I'd think anyone left would take off."

The reason for the question was obvious.

It wasn't that we gave a damn about the men. I was fine killing just as many as I needed to, but I wanted to follow Nem, to make sure she was safe, to protect Kenz. That was our whole fucking point! Having to stay put and deal with stragglers while having no idea if Nem was okay tore at me. Jarrod had pulled himself up and taken off seemingly between blinks. Even if he'd taken a bullet for Nem, I didn't trust him a bit, and him taking off already made him look like a coward.

"Another?" Rune asked with what sounded like a feral growl. "For fuck's sake."

I snorted softly before swinging my booted foot against the face of a man on the ground, to ensure he wouldn't get back up. "We've got to be almost through."

"We need to get to Nem," Bray snapped. "She might need us."

I didn't disagree. That was where I damn well wanted to be.

Then I remembered her expression as she'd taken Jarrod's gun, that determination of hers shining in her eyes. "She can do this," I said softly.

Bray met my gaze across the room for a moment. His chest rose and fell before he nodded.

Staying put wasn't easy. It wasn't what any of us wanted. But, damn it, it was what Nem needed, and that was what really mattered...

You'd better live up to your promise, Nem. I'm not ready to lose you yet...

Nem

Exhaustion tugged at me as I forced myself to walk back to the tent, back to where everyone else was. All the energy I'd had earlier, when the panic had hit me, it had drained away and now I wanted nothing more than to crawl into bed and close my eyes.

I walked through the tear at the back, the one I'd gone through earlier, but it all felt so different. When I'd run out of it, when I'd chased Kyler, it had been wrapped up inside that moment, inside the fear and the anxiety and the anger.

I didn't feel cold, not like I'd spent so many years of my life. I wasn't frozen, just...tired. Those feelings had all balled together then drifted away, dissipating until I felt like a balloon that had lost all its air, that hung just above the floor, crinkled and barely recognizable.

I'd spent so many years of my life headed here, and I struggled to find any joy in the moment. I didn't feel as if I'd won, didn't have any elation at the outcome. I'd never expected to end up on the other side of it, had never considered what it meant, where it would leave me.

Inside the tent, the chaos from earlier had ebbed. There were bodies, wounds being treated, but it only took a moment to identify those I knew, the ones I cared about.

They all still stood.

Bray was the first to notice me, and he was in front of me a heartbeat later, grasping my chin to check my face for injuries. He narrowed his eyes at the blood on my hands, but it clearly wasn't mine — at least, most of it wasn't.

Rune walked over next, Colton and Dane behind him. The four flanked me, no one speaking as if no one wanted to ask the questions — or better to say, no one wanted the answers.

I'd come back alone. There weren't many reasons for that to happen, not many outcomes that would leave me by myself.

I swallowed hard, the words ones I never wanted to utter.

I stepped past the men, grateful when they parted, when they let me through, and even more thankful that they stayed at my side.

The first time I opened my mouth, nothing came out. I shuddered, then tried again. "Thank you," I said, my voice soft. "Thank you for trusting me when you didn't have to, and I'm sorry for everything Kyler did, for all the pain he caused. He can't hurt anyone else, though. He's gone."

Murmurs came from the crowd, but I expected that. Kyler's death was important. Even if he was a piece of shit — and we seemed in agreement on that point — he was also an influential player in our world.

That didn't matter to me right then, though. "I killed him. I gave him the chance to run, to leave Kenz alone and escape, but he refused. He couldn't walk away from this life, from what he'd built, couldn't stand to think that he wouldn't control everything. When he couldn't own and control it, he decided to it was better to destroy it."

Just saying the words hurt, like they were sharp and sliced me as I uttered them. "Mackenzie deserved to have whatever she wanted, to live her life how she wanted to, and Kyler was determined to steal that." I took one more deep breath, then said the hardest words I'd ever had to utter. "He shot her. Mackenzie Williams is dead."

Rune pulled me into a hug, and it made me feel like I'd fall apart the moment he let me go.

After everything I'd done, after all my work and risks and suffering, this wasn't how I expected it to end…

Chapter Twenty

Bray

Nem tossed and turned in her sleep, the noises drawing me to her room. They were quiet and the pain in them shattered me.

That was the thing, in the days since the wedding, the days since everything had changed, Nem had changed as well. It was as if the walls she'd created had started to crumble, as if without her mission, she couldn't hold herself together like she had before. It was as if she could now breathe, could become who she was instead of just a list of steps.

Everyone else slept, but as usual, I was still awake even at almost two in the morning. Staring down at Nem almost made it worth the lack of sleep.

Her red hair was braided back to keep it out of the way, and she wore a tank top with shorts. Without her makeup, she appeared so different. When awake, when in the armor of her makeup and her leather and her attitude, she was larger than life. In my bed, though, she was mine. She was the girl I'd loved for years, the only one I'd ever really let my guard down around, the one I trusted even after I'd sworn to never trust again.

She let out a thin, frightened sound as she reached over and grabbed at the scar on her chest, the place where she'd been shot so long ago.

The sound tore at me, one that forced me to remember that no matter how tough Nem seemed now, she'd been through hell. She might have come through it, might have turned into one scary bitch, but she still had those same old wounds, and she'd never gotten to really tend to them, to let them heal right.

I set my hand on her arm. "Nem, wake up." I kept my voice low, not wanting to startle her.

For one, it wasn't a good way to wake from a nightmare and for two, Nem was the sort of girl who might just have a weapon in the bed. I would take a bullet for her, but avoiding it would have been preferable.

She made another sound, one full of even more fear, as if my intervening had only made it worse. I shook her harder, adding a snap to my voice as I repeated her name.

This time, her eyes opened and she bolted upright, nearly colliding with me. She reached for the scar again, something I'd noticed she did when upset. Her chest rose and fell quickly as she darted her gaze around. I could see her pulling herself together, grounding herself in the now, telling herself that she wasn't in that house, that she'd survived and killed the people responsible for that.

Her eyes settled on me, but she didn't speak at first. She traced her bottom lip with her tongue, took a deep breath, the blew it out slowly. "Nightmare?"

I nodded and took a seat on the bed beside her. "I figured waking you up was probably the best bet."

She crossed her legs as she leaned forward. It was odd how casual she looked there, in my bed, as if she belonged nowhere more. "I didn't used to have so many nightmares," she said. "And even when I did, they weren't this bad."

"No?"

She shook her head. "Jarrod said it was weird, that he would have expected it, but they just never happened. They didn't start until I came back. I don't know why they're getting so bad now."

"Because you're safe."

She lifted an eyebrow as she looked back at me, as if that might have been the dumbest thing I'd ever said.

"I'm serious," I pressed. "People react the way they have to when they're in danger, when things are going wrong. It's a trauma response. Things like nightmares, they happen once you're in a place where you can deal with the scars that shit leaves behind."

"And you think safe means here with you?"

I shrugged. "You're sleeping in my bed, aren't you?"

"Only because you don't use it."

I let the lie go, feeling no need to call her out on the fact that even if I didn't use my bed, she had her own in the house. Instead, I pulled my shirt off and tossed it into the hamper.

Nem had a moment of lust as she looked at me, the sort of expression I didn't think I'd ever get used to. I knew exactly what I was, and traditionally handsome wasn't it. I was smart, but I wasn't the man that women lusted after.

Then again, Nem had never done what others thought she should—falling prey to traditional standards of beauty was just one thing in a long line of rules she'd ignore.

Still, that wasn't my point. I rose so I could remove my pants, my feet already bare. After taking off my boxers as well, I crawled into bed, wanting nothing between us, and Nem scooted over to make room.

Her lips found mine, as if she were already halfway down that track. Not that I would complain—anything that got Nem's lips on mine, anything that had her wrapping her leg around my hip like this was something I could get behind.

Except, that wasn't what I was going for.

I set a hand on her hip and twisted her, then tugged her until her back fit against my chest. Her skin was hot, and even the roughness of her scars had a wonderful familiarity.

"Cuddling? Really?" She let out a long sigh as though she had to suffer through it.

I nipped her shoulder in punishment for her smartass remark before throwing my arm around her to keep her close. "You need more sleep," I said.

"Coming from you?"

"Yes, coming from me, since I'm the one who knows how much sleep matters and how badly it affects you when you don't get enough."

She didn't say anything back at first, and slowly, the tension inside her body slid away. It had to be ten minutes later when her soft voice filled the dark room. "I thought you didn't sleep beside anyone."

"I don't," I answered. "People aren't ever at more risk than when they're asleep. Sleeping next to someone means letting down all your guards, means trusting them entirely. I've been burned too many times."

"So you're going to just lie here awake all night?" She huffed, a sound that was oddly similar to hurt.

Instead of answering her question, I focused on what was beneath it, on what she really meant. "You know, you pulled the trigger once."

"Hmm?"

"When we found you at Carlos' house, you pointed the gun at us, and you pulled the trigger."

"Oh. That." She snuggled back closer to him. "Can you blame me? I had no idea how you were going to react."

I let out a soft laugh at the way she phrased it, as if planning to shoot me wasn't that big of a deal.

Then again...it sort of wasn't.

"If you hadn't pulled that trigger, I'd have questioned you. The thing is that I do trust you. I know exactly where I stand with you. I remember when I was betrayed, when Theresa sold me out. I never saw it coming, never suspected a thing. I figured after that, it was a good idea to never let it happen again."

"So what are you doing here?" she asked around a yawn.

I pressed a kiss to the spot I'd nipped earlier. "I don't need to worry about you like that. I know damn well that you're dangerous, that if you wanted to kill me, you could, but you wouldn't trick me. You wouldn't kill me in my sleep. If I did something you thought killing me was worth, you'd wait until I was ready for you."

She twisted slightly to side-eye me. "I wouldn't kill you."

"You might," I responded, "but I'd probably deserve it then."

She huffed, then shifted once more, settling in.

I pulled her against me tighter, enjoying how she fit into my arms, how she fit against my chest. She was perfect there, so much more than I ever thought was possible.

I closed my eyes, and for the first time in so many years—maybe the first time ever—I fell asleep beside another person, managing to sleep better than I ever had before.

This wasn't what I expected, what I'd planned, but damn if it wasn't exactly what I needed.

* * * *

Nem

I closed the door to the rental house behind me after I walked in, the last few days having passed in a blur. Who knew there was so much damn work to do when someone died?

I sure hadn't since I'd expected not to be there anymore. I'd planned on being dead, so issues like bodies and funerals and estates hadn't meant a damn to me.

It was one of the times when the prospect of living seemed far too difficult.

Another was knowing I wouldn't have the future with my sister I had finally realized I really wanted.

Still, as Dane had reminded me constantly over the past week, I'd made good on my promise and not died—now I had to actually live.

The door from the bedroom of the suite opened and I went still as someone walked through it.

Kenz stared at me, hesitating, watching me carefully.

Was she afraid of me? Was it residual from what had happened? I lifted my hands to show I wasn't a threat, that I wasn't armed.

I hadn't seen her since Jarrod had shown up after she'd been shot, when he'd sworn he could get her out of there safely. They'd both taken bullets, so it seemed a good enough idea for them to go get medical care together. Both would be safer if they left as soon as possible.

I'd gotten a message from Jarrod later that night, assuring me she was safe, that she'd only been grazed. He'd gotten the worst of it, but Jarrod wasn't the sort to let something as insignificant as a bullet to take him down, nor was he the kind to complain.

Which meant despite the week apart, I hadn't reached out to Kenz.

Now that she knew the truth, would she hate me? Would she fear me?

The fear on her face said yeah.

As quickly as it happened, though, that fear slid away. She didn't come closer, tucking her hands into the front of her hoodie as if she wasn't sure what to do with them.

"I can go." I nodded back toward the door. "I don't want to impose if you don't want me here. Jarrod just wouldn't stop bothering me, telling me I needed to come, and it's easier to just give in to him most of the time."

She furrowed her eyebrows, then shook her head. "What? No. Of course not. I was just surprised because I didn't expect anyone to come over. I was afraid..." She trailed off. Her meaning was clear—she was afraid it was Kyler, afraid it was someone else, just afraid of the entire world.

I nodded, shutting the door behind me and locking it. "How's the wound?"

She shrugged. "Not too bad. It didn't hit anything vital, at least according to Sasha."

I couldn't help my smile at the name, a reminder of how nice the nurse had been when she'd helped me. Of course Jarrod had gone to her again, and it made me happy to know they'd both been in good hands.

"Jarrod said it'll be another week before all your documents are ready." I took a slow breath before finishing that statement, knowing I needed to even if it was hard. "Then you'll be able to go wherever you want."

"Jarrod seems nice." She went and sat on the couch, pulling her legs up to cross them in the same way I'd often done. It was strange to see the same mannerisms I had. Still, her moving around, walking without any visible pain eased me.

I sat down beside her, but far enough over on the couch to give her space. I didn't want to crowd her. "He isn't, actually." I thought back to when I'd first met Jarrod, to the way he'd sat there, beside my bed, watching me silently each time I'd woken. He hadn't cracked a smile, hadn't reassured me at all. "But you can trust him," I added.

She smiled softly. "He's not so bad. He rented a chick flick for me to watch the first night."

I narrowed my eyes. "He what?"

"I think I was talking too much, and he wanted some silence."

Now *that* sounded like the man I knew. Jarrod wasn't a man who liked to talk a whole lot, and Kenz seemed the type to narrate everything. Not to mention Jarrod was injured, which meant he probably wanted to rest. Still, the thought of him picking out a romcom just for a little silence made me smile.

Jarrod and I had an odd relationship, one that had been built off my own trauma. Kenz, on the other hand, might have dealt with her father trying to kill her, but it hadn't changed her as it had me. Maybe that was what it was? Maybe Jarrod saw something in her that had been driven out of me? Maybe she offered him some kind of relationship that wasn't possible for us.

Whatever it was, Kenz having anyone made me feel better. This world was a hard place, and it was impossibly harder when a person was alone.

"I'm sorry I lied to you," I finally said, forcing myself to address the thing I really didn't want to.

"It's okay. I get it." After a moment, she paused, then shook her head. "No, I mean, it isn't really okay, but I understand why you did it. I'm not mad at you about it, but that doesn't mean I like it. It doesn't mean it doesn't hurt."

"That's fair." I shifted, unsure what else to say. Even this was better than I would have expected, better than I deserved.

What was I even doing here? I'd done all of this to give her a better life, a future, and where did I fit into it?

I don't.

I sighed, then went to stand. "Look, I'm sorry — I shouldn't have come."

Something wrapped around my wrist, and I looked down to find Kenz holding on to me. Her eyes were locked on me. She didn't speak right away, as if trying to figure out what to say.

Boy, I understood that. Worse, I didn't care for the stress on her, for her confusion. "It really is okay," I said softly. "It wasn't fair for me to just show up out of the blue after everything."

"Did you really come back for me?"

I frowned. "Of course, I did."

"Why?"

I felt like if Dane was there, he'd have answered that with 'are you fucking stupid?' Her question made no damned sense. Why would I? How could I *not*? Kenz was the only person in the whole damn world I'd come back to this mess for. She mattered to me, and the future she could have, the one she deserved, meant everything.

But I had no idea how to explain that to her.

Finally, I offered what was probably a piss-poor response. "Because you're my sister..."

She pressed her lips together and dropped her gaze. "Maybe that's the thing, I haven't known I've had a sister in a long time, so I don't know what that should feel like. I'm just a bad example of it. I feel like if it were me, if I got out of this life, especially after going through what you did, I wouldn't ever look back. I'd run as far as I could and not giving a damn what was left behind. You never thought about doing that?"

"Never."

"But you escaped. You don't even *know* me."

I wanted to deny that, to tell her I'd always know her, but she wasn't wrong. I sighed and leaned forward. "There have been times Jarrod asked me the same thing, when I healed, when I worked so damned hard to be ready to come back, and he asked me why I'd do it. Even the Quad asked me that, wondering why I'd try to get you out of the situation, reminded me that you might want that life, that I didn't know you anymore."

"So why do it? Why risk so much?"

"Because I couldn't not risk it. I remembered you — remembered me before everything happened — and I couldn't let Kyler or this life tear you apart. Do you remember when you were around five? And Bray brought home those cake pops?"

Kenz went still for a moment, as if she had to think back hard for it. Then again, I'd been older when it had happened, and it was one of the few good memories I had. I probably meant nothing to her. After a pause, a smile tugged at her lips. "They were in the shape of a fox, right?"

I nodded, laughing. "Yeah, they were. You started crying, and I couldn't figure out why at first — you *loved* foxes. Then I realized what it was — you didn't want to eat the fox because it was too cute. The person you were — the person you *are* — has a good heart. You care about other people, and you want the best for others, and that sort of thing doesn't survive in this world. I had a little of that too, but Kyler drove it out of me. I couldn't let him or this world do that to you, couldn't let you lose that goodness that's still inside of you."

"I told you this before, but it's still true. You're not as bad as you think."

"I get why you said that before—you didn't know the truth. How can you still say it now? Knowing what I really am, knowing everything what I've done?"

"Because I know you. Everything you've done has been to protect me. Sometimes people do bad things for good reasons."

"I've killed people, Kenz. I never really wanted you to find out about me, but now that you know, you should know it all. I won't pretend, won't lie to you anymore, not even to make you comfortable. I've done horrible things. I came back with a list, and I killed every single person on it."

She dropped her gaze, lines etched into the space between her eyebrows. "They were the people who killed Mom, right? The ones Dad hired to kill you both? Then they deserved it."

That hurt worse than anything, one of the cracks that she never should have had to carry, proof that even already she was changing, that she was hardening.

I shook my head. "It doesn't matter if they deserved it. That doesn't change what I've done."

She reached out and caught my hand, gripping it tightly. "I can't say I'll ever really know what you've been through, or that I'll ever be the person you are, but I know that you helped people when you didn't need to. I remember one time when I went the bathroom and found Rune's shirt covered in blood. I'd run to Mom, crying, scared. She sat me down and explained that the world has monsters in it, and that sometimes people have to fight those monsters. She told me Rune was one of those fighters, that he did things that were hard and scary but he did them to keep us safe, to make the world a better place. That's what you are, too, Nem. It's not easy, I'm sure, but I've seen you now, watched you face down Dad. You're just like the Quad. Maybe it isn't comfortable for people, maybe it's easy to question, but I know the truth. You do things that need doing, even if they're hard, even if they're scary and dangerous, and you did them to keep me safe."

I swallowed down the tears the threatened to spill. I'd never really thought I'd have this, that Kenz would ever look at me as if I were something worthy. I'd worked so damned hard to save her, to get her out of this life, and I'd expected her hatred for it if she ever really understood what I was.

I wasn't the sort to cry, though, so I glanced up at the ceiling to try and clear away the tears.

"Do you really think everyone believes I'm dead?" Kenz asked, no doubt seeing that I needed a break from the personal stuff.

"Yeah, I do."

"What if someone figures it out? Dad made a lot of enemies."

I shook my head. "You don't need to worry about it."

"How can I not?"

"Because I'm going to handle it. I'm going to make sure you're safe, that you get to have the life you want. It's why I came back, why I crawled out of that house, why I survived when I shouldn't have. I've done so much already—I won't let that change now. Trust me, Kenz, you'll be safe, no matter what I have to do."

She sighed but nodded. "So is this it? I take off with my new identity and never see you again? It's like I'm dead now instead of you…"

I'd planned to say yes.

I couldn't get the words out, though. Maybe it was the way she still held my hand, or the fact that she hadn't rejected me, or the way she looked at me, as if I wasn't the monster I'd thought I was. Instead, what I said took me by surprise. "It doesn't have to be. You still need to go—it's not safe for you here, not yet at least. Someone could still try to target you. You should go to college, figure out what you want and finally live your life. It's safer if we don't talk, but if you want, we'll stay in touch."

"Promise?"

"I came back from the dead for you, Kenz. I'm not going to abandon you now."

* * * *

Rune

I waited in living room of our place for Nem to get back, giving her time alone with her sister. I'd already seen Kenz, visited with her on my own, just as Bray, Colton and Dane had. Nem had told us as soon as we'd been alone that Kenz hadn't been killed, explained that the lie was for her safety.

I got it, even if I didn't like it.

Nem, the ever stubborn one, had taken the longest to decide to go see the sister she'd done so much for, that she'd risked so much to save.

I didn't really understand why, but I didn't need to. If there was one thing I knew for sure, it was that people did things in their own time. There wasn't any rushing them, no forcing something they weren't ready for.

It made me think back to Nem, back when she'd been younger, to the way she'd tried to kiss me. She hadn't been ready back then—neither had I.

It had taken ten years and a lot of hell for us to get where we needed to be. It was the same for Kenz and Nem. They'd had to grow, to get ready. Hell, they'd still need more years, time for Kenz to grow into her own.

The door squeaked open, and I noticed her red hair before the rest of her. She took quick steps, her face down, her arms wrapped around her.

She closed the front door with a bang and didn't look my direction.

Which wasn't exactly unusual. Nem was as good with feelings as she was with forgiveness.

Which was to say not at all.

"You good?" I asked, already knowing her answer and that it would be a lie.

"Yeah."

I caught her chin and turned her face to me after I closed the distance. Her eyeliner was smeared, a sure sign she'd shed some tears on her trip back. That was probably why she'd wanted to go alone, to hide any reaction she had. They tore at me, made me want to go murder someone for making her cry, but there wasn't anything for me to fight.

"What happened?"

She let out a long, slow breath before meeting my gaze. "Nothing. It was good, really. I promised her we'd stay in touch, though."

"Course you did. There's no reason to cut ties totally, and it'd be good for you both."

"It'd be safer for her if she never saw or spoke to me again. Each contact increases the odds that someone figures out she's still alive, that someone puts it all together and tries to use her. It was stupid and selfish for me to say yes, all because I don't want to lose her."

I huffed a soft laugh at the way Nem's mind worked, at how she took too much onto her shoulders, how she thought she needed to be responsible for everything and everyone around her. "Kenz is just about an adult, and you did all this for her to make her own decisions. If she wants you in her life, if she's willing to take that risk, well, isn't that the reason you came back in the first place?"

She pressed her lips together, that hard head of hers no doubt trying to figure out a way to tell me I was wrong.

I didn't give her a chance, leaning in to take a kiss from her, to soothe myself with her taste. Funny how a girl as wild as she was could somehow taste so damned sweet.

After a moment, I broke the kiss, smiling when she tried to follow.

Though, the second she realized what she'd done, she sat back, clearly annoyed by her own desires.

"I think you and Kenz need each other. No one else in the entire world can understand what you've been through like her, and no one else can help her the way you can. Taking that away from her would be cruel."

It was *cruel* that did it, that seemed to cement my point.

"I guess you're smarter than you give yourself credit for," she muttered.

The comment would have bothered me before, back when I'd wanted to impress people, when I'd worried about my place in the group. Now, though, I didn't feel the same.

Maybe I'd worked through my own issues, or maybe I'd realized they weren't issues at all. "You know those books in my office?"

"The ones that clearly weren't yours?"

I nodded, not bothering to hide my laugh. "Yeah, those. I took them from the other guys' libraries because I felt like I needed to read them, to enjoy them, to be more like the others. I needed to be as smart as Bray, as good at reading people as Dane, as clever as Colton. I always felt like I didn't really fit in, like I was this idiot who was only good for using his fists."

"You're the size of a truck. You can't really pretend that isn't a benefit."

"Yeah, I know. That's my point, though. I never really felt like I was needed, like I mattered a bit. I kept trying to be different so I could hold my own, so I meant a damn."

She opened her mouth, and I could see the words on those lips of hers. She wanted to reassure me, but that wasn't what I needed.

I held my hand up to silence her, wanting to get out what I needed to say. "I'm not looking for you to tell me I'm good, or about my skills or anything like that. Maybe I needed that before, but I don't now. I don't need you to reassure me, to make me feel better, because I finally figured it out."

She lifted one of her eyebrows. "Oh yeah? And what did you figure out?"

I tugged her closer to brush my lips against hers. "I figured out that I don't need to be something other than I am. I don't need to be smarter or cleverer or any of that shit. I didn't think I had a place, but I do."

"And where's that place?"

My lips curled further. "Right here."

She pulled back enough to give me one hell of a glare. "You are an idiot."

"Not really. In fact, for the first time ever, I think I've got this all figured out. When I was trapped, when

Kyler's boys got the jump on me, I sat there thinking about what to do, about how to deal with it. You know what I did?"

"Something really clever?"

I shook my head. "Nope, not even a little bit. I charged the fucker, and it seems like seeing me headed his way was startling enough to take him off balance. It made me realize that what I do, who I am, maybe it ain't so glamorous, but it fucking matters. Besides, having you is more than enough for it to be worth it."

She offered me a look that said she thought I really was an idiot, and for the first time, that was just fine by me.

I leaned closer. "Besides, there're some benefits to what I've got."

"And what are those?"

I grabbed her hips and lifted her, pressing her back against the wall and grinding my cock against her. "I can use it to fuck you just about anywhere I want, and I can't really think of a better way to use my particular skills."

She probably would have argued with me—Nem was one hell of a stubborn woman—but when I ground against her harder, when my cock teased her clit even through her slacks, she moaned against my lips.

This was my place in the world, right here, and for the first time ever, I felt damned lucky. I'd do whatever it took to keep it.

* * * *

Colton

Nem stared up at the sky, her arms wrapped around herself, the light of the moon pouring over her. She was silent, had sat there for a few minutes without looking around.

Was she thinking? Lost in thought about all that had happened over the last few months? Regretting her choices or celebrating them?

Whatever it was, she'd taken a walk out in the open space behind our place, into the desert, then stopped and taken a seat on a large boulder. She shouldn't have gone out like this, without a word to us, but if there was one thing I'd learned about Nem, it was that she did as she damn well pleased. If anyone tried to stop her, well, they just ended up in her sights as well.

I approached slowly, masking my steps by habit more than purpose. The chance to watch her when she wasn't hiding, when she wasn't putting on some brave face or otherwise lying to me was oddly nice. She didn't hold her body tense, didn't seem to want to fight. She just was, and I found myself drawn by that.

I reached a spot behind her, then stared out at where she stared. The open space spread out, the moonlight enough to pick up many of the details of the sparse trees and wiry bushes. It was pretty, and since our place was located on the edge of a preserve, we had far more of a view than most other homes in town.

"Nice view," I said softly, expecting her to jump, for her heart to race. That was the common response I got from people, but especially women. They tended to watch me warily, to see me as my reputation. It had always chafed, but I'd accepted it as the reality of my situation.

Nem didn't turn her head toward me, didn't react with fear. Instead, she nodded and pointed toward a spot ahead of us. "There's a coyote out there. If you watch, his eyes catch the light sometimes."

I tried to look farther, to spot what she did, but without movement from the creature, I couldn't catch it.

She patted the boulder beside her, and I took the seat she offered. When I sat, she leaned against my side.

Which was...strange. I struggled to get comfortable, to relax.

"You'll scare him off if you keep squirming," she said. "What's wrong?"

"I'm not used to this."

"This?" She lifted her eyebrow despite not turning to look at me.

"Sitting beside someone."

She made a soft sound, then shook her head. "I remember growing up, how you were always on the outskirts. When the rest of us sat down, when we relaxed, you were always perched somewhere not quite in the group."

She didn't ask me why, but I knew that was what she wanted to do. Still, she gave me the chance to decide whether or not to say anything. After a long moment, I let out a sigh, broken by her not fighting with me. "I thought it was better if I stayed back."

"Why?"

"Because you and Mackenzie were young. Caroline, she knew what I was, but I never wanted to frighten either of you."

"Frighten?" she asked with an amused tone.

"I'm a killer, Nem—I always have been. I'm used to how people react to me, how they see me. They're afraid. I accept it, I understand it, but that doesn't mean I wanted to see that in your eyes, in Mackenzie's," I admitted quietly, something I'd never said out loud.

I liked my reputation. It allowed me to protect what mattered to me, but it was hard for people to see through. Hell, I wasn't sure anyone had ever really seen through it. My brothers, they understood it, but that was different.

"I was always afraid that if I got too involved, too close, you'd see what I really was. I figured you'd never relax around me again if you did."

She snorted. "I know what you really are—I've always known. Do you really think even when I was younger that I didn't hear the whispers? That I didn't know exactly what you did? What you'd done?"

I sighed. "You weren't supposed to know that. Those things were adult problems, and you should never have been exposed to them."

A weight on my thigh made me drop my gaze to find Nem's hand there, though she still hadn't turned toward me. She spoke softly. "What you did wasn't ever the point. It never mattered."

"How could it not matter? You were a kid, and I was a killer." Even saying it caused an ache inside me. I never admitted to anyone the struggle I had, the balance between what I did and who I was. "You should have been afraid of me." I let my shoulders drop. "I wouldn't blame you if you still were. Don't get me wrong, I don't want that, but I couldn't blame you for it."

She squeezed my leg, and I realized I'd started bouncing it, the nerves running through me. Honesty was a terrifying thing, and I was opening wounds for her that had been infected for years, ones I'd never expected to heal.

"Is that what you're worried about?" She turned until she looked at me, but I kept my gaze forward.

"Wouldn't be the first time."

She didn't respond right away, and the weight of her gaze was stifling. I was used to wielding silence as a weapon, to using it to my advantage, yet I felt like an amateur at the moment compared to how she used it.

Finally, I sighed and turned to look at her.

When our eyes met, the corner of her lip curled up into a smile. "I'm not afraid of you. I never was, not even when I was younger."

"That's just because you're a fool who doesn't worry about yourself enough."

She set a hand on my cheek, the touch surprisingly gentle between us. We had tended to be violent, angry and broken, which was nothing like the warmth of her palm. "That's not why. I know you, Colton—I've always known you. I don't have any fantasies about the person you are, about what you do, about what you've done."

"So how can you be comfortable around me like this? Even people I know well, they still flinch when I reach for them. They don't turn their backs on me."

She let out a soft laugh and shook her head. "Well, I don't do that, do I? I remember *not* flinching, even when you showed up in my room unannounced." Her smile turned mischievous. "In fact, I recall turning my back on you quite a few times."

That took me back, reminded me of just how close we'd gotten that day. It made me frown. "Why didn't you stop me? Why trust me? You were a virgin, Nem, so how could you be that brave? Or that stupid?"

"Brave and stupid usually go hand in hand." When I didn't speak, she let the smile disappear from her lips, as if she realized a joke wouldn't fix this. "Even back when you turned me down, I think I loved you. I knew you wouldn't hurt me, that you'd do whatever you could to protect me. Even when I came back, when I thought you might have been behind my attack, I think I still knew somewhere deep inside me that you wouldn't have done that."

"I'm a monster," I said, trying to make her understand.

"Yeah, you are." Her words lanced through me, but she twisted, sliding into my lap so only she filled my vision, then grabbed my chin so I had to look at her. "But so am I. We're the same sort of monsters, so you don't need to worry. You don't need to keep that distance. If you aren't scared of me, I'm not going to be scared of you."

It was everything I'd wanted to hear. If she'd told me I wasn't dangerous, that I was a good man, that would have been a damned lie and we'd both have known it. I would have known she didn't understand, that she was either lying to herself or to me—or possibly both. However, as she spoke, as she stared into my eyes denying nothing, I knew that wasn't the case.

I tested it, reaching for her, a part of me still waiting for her to reject me, for her to pull back, to watch me with hesitation and distrust. Instead, she closed the distance as well. She leaned her cheek against my hand, a mirror of how she'd touched me earlier, a sign of her trust.

And that undid me. I shifted my hand to the back of her neck and pulled her in, gave her a kiss meant to tell her how damn much I cared for her even if I didn't know how to say it.

Nem meant the whole fucking world to me. She'd been the love of my life before I'd ever realized it, and now that she was back? Now that I had her? I never planned to let her go.

We were both monsters, both broken, but that didn't matter a bit. The world was a dark place, a dangerous place, and I doubted anyone else could ever survive it.

Her bare skin against mine, her lips deepening our kiss, her seeking hands all made me let go of my worries, let me stop pretending, stop keeping any distance between us.

I'd wanted nothing more than the woman in my lap, my perfect partner who made things matter to me again. If anyone threatened what I'd finally found, I'd show them the monster I really was.

* * * *

Nem

Why finding random people in my room surprised me anymore I had no idea. Places in my world were only private for as long as no one could break into them, and I had some exceptionally talented folks in my life.

"You're supposed to be resting," I scolded Jarrod as he sat on my desk.

"I don't like downtime."

"Neither do I, but when I almost bleed out, it's time to deal with it."

"Sasha cleared me."

I lifted an eyebrow at him, knowing damned sure he was lying through his teeth.

"Fine—she didn't exactly clear me. She said I wasn't going to die, and that is pretty much the same thing. Staying in one place makes me anxious, anyway."

"Bet you wish you'd worn a bulletproof vest now, huh? Maybe you'll start listening to me." So, playing 'told you so' wasn't the most mature response, but it did ease my worries.

"I think I'll just not get shot anymore."

I shook my head at his joke before moving on, since I doubted Jarrod would ever change his behavior unless he damn well wanted to. "Kenz said you watched a romcom with her."

He snorted. "She was nervous and wouldn't quit rambling. Figured that was the best way to get a little shut-eye." He paused for a moment, then added, "She's a good kid, you know?"

"She really is. Thank you for everything — for what you did for me, what you're doing for Kenz."

He looked me in the eye, and it felt odd. Jarrod and I danced around things, having the closest thing to 'real' talks on the gun range or at some other inopportune times. It meant the weight of his gaze made me want to pull back. "Don't do that," he said.

"Do what?"

"Don't thank me. I don't deserve that."

"You took a bullet for me. You deserve a hell of a lot more than a thank you. You took me in, taught me, kept me safe, then helped me and ended up risking your life to save me."

He shook his head. "That's like thanking me for cleaning up the mess I fucking made."

I didn't ask him what he meant, knew if he wanted to tell me he would and if he didn't, nothing I could do would change it.

Sure enough, he kept going. "You know why Caroline married Kyler? Why I wasn't there? I never really told you the full story, but I owe you that."

"I figured you guys just didn't work out."

He shook his head. "That would have been easier. No, that wasn't it. Caroline wanted to settle down, wanted us to have a real relationship. She'd said it a few times, then she ended up pregnant, and I guess that made her push it. She wanted to tell her parents about us, wanted us to do the whole picket-fence bullshit. She didn't tell me about you—fuck, I don't know if that would have even changed my mind. I told her it wasn't possible, that it wasn't safe, and she left me."

"Why wasn't it possible?"

"I fucking loved her, you know? More than I thought possible, more than I ever admitted even to myself. The thing was, I know what I am—nothing. I'm good at what I do, but it's dangerous. I'm best when people don't know shit about me. My name couldn't have given her the life she wanted. She would have been in danger constantly, would have had to look over her shoulder always, would have had to hide in the shadows. I was afraid of losing her, afraid of having to watch her die." He let out a laugh that held no humor. "I didn't think I could survive that, or fuck, maybe I was afraid of seeing disappointment and resentment in her eyes one day. It happened anyway, though. If I hadn't made that choice, Caroline would have been with me. None of you would have been in Kyler's path, none of you would have had to suffer like you did."

"You couldn't have predicted any of this. You don't know what would have happened, if it would have gone any better."

"No, I don't, but I know I could have tried. Instead, I was a coward, and I let her go, and even after I realized you were mine, I left you where you were. I was still a fucking coward, still so damned afraid of failing that I let Kyler take Caroline from me and nearly lost you too. So don't thank me, not for trying to clean up the mess I made, for trying to fix what I fucked up. I failed Caroline, failed you, and not even a bullet can fix any of that."

I stared at him, surprised by just how human he sounded. Jarrod had seemed invincible for so long, like he'd stopped being a person and had become a weapon years before, that it was strange to see him broken, to see him carrying so much regret.

"If there's one thing that I've learned so far, it's that nothing is set, that all that shit we don't like in our past, that's what brought us here. I spent a lot of years thinking that what I went through in that house had ruined me, that it had literally killed me and I was just this corpse still moving. I would have done anything to take that back, to change it, but you know what I found out? I won't say it was worth it, that I'm happy about it, but I wouldn't be *here* without it. I wouldn't have Kenz safe, wouldn't have the Quad in my life, wouldn't have you if none of that had happened. I'm not going to tell you how to feel or how to think about what happened, but I'm going to say you can't change it. You're where you are, and all you can do it figure out where you want to go from here."

He stared at me in silence for a minute, as if he had to figure out whether he wanted to accept my point or not. Then again, truth took a while to sink in, for a person to realize how they felt about it.

Kenz would take time to figure out what she wanted, to find herself, and the same was true of Jarrod. Nobody heard good advice and just took it. They had to live it, had to find their own path, their own realities.

"Maybe," Jarrod said as he pushed himself off the desk, his slow movements telling me he wasn't quite as well off as he wanted me to think. "Guess I'll figure it out."

The way he spoke made me take pause. "You're not sticking around, are you?"

"You always were smart," he said, offering me a strained smile. "No, I'm not. I haven't stayed in one place this long ever, and now that you're settled, it's time for me to head out."

"You don't have to. You could settle here, too."

"That's not a life for me. I need to get out there, get my head back in the game, you know? I'm going to get Kenz safely to where she's headed, make sure she's settled in, then take off. You need me, you know how to contact me, but I figure it'll be a pretty long time before I head back this way. Too many people have seen me, especially after the wedding." He tucked his thumbs into the pockets of his jeans, as if he wasn't sure what to do with his hands, then took a step toward the door. "You be careful, okay, Nem?"

When he tried to move past me, the awkward tension thick, I did the impossible. I reached out and wrapped my arms around him.

It was weird and uncomfortable and we both froze. We hadn't ever hugged—that wasn't *us*. Still, I did it anyway, and after a moment, he wrapped his arms around me too.

He held me tight, his fingers curling in as if he couldn't help it. It was so not like us, but maybe that was the point.

I'd grown, changed from the angry, empty corpse he'd met a decade ago. I'd been powerless, a pawn in other people's games, feeling as if I were a name and nothing more. He'd helped me grow, given me a place while teaching me how to create my own safety. He'd taught me I could become more, that I could be the person I chose to be. In exchange, I'd helped him move forward, helped him have something in a world when he'd thought he'd lost everything.

"I know you don't want to hear it, but thank you," I whispered.

Jarrod hugged me tighter, the feeling the sort of thing I hadn't realized I needed. "Thank you, too."

I didn't bother asking what he meant by that—it didn't really matter. I was pretty sure it was less about telling me and more about him wanting to have said it.

It was fitting, though, just like the two of us. Awkward, and we didn't really fit in, didn't do what was expected, but we still ended up exactly here, right where we needed to be.

It was two broken people who had made some sort of family when we had nothing, and no matter how it looked to anyone else, it was one hell of a family.

* * * *

Dane

Nem sat on the swing in the backyard, a book in her lap. She looked relaxed, and it drew me outside after her.

I closed the glass slider behind me, then took a spot next to her on the swing. When I set my arm on the back of the seat, she scooted in closer.

It was fucking perfect. The warmth of her, the vanilla that clung to her hair, the weight of her body resting against me.

We sat there in silence, and I wondered if that had ever happened before for me. My life was made up of words, of conversations, always running from the quiet. In my world, quiet was dangerous. Silence was like darkness to most people, a lack of information.

I filled every second with noise, with conversations, with pulling information from others and filing it away for later use.

The urge to do so wasn't here, though. I took a deep breath, pulling in the crisp air, petrichor thick telling me it would rain before morning. Tension slid from me, an odd feeling of calm, something I barely recognized.

"I can't read you," I finally said.

Nem curled in closer and stayed quiet, her book forgotten on her lap.

"I can read everyone. Right on their face is everything they're thinking, but you? You're a blank canvas. It feels like having my eyes closed."

"And you hate that?"

"I did, yeah. I don't trust anyone, and having you there, being unable to understand you at all, it was really fucking annoying."

"Well, I don't know what you want me to say. It's not like I'm doing it on purpose."

"I don't think you're doing it at all," I said. "I think I am. I think I knew I needed that. It's exhausting to constantly have to read people, to know what they're thinking, to try and identify it all, but I don't have to do that with you. I think I knew somewhere inside me that if I didn't do that with you, if I didn't have to read you, I would get what I really needed."

"And what's that?"

"Peace. I needed to be able to fucking relax, to sit back and not have to try and figure out what you're thinking, to be able to just hear what you say and take it at face value. I've never had that before, never been able to let that all go. I can't read you, have no fucking idea what you're thinking, and I don't think I've ever been happier."

She twisted to look at me, the moonlight catching on her eyes. "You're impossible."

I nodded and tugged her against my side again, making the swing move with my feet. "Yeah, I know, but so are you. The girl who died, the one who came back from it and did what no one else could. Maybe we're both impossible, and it's why we work."

"What are you, a fucking romantic now?" Her words were colored with amusement.

"Looks like it. Now shut up and enjoy the view."

"I didn't think you liked the quiet."

"Guess I just never had someone to enjoy it with."

Instead of responding, Nem shifted so her head leaned against my shoulder, her legs stretched out beside her, then let out a long breath as she eased into the moment.

And that moment was fucking perfect.

* * * *

Nem

I tried to not look nervous. I really did. I'd faced down so many things that I felt like I should have been immune at this point.

Rune and Bray stood to my left, both dressed in suits that made them look just as dangerous as ever. To my right were Colton and Dane, similarly dressed and with

Dane offering me a side glance along with a grin and a wink.

I held on to that, to the fact that they were by my side, that I wasn't here alone.

"Relax," Colton told me as I stared at the large desk. "You'll be fine."

"What if people don't respect me?"

"Then we'll kill them," Rune said with a shrug.

Then again, that was as simple as he would find it, no doubt.

"Great business plan," I responded.

Bray took off his backpack with his laptop in it, setting it on the shelving on the side of the office. "You'll be fine," he assured me.

"How can you be sure?"

"Because I know you. You outsmarted us, outmaneuvered Kyler and have proven yourself quite resourceful. You can handle this."

"I guess I don't have any other options," I muttered.

Dane turned to look at me. "That isn't true, Nem. You've got choices—always have. You picked to come here, to save Kenz, to face Kyler. You can still walk away, but you're choosing to stay."

That was true, and that reminder actually helped. He reminded me that I was here because of all the choices I'd made, that I'd reached this point not by chance or fate but by my actions. I'd followed through and dug in, and I was here now.

The reminder had me pulling my shoulders back as I took a seat at the large desk, flanked by the Quad, by the men who had my back no matter what we faced.

Colton let out a soft laugh, drawing my attention to him.

"What's so funny?" I asked.

"Just thinking about how you used to think you were dead. Guess things have changed, huh? Did you finally figure out you were wrong?"

I paused, thinking about, then shook my head. "No, I wasn't wrong."

Colton's expression darkened, disappointment there, but before he could say anything, I lifted my hand to let me finish.

"I *was* dead. I was just going through the steps because I didn't have anything. I'm different now, but it isn't that I was wrong, that I wasn't dead. I'm different because of you all, because you gave me something worth changing for." I forced myself to tell them the truth, to admit it to them no matter how terrifying it was to bear my wounds to them, to let them see how much they mattered to me. "I came back as just a corpse, but somewhere along the way, you four resurrected me, you gave me a life I thought was gone. So, no, I wasn't wrong, but you helped me become more."

The softness in the expressions of the Quad, of four men who could terrify damn near everyone, made me realize I'd done the same for them. We'd changed each other, relied on each other, taught each other that we could have whatever we wanted. Just like how I'd done that for Kenz, had told her she was free, the Quad and I had freed each other so we could have the life we wanted.

And now, we were about to face a lot, but for the first time, that was okay. I took a deep breath, centering myself, before nodding. "Okay, send in the first."

Rune offered me a smile before walking to the door and opening it. A moment later, he returned with a man in front of him, one I recognized from the wedding but couldn't name. He was in his forties, dressed well and with that same arrogance I was used to. He was a man who hadn't looked at me twice so far, one who had dismissed me as unimportant to him.

It was different now, though. His gaze didn't skirt over me, didn't dismiss me. He didn't meet my eyes directly, his gaze on the floor, his gait far less confident than before.

When he approached the desk, he stopped just before and stared at me, his posture showing someone intent on proving himself not a threat.

"I came to ask for your help, Madam Nemesis," he said, dropping his head forward in respect.

It was funny that after so much work, after so much suffering and pain, I ended up here. In control of the very machine I'd wanted to destroy, having taken everything Kyler had had, with the men I'd been sure were trying to kill me by my side.

Maybe it wasn't the straightest of roads. Maybe I'd fucked it up a time or two. But I'd done it as *me*. I'd done it as the person I'd created, the one I'd chosen to be. I wasn't a Hester or a Williams or anything else others tried to shape me into. I was flawed and temperamental and vicious as they came, but damn it, I was me.

I was Madam Nemesis, and anyone who wanted to fuck with me or those I cared about would find out exactly why I'd chosen that name.

Want to see more from this author? Here's a taster for you to enjoy!

Dark Sanctuary:
Trapped by Doubt
Jayce Carter

Excerpt

There was something about the courthouse that Ell both loved and hated. She loved the clear rules and the regimented way it ran. There was never a question about what the next step should be, about what was and wasn't allowed and about how a person went through those steps.

However, another part of her remembered coming as a child and the crushing disappointment that happened no matter how it went. Being there as an adult was different, gave a person a sense of power, but as a kid?

She recalled sitting beside a social worker, trembling, never sure how it would go or what that meant for her. Would they hand her over to her mother? Her father? Some relative she'd never met who wanted good karma points for taking in the poor, destitute child? Or would she take the gamble that was foster parents?

It was terrifying—always.

Which was exactly why Ell handed a closed cup of hot cocoa to the boy sitting on the bench in one of the many long hallways.

Donnie Denton, the first case she'd ever been assigned on her own. She could still remember walking in to see him, black eye but ready to take on anyone he needed to to survive. It had broken her heart to see him like that, to know he'd lived a life where he'd needed that hard edge.

He took the hot cocoa and offered a rough thank you. While other case managers had had trouble with him—they claimed he lied and was disrespectful and labeled him a lost cause—Ell had taken to him right away. She still smiled each time he went to respond with cursing but stopped himself, as if he knew it wasn't appropriate to say in front of her.

At fourteen, Donnie stood taller than her and had started to put on more bulk. Even still, she couldn't help but see the kid he'd been when she'd first met him.

"I'm sorry," he muttered softly, holding the cup between his hands.

"You don't need to apologize." Ell took her seat beside him.

"Yeah, I do. I fu—I screwed up. You shouldn't have to waste your time cleaning up my messes."

Ell shook her head. "I know you—if you got into this fight, you had a good reason, right?"

The color leeched from his lips as he pressed them together, the universal signal for 'I'm no snitch' that he got whenever she questioned anything. Then again, he was going to have to go back to that life, to those streets, and the sorts of people who existed in that world didn't forgive betrayal.

"I'm not trying to find out who it was," she pressed, gesturing at his split lip and his black eye, all signs he'd taken a hell of a beating. "I'm just saying, I know you have a good heart. You wouldn't be out there attacking random, innocent people. So for this to happen, you had a good reason."

He let out a long breath before taking a sip of the drink. He held it in his mouth for a long moment, as if thinking, then swallowed. "Someone wanted me to do a job, but they didn't tell me the real job. When they did? I told them to fu—I told them no. Well, he didn't take no very well."

Ell set her hand on his back and rubbed, knowing there wasn't much she could do for him. It was like his path had been made for him before he'd ever been born, and no matter how hard she tried, she had no idea how to get him off it.

The creaking of a door caught Ell's attention, and sure enough, Jeff Jadzen walked out of his office. Exactly the man she'd been waiting for.

Ell rose to her feet after nodding at Donnie, her way of assuring him she'd handle it.

Jeff took one look her way and walked faster.

Too bad Ell was perfectly fine with running in heels.

"Jeff, I need a minute—"

"Sorry, Ell, but I'm really busy. Set something up with my secretary."

"I tried. I haven't heard anything back in a week, and I've called every day."

"Like I said, very busy." He reached the men's room, then smiled like he'd won some prize. "It was nice to see you. Call the office and we'll try to get together next week." He ducked into the bathroom, his voice floating out as the door swung closed.

Next week would be too late. The pretrial was set for Friday of this week, and she shuddered to think about

Donnie ending up in juvie, of how quickly the rest of his options could float away.

Which was the exact thing that had her walking into the men's room. She'd been in far worse places in her life for far less noble reasons.

"Please tell me you didn't follow me into the men's room." Jeff spoke through a closed stall door, the annoyance palpable.

"I wasn't finished talking with you. At least now, you can't leave."

The longest sigh came from the stall. "Which charity case are you here about this time?"

"Donnie Denton."

"*Him* again? Come on, Ell, you run yourself ragged and for what? Donnie isn't some six-year-old who needs you to save him—he's basically an adult in his world. Stop seeing him as something he isn't."

"He's fourteen—that's still a kid. He isn't a bad kid, either."

"You say that because you didn't see the other person in the fight. Donnie shattered his eye socket with a bat."

That took her off guard, the level of violence new. Still, Ell shook her head, reassuring herself that she knew Donnie. He didn't lie to her. If he didn't want to tell her something, he just wouldn't, but he didn't lie.

"You know what it's like for people who live in that area."

"Yeah, I know, because I see what happens to the victims."

"Some victim. They wanted Donnie to do a job that was bad enough he turned it down once he knew the details."

"Is that what he told you? Well, his 'turned it down' moment ended up being *inside* someone's house as they robbed it. Did he leave that part out? That the woman walked in and saw them there."

Ell cringed at the little detail that, well, yeah, Donnie had left out. Still, it didn't change the rest. "Well, did Donnie touch the woman?"

Silence let her know she was right.

There was the flush of a toilet, then Jeff walked out and headed for the sinks. "No. According to her, Donnie's friend pulled a bat, and when Donnie objected, the two got into a fight. Scared the poor woman half to death, and when Donnie won, when the other man took off, Donnie said sorry and escaped through a window. We caught him down the street."

"You see? He was trying to help."

Jeff dried his hands, then turned to face Ell. "You see the best in people, Ell, and that's great, but it's going to get you killed. These kids you help, they aren't innocent and fragile. By the time they hit their teenage years, a lot of them are already killers. They're dangerous, and they're manipulative, and if you're not careful, it'll end you."

How many times had she heard that sort of warning? People who told Ell that she should pick a safer job, that she should do something else?

It didn't matter. She knew exactly why she did what she did. "Donnie has a shot. If you throw him into juvie, you're just going to solidify this path for him. Prison doesn't rehabilitate kids. It just makes them into better criminals."

Jeff rubbed the corners of his eyes. "What do you want me to do? He broke into a woman's house and put someone else in the hospital. I can't just look the other way with that."

"Community service."

"What?"

"He needs to see there are options for him, that there's a life he can still have that isn't on the streets. Assign him community service hours, and I'll make sure to find him a place to work them where he can do some good, where he can see a different life is possible."

Jeff's expression twisted the way it always did when he was in thought, when he was trying to see all the possible outcomes. His job had jaded him, but he wasn't a bad man.

Finally, he nodded. "Okay. I'll get it all drawn up and present it to his public defender. Make sure he understands that this is it, though. This is his one big shot. If he gets involved in something else like this, you won't be able to save him again."

Ell agreed, thanked Jeff, then exited the men's room. A quick conversation with Donnie outside let him know the details, and even though he wasn't the sort to admit to being nervous, the shuddering breath he released said he had been. He thanked Ell, then took off.

She would have driven him home, but Donnie was used to using the bus system. He always refused when she tried, saying he'd meet her wherever it was.

A glance at her watch told Ell that she didn't have another appointment until later, which gave her time to gather herself. When she slung her bag over her shoulder and turned, however, she ran directly into someone else.

Hands grasped her arms to keep her upright, and Ell glanced up to find a familiar face grinning down at her.

Ethan Jaymes, a detective she'd dealt with more than a few times. He was tall, dark and handsome—all the things that made her certain he was also trouble, especially when he smiled at her the way he always did. His green eyes danced with an amusement that his voice mirrored. "Aren't you in a hurry?"

She pulled away, extracting herself from his strong grasp. "You were the one standing far too close."

"I said your name, and you didn't hear me. Distracted?" He lifted an eyebrow.

"Well, believe it or not, my world doesn't revolve around you."

He let out a soft laugh, the way he always did when she soundly rejected him. It was odd, because sometimes it seemed the meaner she got, the more Ethan liked her.

And, just like clockwork, Ethan's shadow came around the corner.

Clint Faire, Ethan's partner, and an unnerving presence who had always made Ell fidget under his intense stare. He peered at her, no pleasure or surprise showing in his hazel eyes. He had a light brown beard and mustache, both well groomed, but shaved his head. If he weren't dressed so well, she'd no doubt think he was some muscle-head up to no good. "Ms. Hayden," he said, his tone as respectful as always.

Ell nodded back, still trying to calm her racing heart from her surprise at seeing Ethan. It shouldn't have surprised her that much — the two detectives were often at the courthouse — yet they always managed to make her feel out of control.

Which was about the worst feeling she could imagine. Ell was the sort of woman who preferred everything in its place, everything well-regulated and scheduled. Ethan and Clint managed to make her feel the opposite, as if she couldn't quite get a hold of all the pieces of her life, as if she couldn't make sense of it all.

And why, she had no idea.

She'd known the two men for years, though never well. She wouldn't call them friends by any stretch of the imagination, but they'd worked together from time to time—both on the same side and not so much.

"So who are you harassing today?" Clint asked in his matter-of-fact way that always made Ell's cheeks heat.

"I wasn't harassing anyone. I was doing my job."

"And who did your job require you to harass today?" Clint pressed.

"No one." Ell crossed her arms and tapped her foot, trying her best to make her annoyance as clear as possible.

"She followed me into the men's room," Jeff answered as he walked past, not slowing down to talk, seeming more than happy to rush across the hall so he could hide in his office again.

Ethan let out a hard laugh at that, and the fact he accepted her actions without question annoyed Ell. Yes, she was dedicated, but he could have had a second of 'Are they being serious? Would she really do that?' doubt.

"I needed to discuss something important with him, and he wanted to hide in the bathroom."

"You're going to get yourself into trouble one day," Ethan said as he caught his breath from his laughter. "It's good to go to bat for your kids, Ell, but be careful that you don't put yourself in a position you don't want to be in."

His words ran through Ell like they always did, tinged in something she tried so hard to ignore. Why was it that Ethan managed to get beneath her skin like this? His voice was like honey, something sweet enough to draw her closer, but also sticky enough she feared it might trap her.

All the reasons it was a bad idea had gone through in her head on nights when she stayed up thinking about him, even about Clint. She had her life in order. She'd perfectly crafted each part of it, fitting the pieces together, making exactly the picture she wanted. The idea of anyone else coming into that, of them possibly tearing apart everything she'd worked so hard to put into place, terrified her.

Life was hard and scary and dangerous, but if she kept the pieces in their spots, if she made sure everything went where it belonged, she could avoid the pain and fear she'd known so well as a kid.

So Ell offered a quick goodbye before she risked falling any further into either man, before she risked everything she'd built, her perfect house of cards.

The last thing she needed was to let either of these men blow down all the hard work she'd put in.

Clint watched the social worker scurry away, her heels loud against the tile floor. He stared at her ass, at the way it looked in her slacks.

Knock it off, you pervert.

Despite chastising himself, he never fully shook that. Sure, she was *way* too young for him, and there was no doubt she was strung too tight. None of that changed that each damn time he spotted her, his pulse sped and his cock hardened.

Hell, he was pretty sure his cock was like a barometer for that girl—it took notice even before *he* realized she was around.

"She's not interested," Clint said, and yet again, Ethan wished the other man developed some sort of a filter on that mouth of his.

Then again, if he hadn't in twenty years, it probably wouldn't happen now.

Clint said what he thought, no matter the consequences. Teaching him tact was a pointless endeavor.

"Even if she was..." Ethan said.

"She's too young."

Ethan nodded. "Yeah, she really is. She's grown up a lot in the last few years, though. Did you see Jeff all but run away? I can't remember the last person who got him moving like that."

Clint hooked his thumbs into his pockets, staring down the hallway in the direction Ell had scurried off in. "She's got too many hang-ups anyways."

Ethan snorted at the understatement. "That girl has more baggage than could fit on a plane."

Still...

Still what? Ethan couldn't help the fact his brain did that, locked onto her, and each time he came up with all the reasons it was a piss-poor idea, his mind seemed to rebut it.

Not that any of it really mattered. All the whys didn't change anything — she wasn't interested. Ethan hadn't actually asked her out, hadn't tried seriously to pursue anything, but Ell made it clear enough without that. The second their conversations turned to anything remotely personal, when an opening might occur where he could ask her, she shut it down and ran.

He had no idea if that was due to his age, his profession, her background and if she was just so terrified of the world that even the consideration of dating wasn't there.

In fact, he didn't think he'd ever seen her with anyone, or with any sign of dating at all...

Which seemed like a pity.

Ell was the sort of woman who should have a man — maybe more than one.

But since she didn't seem on board with that plan—and he reminded himself again that neither was he—Ethan tried to put it behind him. He looked over at Clint and gestured toward the elevator. "Come on, let's go get some lunch. We can ponder the direction of our love life over food."

Clint nodded and followed Ethan's lead.

Why not drown his disappointment in carbs?

About the Author

Jayce Carter lives in Southern California with her husband and two spawns. She originally wanted to take over the world but realized that would require wearing pants. This led her to choosing writing, a completely pants-free occupation. She has a fear of heights yet rock climbs for fun and enjoys making up excuses for not going out and socializing.

Jayce loves to hear from readers. You can find her contact information, website details and author profile page at https://www.totallybound.com

Home of Erotic Romance

Sign up for our newsletter and find out about all our romance book releases, eBook sales and promotions, sneak peeks and FREE romance books!